THE SWORD OF
SAMURAI CAT

Look for these other Tor books:

THE ADVENTURES OF SAMURAI CAT
MORE ADVENTURES OF SAMURAI CAT
SAMURAI CAT IN THE REAL WORLD

THE SWORD OF
SAMURAI CAT

MARK E. ROGERS

TOR
fantasy

THE SWORD OF SAMURAI CAT

Copyright © 1991 by Mark E. Rogers

A Tor Book
Published by Tom Doherty Associates, Inc.
49 West 24th Street
New York, N.Y. 10010

Library of Congress Cataloging-in-Publication Data

Rogers, Mark E. (Mark Earl)
    The sword of Samurai Cat/Mark Rogers.
        p.   cm.
    "A Tom Doherty Associates Book."
    ISBN 0-312-85156-1
    I. Title.
    PS3568.0449S37   1991
    813'.54—dc20   90-48774
                                                            CIP

Printed in the United States of America

First edition: April 1991

0 9 8 7 6 5 4 3 2 1

To Steve, and that guy out in Latrobe,
for sitting through the whole thing.

THE SWORD OF
SAMURAI CAT

Red Dawn of the Dead

That which does not kill us must have missed us.

—Friedrich Nietzsche

Just off I-95 in Delaware, midway between Newark and Wilmington, stood Christiana Mall. It could have been any mall, anywhere, except for the fact that it was located where it was. You would've felt quite at home there, if you were the sort who lived in a mall. Amidst such prosaic surroundings, what shopper could possibly have expected the carnage that was about to erupt that spring afternoon in 1987? Who, waiting to pay for anti-itch medications at the CVS store, or buying the newest Samantha Fox record at Musicland, would ever have dreamed that thousands of Bolshevik zombies were about to make an extreme nuisance of themselves? Even Tomokato and Shiro, alert as they were to signs of danger, hadn't the slightest inkling of the storm that was about to break—but hell, I'm getting ahead of myself here.

The facts speak for themselves, yet one thing is indisputable: the cat and his nephew were looking for Meister Rodgerz, aka Gruppenführer Friedrich Rudegerz, "The Beast of the Balkans," the right hand of Kurt Waldheim in a string of Nazi atrocities. The famed kidshow host was lecturing a crowd of tots on the moral

1

and psychological dangers of Samurai Cat merchandise when the felines found him.

What horrible twaddle, Tomokato thought. Occasionally glimpsing Rodgerz on American TV, even before learning his true identity, Tomokato had always found the man's persona disturbing, indeed downright sinister. The revelation that all that benevolence was really just a front had not come as much of a shock. The cat wondered if any of the kiddies in the audience, or their parents, fathomed Rodgerz's true aim: to weaken Allied youth and render them vulnerable to Fascist attack.

The cat also wondered if Rodgerz realized that the Big One had been over for some time.

But no matter what, Rodgerz's monotonous bleat-and-whine had been used to numb Lord Nobunaga's troops into insensibility that fateful day when the assassins had descended upon Azuchi Castle; and Rodgerz would have to pay.

The Nazi's traveling troupe had set up "The Reich of Make-Believe" on a stage next to McMahon books. Finishing his spiel, Rodgerz turned to hear König Freitag and Chef Von Brokett do a little ditty on the dangers of flame-throwing toys. The mild-mannered war criminal never saw Tomokato and Shiro shouldering their way through the crowd.

"Mom, I hate this stuff," Tomokato heard one youngster say.

"Why do you think you're here?" Mom replied. "One more letter bomb, and I'll make you watch his show every day for a month!"

And what did the other children do to deserve this? Tomokato thought, looking out over the crowd.

Up on the stage, Chef Von Brokett produced a puppet-sized flamethrower and sent König Freitag flying back through the asbestos curtains in a blast of napalm. Stricken with remorse, Von Brokett turned to Meister Rodgerz, and they began to sing a wretched little piece about repentence. Miraculously healed, apparently by the glow of Rodgerz's good intentions, König Freitag reappeared and joined in.

Shiro tugged on Tomokato's mailed sleeve. "This stinks," he said.

Tomokato nodded.

Tuneless and witless, the ditty was a perfect evocation of eternity. Seconds were transformed into eons. Tomokato found himself wondering how many species, indeed, how many orders of life had become extinct since the song began. Somehow he could not quite believe a wall clock that kept insisting that only minutes had passed.

When at last Lord Buddha took mercy and the horrid song whined to a close, Rodgerz faced the audience once more.

And finally spotted the cat.

"Miaowara Tomokato," he said.

The kiddies gasped, turning towards Tomokato, faces ablaze with joy. Tomokato drew his sword.

"Kill him!" the children cried, pointing to Rodgerz, hopping up and down. "Kill him!"

Tomokato advanced to rabid applause.

"You won't stop me from carrying out my mission for

3

das Vaterland," Rodgerz said blandly, pulling a silver-plated Walther P-38 out from under his sweater.

"The *Vaterland?"* Tomokato asked. "Germany surrendered back in '45!"

"So did Japan," Rodgerz needled.

"We were nuked," Tomokato said. "How could we continue?"

"That's it, make excuses. You're all a bunch of wimps."

"Takes one to know one!" Shiro cried.

"I'm not a wimp," Rodgerz answered, grinning his patented watery grin. "I'm just extremely diluted." He pointed the gun at Tomokato. "I'm going to blow your brains out. Can you say *exit wound?"*

"I knew that stuff about being neighbors was all hogwash," Shiro said. "Grease 'im, Unc!"

Rodgerz snapped off a shot.

Tomokato ducked.

The slug hit a little Sicilian kid who'd been brought to the show for doing unauthorized hits. The boy went over on his butt.

But he was wearing a Kevlar T-shirt; leaping back to his feet, he unlimbered a Thompson submachine gun, and as Tomokato neared Rodgerz, the little fellow scooted between the cat's legs and unloaded half a clip into the most unwatchable phenomenon in television history. Sweater blasted to blood-sodden rags, Rodgerz catapulted back into the Reich of Make-Believe.

And twenty demons came out of him, entered a herd of swine down in Smyrna, and promptly forced them to cross the border into Maryland.

"Wow," Shiro said, looking admiringly at the little

mafioso, impressed by his technique with the chopper.

"You killed him," said Chef Von Brokett and König Freitag together.

"It was self-defense," said the young Sicilian, almost apologetically.

"Good," they replied. "We're glad you killed him."

The kid's mother ran up on stage.

"You didn't see any of this," she informed the audience, a wonderfully menacing tone in her voice.

"Hell no," the kiddies replied, with much more enthusiasm than she apparently had expected. She hustled her young one away, the other kids patting him on the back.

Shiro looked at Tomokato. His uncle was staring off into space with a stunned expression.

"That child beat me to the kill . . ." Tomokato said, his voice trailing away.

"Of course, Uncle," Shiro said cheerfully. "Let's go get something to eat."

"How can you think of food when I've been so humiliated?"

Shiro shrugged. "I'm hungry."

And so they headed off to the mall's restaurant court, which was over by the threaters and the eastern exit.

"What do you feel like, Shiro?" Tomokato asked. "Chinese? Italian?"

"Greek, I think. I'd like a gyro, Uncle."

"Me too."

While they were waiting in line, Shiro glanced over at the exit doors. Night had fallen.

He was starting to look away when the sky reddened; a line of fire slanted earthwards.

Shooting star, he told himself.

The streak descended behind a distant hill. A yellow flash silhouetted the crest. He blinked; the light was gone. Had he seen anything at all? Everything was over so quickly. . . .

He heard a *crump!,* the delayed sound of impact. That convinced him.

"I think I just saw a meteor land," he told his uncle.

"Where?" Tomokato asked, somewhat distractedly. Shiro guessed he was still brooding on the little *mafioso's* coup.

"Out across the parking lot," Shiro said. "You didn't notice that flash?"

"No."

"Well, I think I'd better go investigate."

"Don't you want your gyro?" Tomokato asked.

"Save it for me," Shiro said.

"You be careful now."

"Aww, what could happen to me in Delaware?"

Tomokato made no effort to argue, knowing that if there was trouble to be found, Shiro would wander into it no matter what. And since it was frequently very nasty trouble, there was no point wasting time on preliminaries.

Shiro wandered off.

"Help you, sir?" the guy behind the counter asked Tomokato.

Tomokato ordered the gyros. "And do you have diet Dr. Pepper?"

"Hey," the man beamed. "Are you a Pepper too?"

"Not exactly," Tomokato replied.

6

"Then drop dead!" the man shouted, and snapped a steel shutter down over the counter.

Tomokato went to the pizza place.

Crossing the parking lot, Shiro entered a field overgrown with weeds. Ahead was the hill, not so distant as he had thought. Red light pulsed behind it. He guessed the meteor had started a fire.

Reaching the foot of the incline, he started up. As he climbed, strange words and thoughts began to enter his head, phrases about "Dialectics," and "Left Deviationism," and "Periods of Peaceful Coexistence." Before long he found himself whistling snatches of Prokofiev and Khachaturian—*that* puzzled him immensely. He hated classical music, much preferring loud, vicious rock and roll, Billy Idol whenever possible.

"Communism equals Soviet power plus rural electrification," he muttered to himself—and halted in his tracks. What on earth was he talking about? He waited a few seconds, wondering what he was going to come out with next.

His lips just sat there. Yet somehow he was sure they were merely biding their time.

He continued up the hill, only to find himself announcing, with some passion: "Treaties are like piecrusts, leaven to be broken." There was a brief pause, then out popped: "Questions of revolutionary morals are fused with questions of revolutionary tactics," followed by: "What do you *mean* they won't let me go to Disneyland?"

7

He halted once more, clapping a paw over his mouth, stifling a command to "bring on the dancing bears." He had come to the top of the hill.

Before him stretched a huge graveyard, looking like something out of the "Night on Bald Mountain" sequence from *Fantasia*; it was full of ornate Eastern European–looking tombstones and massive mausoleums sporting onion domes capped with red stars.

But as weird and interesting as the scene was, he could not keep his mind on it. Thoughts about five-year plans and backyard steel production kept rampaging through his mind.

Suddenly he had a brainstorm: what if, upon becoming General Secretary, he made all the rivers in Siberia run backwards, into central Asia? He could not think of any reason for doing this, but surely no one would dare call the Socialist Motherland backward after such a feat. . . .

Why was he thinking all this stuff?

Especially when there was a big fat extraterrestrial mystery in front of him?

The meteor had not blasted out a crater. It had cut a thoroughly unmeteorish trench in the earth. Metal debris was scattered all around, glowing with a garish scarlet light.

Beautiful color, red, he thought. *How nice it would be to have a nice red flag, with a big yellow hammer and sickle on it, and lots of tanks, T-80s, not crappy old T-55s, and boxes and boxes of mines shaped like toys, and fifty divisions of dancing bears . . .*

He glanced at a piece of debris. It had funny writing

8

on it. Kind of like Western writing, only some was backwards. One bit said CCCP.

He had seen spaceships on TV marked with that. Russian spaceships. And he had heard that there was a Russian Venus probe returning to earth. . . . Could this be its wreckage?

"Hooray!" he cried. "Another triumph for the *Rodina!*"

He caught himself. A crashed probe was hardly a triumph.

Moreover, he was a little Japanese fellow. What did he care about the *Rodina?* What *was* happening to him? Was the ruined probe doing something to his mind? Was that red glow radiation? Communist radiation? Was he being turned into a little commie? Had he wandered into some kind of fifties paranoid science-fiction flick like *Invaders from Mars,* except there weren't any Martians, there were Commies, and they were *him?*

He remembered that bit in *Temple of Doom* where Indiana Jones was saved from brainwashing by being burned; the scene had struck Shiro as pretty dumb, but now it seemed like his only hope. Pulling out a cigarette lighter, he struck a flame, and held his little wrist over it.

"Woo-HAH!" he shrieked, or rather, Japanese sentiments to that effect; the pain was exquisite. His scorched hair smelled as bad as only scorched hair can smell; slightly worse, even. Still, the gamble paid off. Wincing, he clicked the lighter shut, blowing on his burns, mind purged of Marxism-Leninism.

He still remained skeptical of virtually everything else in *Temple of Doom,* though, particularly the bit where they go down the mountainside in the raft.

9

But there was no time to worry much about the decline of Lucas and Spielberg. All those living-dead communists rising from their graves by the thousands seemed a more pressing problem.

Rotting heads and hands thrust upwards through the turf. Grinning skeletal mouths burst forth with gargly renditions of the "Internationale." Shreds of rotted flesh dropped from hanging jawbones onto uniformed chests decorated with campaign ribbons from the battles of Stalingrad and Kursk. The barnacled barrels of rusting T-34 tanks cracked through the lids of sealed concrete graveliners.

Realizing he was surrounded, Shiro raced straight up a tree and hid in a clump of leaves. Primarily for reasons of plot, none of the corpses had seen him yet. Yanking the bolt back on his Ingram Mac 11 Tiny Tim, he peeked out, watching the horrid tableau unfolding beneath.

Spetsnaz airborne units clawed their way into view, alongside KGB border guards. GRU married couples emerged, asking how to get to Silicon Valley. Khmer Rouge appeared, along with North Vietnamese regulars, little gymnasts named Natasha, chess players, ballet dancers, SS-20s, huge rotting Aeroflot planes, and kindly vigorous reformers complete with wives who were the spitting image of Jackie Kennedy if you could just ignore their more potatolike qualities. All glowed with that strange red light, and none of them smelled too good. Even thirty feet above them, Shiro was practically being wafted out of the tree on a sea of stench.

He began to gag and cough. Violent spasms wracked him. He brushed a dead branch just hanging by a splinter; dropping, it landed square on the decaying sable hat of a maggot-infested Minister of Culture. Craning his head back, the red noticed Shiro before the kitten could pull his face behind the leaves.

"A live one!" the corpse croaked.

"Borscht!" a hundred ragged voices replied. "Borscht at last!"

Borscht? Shiro thought.

The tree began to sway and shudder. The living dead were scrabbling up the trunk. He stuck his head back out.

"Borscht!" they cried below. "Collectivize the borscht!"

"You collectivize it!" Shiro replied, and opened up, Tiny Tim sputtering slugs in a murderous parody of Dickens. Ripped across the top of the head and shoulders by the nine-millimeter spray, the first corpse up the tree lost its grip and fell backwards in a flurry of putrescent pureed brains.

It was swiftly replaced by a North Korean MiG pilot with a worm the size of a weasel hanging from its mouth; the Korean took five hits in the center of the face and slid straight downwards, knocking the cadavers beneath to the ground.

Shiro felt a cold semiliquid touch at his back. A mold-covered Pathet Lao in a "Better Red and Dead" T-shirt had come up the other side of the tree; the kitten whirled just in time to sever its neck with a scythe of hot bullets.

Next to confront him was one of those Moscow Jackie K's.

11

"What do you think of my trousseau?" she asked, halting as his smoking barrel trained upon her.

"Stunning," said Shiro, and spackled her fur stole with little bits of lead.

That was the end of his first clip. He had two more, but realized that staying up that tree was a losing proposition. Especially with three thousand zombies still waiting to collectivize his *borscht,* whatever in Buddha's name that was.

He heard the roar of an engine, and the *whup-whup-whup* of great propellers. Peering out through the leaves on his left, he saw a massive MI-24 gunship looming his way, attended by a flock of carrion birds ripping and tearing at its rank, corrupted flesh. Shiro leaped up and grabbed onto a weapons pod just as a half-dozen decomposing hands thrust up into the clump of leaves.

The MI-24 made for the mall and set down on the roof. Letting go of the pod, Shiro raced off into the darkness, pausing only for a look back. In the glow of several plastic-domed skylights, he could see a squad of Spetsnaz commandos pouring out of the helicopter's yawning hatch.

Got to warn Uncle, he thought.

He found a skylight directly over Tomokato's table, but thump as he might, he couldn't attract his uncle's attention. Infuriatingly unaware, Tomokato sat munching tranquilly on a slice of pizza—pepperoni and mushroom by the look of it, even though it was hard to tell from such a distance.

What happened to the gyros? Shiro wondered.

Feet scuffled behind him. Turning, he saw the Spetsnaz shambling near, shadows against the dark blue sky.

"Don't shoot!" a thick bubbling voice cried. "We don't want to spill any of that lovely *borscht!*"

Popping a new clip into his gun, Shiro let off a rattling fusillade, hammering the onrushing shapes to a standstill. Then he blasted the skylight dome to pieces and hopped down into the opening, crashing through a thin glass window below.

"Heads up, Uncle-*san!*" he shouted.

Tomokato's face lifted. His eyes widened slightly, but he betrayed no other hint of surprise. Shiro fell directly into his mailed arms.

"Shiro!" Tomokato said. "I was wondering what all that shooting was!"

"I was fighting zombies, Uncle!" Shiro answered breathlessly, clambering out of Tomokato's grasp. "Communist zombies! The meteor was a Russian Venus probe, and it brought all these corpses back to life and turned them into Communists!"

"Oh," Tomokato said.

"Borscht!" growled a chorus of rotting voices. Tomokato glanced up to see the Spetsnaz troopers grinning hellishly at him. Even as he looked, a Soviet eyeball landed in his Dr. Pepper.

Shiro emptied his gun at the skylight. Heads exploded. Bodies rocked back from the opening. Hideous fetid garbage rained down all over the table, as if the shark from *Jaws* had just thrown up.

"A bit much even for me," said Shiro, all but barfing then and there.

13

"How many more up there?" Tomokato asked him.

"Don't know for sure. But a couple thousand came out of that graveyard . . ."

There was a peal of shattering glass. Customers scattered as fifteen scabrous armored personnel carriers smashed through the eastern exit, disgorging swarms of Red Guards and Young Pioneers.

"Collectivize the borscht!" they cried, flinging shoppers to the floor, ripping into their stomachs with ragged fingers and teeth, burying their mouths in hot, reeking guts. But their dripping faces came up twisted with disappointment.

"No borscht?" the corpses mumbled, shaking their heads.

"What's borscht, Uncle?" Shiro asked, eyeing the scene in horror.

"Beet soup," Tomokato replied grimly. "Most Americans don't eat it."

"Borscht!" the dead shrieked, rising. "Give us borscht!"

A solid zombie wall advanced towards Tomokato and Shiro.

"Time to leave, Uncle," Shiro said.

"Can they be killed?" Tomokato asked.

"Haven't you ever seen any zombie flicks?"

"No. I haven't been to any films in a while. Movies have been getting too stupid lately."

"Well," Shiro answered, "all you have to do is get the stiffs good, right in the head."

"Then why do we have to flee?"

"Just a thought," said Shiro, as the red dead charged.

Tomokato boosted the kitten up onto his back. "Hang on!" he shouted, unsheathing his sword.

The carnage that followed was indescribable—so I won't describe it.

But by the time Tomokato finished with the Red Guards and the Young Pioneers, the whole food court looked like a cross between the battlefield at Antietam and the fiftieth day of a Calcutta undertakers' strike. This time Shiro actually did puke.

Luckily for his uncle, he had gotten down from Tomokato's back by then.

"The worst part is when it goes up your nose," Shiro said, recovering.

"I wouldn't know," said his uncle, looking towards the doors. "Here come some more!"

And this time the zombies weren't fooling around. Five hundred Spetsnaz and KGB troops marched towards them humming "Arise to Arms Ye Russian Folk."

"Uncle, behind us!" Shiro cried.

A dozen decaying Siberian mammoths lumbered into the food court from the mall side, female tractor operators of heroic proportions mounted on their tiny little howdahs.

"Come on, Shiro!" Tomokato said, and ran straight towards the prehistoric elephants. Shiro grabbed onto his tail, skidding along in back of him like a water-skier.

Tucking his sword under one arm, Tomokato reached into a food wallet for one of his extra-energy treats; holding the squirming mouse by the tail, he hurled it at the mammoths.

Squealing with terror, the Bolshevik behemoths

15

bounded to get out of the way, half of them plowing into the ice cream stand on the right, the rest scattering caramels and chocolate-covered cherries by the millions as they bashed into the candy shop on the left. Tomokato went right up the middle.

The corridor adjoining the food court was not yet packed solid with zombies, but scores, even hundreds could be seen, rising from slaughtered shoppers seething with frustration, sunken eyes flaming with borscht-lust, mouths mumbling slogans about socialist realism and the downright rudeness of Afghans. There seemed to be fewer of the shambling corpses off to the left; still dragging Shiro, Tomokato went that way, braining any cadaver that wandered too close.

Yet he had only gone so far as the Macy's when his path was blocked by an army of Khmer Rouge. And while he was hacking their vanguard to pieces, the Spetsnaz and KGB swept up in the rear.

"Into Macy's, Uncle!" Shiro cried. "There's too many of them!"

It galled Tomokato to admit it, but his nephew was right. In through the doors of the department store he fled, the living dead hard behind.

He ripped right through Lingerie and Perfume, but as he neared Sporting Goods, something caught his eye: was that a Gatling minigun nosing out of that duck blind?

"For the *serious* duck hunter," an ad proclaimed.

"Yeah!" cried Shiro, as his uncle dragged him into the blind. "Swiss-cheese 'em, Uncle-*san*!"

And raking the minigun back and forth, swiss-cheese 'em Tomokato did.

17

Blood and slime gushed from inch-wide bullet impacts. Skulls shattered. Rib cages blew apart. Bodies crashed backwards into bullet-riddled display cases. Bits of glass and flesh and teeth whirled through the air. Mannequins spun and exploded.

Decapitated rank by rank, the Spetsnaz and KGB and Khmer Rouge went down. The entire population of Uzbekistan came splattering apart in disgusting colors. The Politburo of Albania landed riven in a stinking swamp of spilled Calvin Klein Obsession; even over the roar of the minigun, Tomokato heard them intone, "Oh, the smell of it," in unison before they succumbed to their head wounds. Bleeding furiously from the sinuses, brow caved in, the Kola Peninsula collapsed in a welter of torn submarine pens.

At last a white flag went up. Tomokato relented with the minigun.

"Can't we just talk about this like civilized men?" called a commissar from across the waste of corpses.

"Will you let us go?" Tomokato asked. "Stop trying to suck our borscht?"

"No," the zombie replied. "But you really should surrender anyway. Think of the advantages!"

"What advantages?"

"I was hoping you'd think of some," the zombie said.

There came a distant bass-drum thump, followed by the bang of a cymbal.

"But seriously, folks," *der Kommissar* went on, "Why is a Muscovite putting his clothes on like what you get on a salad?"

"I don't know, why?" a dozen decomposing voices asked.

"Because it's a Russian dressing!"

Tomokato opened fire again, blowing another five hundred cadavers into stench sauce. When he relented, squinting through the gunsmoke, there wasn't a single zombie left on its feet.

"Gee, Uncle-*san*," Shiro said, "I kind of liked that last joke."

"You will never be a true samurai," said Tomokato.

Taking Shiro's paw, he led the kitten from the blind. Briskly they strode towards the department store's back door.

"Do you think it's all over?" Shiro asked.

"What's the matter?" Tomokato replied. "Hasn't there been enough violence for you?"

"Well, there's quite a big difference between enough violence and enough violence for *me*—"

"Shhh," said Tomokato. "Do you hear anything?"

"You mean, besides that ominous rumbling?"

"No, that's it."

It sounded as though God Himself were roller-skating in the parking lot outside; the wall in front of them collapsed, and in came a scrofulous ringworm-encrusted SS-20 launcher. Its triple-warheaded missile dipped towards them; on either side of the vehicle swarmed mummified Cubans armed with machetes and giant cigars. And up from behind the cat and Shiro stormed the entire staff of Mosfilm Studios, every man jack of them packing a knife-edged Sergei Eisenstein.

"Looks bad, Uncle," Shiro said.

"Weapons, eh?" Tomokato asked the corpses. "Aren't you afraid of spilling our precious borscht?"

"You're too dangerous," a wizened Cuban cried.

19

"I see," Tomokato said, clapping both paws to his hilt.

Shiro fed his last clip into his Tiny Tim. He laughed fiercely, beckoning.

"Who's first?" he cried.

The corpses growled, the ring tightening.

"Just one last thing," Tomokato shouted. "What are you gentlemen going to do after you finish me and my nephew?"

"That's a tough one," the Cuban *comandante* answered. "I suppose we should spread the revolution as quickly as we can. . . ."

"No!" shouted a saturnine Georgian. "We must consolidate our gains. Socialism in One Mall!"

"Stalinist!" screeched the Cuban.

"Trotskyite!" howled the Georgian.

Other voices clamored up: "Stakhtyite!"

"Right Deviationist!"

"Tailist!"

"Fucking dancing bear!"

"It's no wonder they wouldn't let you into Disneyland!"

Machetes rose and fell. AKMs blew heads from shoulders. Gleaming wickedly, Eisensteins montaged. The whole crowd erupted into ferocious fighting.

In the chaos Tomokato and Shiro, completely unnoticed now, slipped over to the launcher.

"Conventional warheads," Tomokato said, looking up at the missile.

"How can you tell, Uncle?" Shiro asked. "The warheads are all covered by the nose cone."

Tomokato handed him a book called *Zen and the Art of X-Ray Vision*. Then he and the kitten got up into the

20

cab and backed the launcher out into the parking lot. Corpses streamed past, rushing into the Macy's to get in on the fight.

Some distance from the building, Tomokato halted the vehicle, got out, went to the control panel, and set the missile's coordinates for an all-but-straight-up-and-down shot back into Macy's. Then he activated the launch sequence.

Crossing to an abandoned MI-24, he and Shiro took off in it just as the missile roared up into the heavens. They hovered for a few moments, watching it climb. Then Tomokato swung round, the Hind hurtling Japanwards.

"Conventional warheads or no, there's not going to be much left of that mall," he said. "There won't be much left of those zombies, either."

"But what about this helicopter?" Shiro asked excitedly. "Can I keep it? I know it's been raised from an unquiet grave, and it smells really bad, but maybe if I cleaned it up . . ."

"Why do you think we took it?" Tomokato replied. "I knew you wanted one of these."

"Oh, Uncle-*san*," Shiro sighed. "This is all like some kind of wonderful dream—"

"Great Buddha in Heaven," Tomokato broke in, pointing. "Bandit, one o'clock!"

Against the bilious disk of the full moon, they saw the descending shape of an F-4 Phantom.

"This is Delaware Air National Guard Phantom Squadron Leader," came a voice over the radio. The jet screamed by. Four more followed. "You are violating U.S. airspace. Please identify yourself."

Tomokato reached for the microphone. The rotted cord broke as he brought the mike up to his lips.

"We can't transmit," he told Shiro.

"Repeat, you are violating U.S. airspace," the American pilot said. "Identify yourself immediately."

"What can we do, Uncle?" Shiro asked.

"Try to land," Tomokato said. He started to ease the Hind down, but the controls disintegrated in his paws. The MI-24 bounced *upwards*.

Tracer bullets ripped past the cockpit. "Halt where you are," said the Phantom jockey. "The next time it won't be a warning."

The MI-24's speed increased. Without any prodding from Tomokato, it wheeled round as if to engage the returning F-4s.

"Uncle-*san*!" Shiro cried.

Flames lit the undersides of the Phantoms' wings. Missiles surged towards the Hind. Just before the first crashed head-on into the cockpit, Shiro saw his name written right on it, just as clear as clear.

Glass showered inwards. The rocket exploded in his chest. He had the very awful sensation of feeling his little kitten head go shooting up, through the canopy, screaming its way straight towards the Andromeda Galaxy. . . .

Howling at the top of his lungs, Shiro sat bolt upright in bed.

"What a nightmare!" he cried, wiping sweat from his furry brow. He glanced over at his clock. It read four A.M.

He looked slowly around the room, still trembling.

Suddenly it occurred to him that he didn't have a clock in his bedroom. As a matter of fact, his whole

22

bedroom seemed completely different. His brothers were nowhere to be seen. And the decor was not at all Japanese; it seemed, if anything, 1950s middle-class American—knotty-pine paneling, Little League pennants, model planes, a "Stevenson for President" button pinned to a wall-hung corkboard . . .

Shiro wrinkled his nose. *Stevenson?*

He heard a loud rushing sound. Running to the window, he saw a reddish streak shoot down from the sky, landing in the sandpit just the other side of the hill, behind that old broken fence.

Wait a moment, he thought. *How do I know there's a sandpit over there?*

The question was driven from his mind as a throng of obviously Martian invaders came pouring up over the lip of the hill, sweeping aside the fence, racing towards the house in the moonlight.

He had to warn Uncle!

Shouting, he ran upstairs to Tomokato's room.

But Tomokato was already awake; there he stood at the window, blazing away with his minigun.

Shiro cried aloud in joy and relief. Everything was going to be all right. He dashed to the window. The Martians were in full retreat.

Rushing with his crack shock troops towards the isolated earth structure, Captain Zork Arggh was completely confident of success. He had no idea of the surprise which awaited him.

All at once one of the apertures in the upper part of the building spewed out a long tongue of flame. His soldiers began to fall, great spurts of dirt shooting up from the ground all around them. In ten seconds half his company was down.

We're not even close enough to use our zorch guns! he thought desperately. The High Command had never told him that the Earthlings possessed such firepower. It was a nightmare!

He blew his whistle, shouted exhortations to his troops. It did no good. Soon they were all in full retreat. There was nothing for him to do but race after them, back towards the ship. . . .

Something ripped across his back like a burning scythe. Blood squirted from his scaly green chest.

For a moment he remained upright. He could no longer feel his legs, indeed, anything below his rib cage. He was dimly aware of the top half of his body sliding off the bottom. He twisted his head, looking backwards.

Yep, there were his legs, still standing there.

The fearsome alien weapon had cut him clean in two. . . .

Howling at the top of his lungs, little Zork Arggh sat bolt upright in his bed just in time to see the strange flying object glowing with a weird cattish light crash into the sandpit just the other side of the hill.

The Dead Lot

Thoroughly annoyed at having expended so
much energy in a mere dream, and someone
else's dream at that, Tomokato and Shiro determined to find themselves a more typical adventure. Traveling to northern Virginia, they visited
various contacts in the U.S. intelligence community, trying to learn the whereabouts of Count
Johnson, vampire lord and all-around obnoxious
person. While in the form of a giant bat, Johnson
had turned the tide of battle at Azuchi Castle,
grossing out thousands of Nobunaga's retainers
with a mind-boggling napalm-and-guano attack;
now he was said to be the head of a shadowy
organization known as the S.I.A. In a furtive
phone conversation with a certain Pat "The
Hardware Man" Meenehan, Tomokato discovered that Johnson and a large contingent of S.I.A.
operatives had located themselves in a Maine
town called Bethlehem's Lot. Tomokato and his
nephew immediately headed north, stopping off
briefly in Boston to pick up some specialized
equipment.

—from *Cat Out of Hell: A Biography
of Miaowara Tomokato* by William Shirer
and A.J.P. Godzilla

25

1

It was called the True-Value Occult Armament Shop, and stood on an old wooden quay in the seediest part of Boston's waterfront: arriving an hour before closing on a damp Tuesday night, Tomokato and Shiro gave the goods in the window a look.

"Think of all the things you could kill with that stuff," Shiro said appreciatively, staring at the rune-graven swords, blowpipes for projecting splinters of the True Cross, and mystic *nunchakus* made from Bruce Lee's humeri and thighbones.

Tomokato grunted, attention drawn by a roach motel of strange and sinister aspect. Even as he watched, a large roach with a fluorescent orange 666 painted on its back vanished inside. The motel began to shake, and sputter out smoke; listening closely, barely able to hear through the window, Tomokato caught a snatch of what might have been a tinny argument about which was the better movie, *Ishtar* or *Ghidrah,* or whether they were, indeed, actually the same film. Then came coughing, and a high-pitched scream, and the roach's legs, minus their body, staggered out of the motel, going a few inches before they fell.

"Come, Shiro," Tomokato said, and they entered the store.

As the bells over the door jingled, the little old man at the cash register looked up from his copy of *S.W.A.T. (Supernatural Weapons and Tactics)* magazine.

26

"Can I help you?" he asked.

"I hope so," Tomokato said, going up to the counter. "The Hardware Man told me this was an excellent store."

"Pat would know, wouldn't he?" the proprietor said. "What are you packing for?"

"Vampires."

"Well, let me show you what we've got. Best line in Boston, or all of New England, for that matter."

The old man led Tomokato and his nephew off to the left, past aisles marked "Cthuloid," "Little People," "Were-Animals," and "Whitney Houstons."

"The stuff that you want is in "Living Dead," as you might expect," the storekeeper went on, turning at last. Beyond racks of salt pellets for poisoning zombies, and maggoty-looking corpse costumes for infiltrating Pittsburgh, they came to a section where the walls were lined with many kinds of crosses and crucifixes; also on display were containers of holy water (anything from hypodermic needles to two-liter plastic jugs), garlic bulbs, mallets, sharpened wooden stakes, and more exotic items.

"Here we are," the old man announced. "Vampires."

"Excellent selection," Tomokato said. "But I'm not after one or two vampires. I'm interested in wholesale extermination."

"How wholesale? If you can wait twenty-four hours, I can get you a PA truck that broadcasts old Joan Rivers routines."

"Will that kill bloodsuckers?" Shiro asked.

27

"It'll kill anything. To give you some idea, those trucks were tested outside Camden, New Jersey. . . ."

"We passed Camden on the way up," Tomokato said. "I was wondering what could have caused such devastation. . . . Joan Rivers, eh?"

The old man nodded solemnly.

"I don't know," Tomokato continued. "Perhaps that's *too* wholesale for my purposes. I'd prefer something less impersonal."

"Well, I think I might have just what you need. Came in this morning—they're still in the crates. I'll go scare one up for you."

The storekeeper hustled away. Tomokato watched him disappear, then turned his attention to several of the pieces on the wall before him.

Particularly intriguing was a holy-water modification of the Entertech Uzi Repeater squirt gun; with a Vatican Underwriter's Seal of Approval pasted on its pistol grip. He took the weapon down, hefted it. It had a good solid feel, and he guessed it performed well enough in the combat situations it was designed for. But he needed something more devastating; holy water was all very well and good for giving vampires one hell of a rash, but he wanted a weapon with stopping power. He put the squirt gun back.

A Van Helsing .357 mag stake projector caught his eye, a real beauty, nickel-plated. He had read in *Samurai Weekly* that this was a very reliable weapon. But the magazine only held six shots.

"Get a load of this, Uncle-*san*," Shiro said, handing him a grenade. In basic design, it was quite similar to the

American pineapple, but instead of being covered with small squares of metal shrapnel, it was lined with garlic cloves.

"Like phosphorus, only for a vampire, huh?" Shiro said.

"What do you know about phosphorus grenades?" Tomokato asked.

"I invented 'em," Shiro said.

"What?"

"Yep. I own a hundred and thirty-two basic arms patents. It's really kind of depressing back in the sixteenth century. Everything's so primitive technologically. So I just thought I'd spice things up a bit. I could kick myself for not thinking of that Joan Rivers truck. Sometimes an idea's *too* obvious, you know?"

"Shiro, you're a very sick puppy."

"Nah, I'm a little psycho kitten." Shiro paused. "You ever see *Blue Velvet,* Uncle?"

"Why?"

"Someone told me I reminded them of Dennis Hop—"

The proprietor reappeared, carrying a steel crossbow with a drum clip.

"Barnett Model 350," he said. "You can go semi or full auto. Kicks out fifteen heart-seeking quarrels a second."

Tomokato gave the grenade back to Shiro and took the crossbow. "Burst control?" he asked, aiming it at an African demon mask hanging on the rear wall.

"Sure thing. Three or five shot."

"How many rounds in the clip?"

29

"Seventy, with telescoping oak shafts. Once they're flying, they spring open, and your vampire gets eleven inches of hard-hitting dowel right through the old ticker."

"I'd like to try it," Tomokato said. "Do you have a firing range?"

"Come with me."

They followed the old man through the back room and into a long annex. At the end of the range stood five werewolf silhouettes, blowups of Lon Chaney, Jr., Henry Hull, Oliver Reed, Michael Landon, and David Naughton.

"But you want vampires, of course," the shopkeeper said, and hit a button on a control box. The werewolf silhouettes went down, replaced by cutouts of Max Schreck, Bela Lugosi, John Carradine, Christopher Lee, and Robert Quarry, all sporting bright red valentine-shaped targets.

"They're all yours," the proprietor told Tomokato.

The cat clicked the burst control to five. One squeeze of the trigger punched the silhouettes over, a quarrel embedded dead center in each.

"I'll take it," Tomokato told the old man. "Do you accept Bank of Kyoto traveler's checks?"

"Of course."

They went back out into the store.

Tomokato added: "I'll also take two of those crucifixes, a package of garlic, another full clip for the crossbow, and one of those holy water Uzis for my nephew here."

The shopkeeper gathered up the items Tomokato had

requested, brought them to the front counter, and asked casually:

"Where you bound with all this ordnance?"

"A small town in Maine," Tomokato replied. "Called Bethlehem's Lot."

"The Dead Lot," the owner said, nodding.

"Why do they call it that?" Tomokato asked. "Because of the vampires?"

"No, just to make it sound nasty. They've got all kinds of supernatural trouble up that way. But I never heard they had vampires."

"Well, if my information's correct," Tomokato said, "they have them now. Have you ever heard of Count Johnson?"

The old man blanched. "Of the S.I.A.?"

"Yes. He's taken up residence there, or so I've heard. And I'm going to kill him."

"A lot of men have tried," the storekeeper said.

"I'm not a man," Tomokato answered, but caught himself before he could add *I'm a little psycho kitten.* Snapping his mouth shut, he wondered: Was Shiro beginning to infect him with his cheerful moral idiocy?

The old man began making out the slip. Tomokato looked round for his nephew. The youngster had wandered off.

"Shiro!" Tomokato called.

The kitten came out of the Cthuloid aisle, carrying a familiar-looking item.

"Look, Uncle!" Shiro said. "Remember this?"

"How could I forget?" Tomokato said, taking the object. It was a strange, unearthly electrum shape, a

31

nearly indescribable cross between a Talking Pee-wee doll and G. K. Chesterton's economic ideas. "Wilbur Wartley's talisman."

Shiro nodded. "The one that killed Great K'Chu."

"Now I know who you are," the storekeeper said. "You're Miaowara Tomokato—the cat who did K'Chu in."

Tomokato nodded, then asked: "How did you come by this?"

"Got it from some Russian whalers who jumped ship. They took it out of a bull sperm. It was all tangled up in a mess of squid."

Recalling K'Chu's huge octopuslike head, Tomokato thought it only natural that they had misconstrued.

"Oh well," the cat said. "It's no use to us now. Put it back where you found it, Shiro."

Dejected to learn that his discovery was not needed, Shiro moped back up the Cthuloid aisle, returning just after Tomokato settled up.

"God go with you," the storekeeper called after them as they headed out with their new equipment.

A half hour later, the old man was leaning back in his seat, feet up on the counter. He had come to the last article in the *S.W.A.T.* magazine; it told how researchers at Duke University had demonstrated that dreams could be Freddy Krueger–proofed if test subjects wore headphones playing easy-listening music during REM sleep. There were only two hitches. Most of the subjects wound up opting for Freddy; the remainder tended to become psychic channels for long-dead painted turtles, developing an irritating penchant for sunning themselves on logs and diving headfirst into the dirt when anyone strayed too near.

Finishing the article, the proprietor closed the magazine and flipped it up onto the counter. For some time he had been aware of a distant, rythmic sound, like waves on a beach; it was quite unlike the usual knock-and-slosh of water against pilings. Swinging his feet down, he stood, cocking an ear. Something massive seemed to be slogging through the harbor, getting closer to his store with every splash.

He went into the back room, and looked out through a window in the rear door. A heavy fog had come down. To the right was the outside wall of the shooting range, disappearing into the mist after a few yards. Ahead and to the left, there was only white miasma, faintly luminous with the glow of the city lights. He could see nothing of the harbor.

The splashing continued, moving off into the fog alongside the quay. Feeling in the crawling marrow of his bones (not to mention in the hidden recesses of his still-latent gooseflesh) that some terrible supernatural presence was approaching, he went back into the showroom.

But there he paused, torn by indecision. Should he make a break from the building, try to lose himself in the fog? Or would it be better to remain inside and attempt to take advantage of the proper occult weapon once the nature of his adversary was revealed?

All at once the question became academic—a situation the old man always dreaded, since he was not

33

an academic type. With a squeal of splintering wood, the roof lifted from the walls, wrenched up and back by an immense fog-wreathed reptilian-looking claw. The old man bolted for the front door.

A second claw reached down and lifted him high into the misty gloom. Two bilious green lights became visible in the fog above him. As he rose higher and higher, he realized they were terrible eyes, located in the midst of a huge octopuslike head fringed with dangling, writhing tentacles. By what power those orbs had picked him out through the fog, he had no idea. But he knew he was dealing with something far beyond his ken, something unguessably eldritch and cacodaemoniacal and non-Euclidean.

"So you think I'm non-Euclidean, huh?" the monstrosity boomed.

"Well, sir . . ." the storekeeper squeaked.

"Do you even know what non-Euclidean means?"

"Doesn't it have to do with the geometry of curved surfaces?"

"Yeah."

"Well, unless I'm mistaken, sir, you're all made up of curved surfaces. Particularly that octopuslike head of yours. And if we drew triangles on you, and computed the angles, we'd get non-Euclidean results."

"Well, so what? That means you're basically non-Euclidean too."

"Very true, sir. But I still was quite correct in applying the word to you."

"What is this, flyspeck? I thought you weren't an academic type."

"I'm not, sir. But we're not dealing with character humor here. These stories rely very heavily on absurdity, and my knowledge expands or contracts depending on whether or not the author thinks he can make a joke."

"Well then. Do you know who I am?"

"Tip O'Neill?"

"Close, but no cigar. And no longer topical, either. The name's Bl'syu. That's *Great* Bl'syu to you."

"The brother of Great K'Chu, sir?"

"The same. Fresh from my sunken isle off Frisco, and mad as hell."

"Why are you mad as hell, sir?"

"Because someone offed my brother, that's why. And that someone was just here at your store, wasn't he?"

"Oh, no sir—"

Bl'syu gave the storekeeper a mild squeeze. The old man's tongue shot straight out like a slug with fifty thousand volts going through it, and his whole head turned a dark shade that would've been beet red if not for the green light from Bl'syu's eyes.

"I can still sense his presence," Bl'syu said.

"Actually, now that I think about it . . ." the storekeeper whispered, barely able to breathe.

Bl'syu relaxed the pressure.

"I think he *was* here, sir. Hot damn, but you're right, sir."

"Of course I'm right, dingleberry. That's why I'm one of the Real Old Ones, and you're just one more wretch paying those outrageous Massachusetts taxes. But enough of that. Where is he now?"

"Can't you read my mind, sir?"

"Yeah, but it's more fun brutalizing you this way. Where did he go?"

"To Maine, sir."

"Where in Maine?"

"A place called Bethlehem's Lot, sir. You're going to try and kill him?"

"What do you think? Ichor's a lot thicker than water, and forgiving and forgetting was never too big where I come from.

"But I didn't leave my lair just to wipe him out. First off, I had some money to deposit down in Panama. Second, I'm going to remind everyone what real horror, *cosmic* horror, is. Things have been going straight downhill ever since the 1930s. What do you have now? Authors getting on bestseller lists with crap about rabid Saint Bernards and people choking on Big Macs. I'm not going to let your children or your children's children live in a world where that sort of stuff's passing for scary."

"Oh, thank you, sir."

"For that matter, I'm not going to let *you* live in that kind of world either!"

"Oh, don't trouble yourself on my account—"

Ignoring the storekeeper's protestations, Bl'syu lifted him even closer to his lambent eyes, and in their depths, the old man saw a vision of such incalculable hideousness, a revelation of such bottomless evil and corruption, that any hope in the basic goodness of the universe was blasted from his mind, replaced by a maddening despair, all itchy and smelly and the nastiest shade of green you ever thought of; and his brain cells, by the millions, by the *billions,* in even greater numbers than he *had* brain cells, began to wither, to melt, to implode, their liquid residue settling mushily in the bottom of his skull and running out his nostrils and ears.

Bl'syu laughed. Echoes rumbled off the facades of buildings nearby. Then, since there were no longer any real jollies to be gotten from the storekeeper, the Real Old One tossed the limp form onto the quay, turned, and strode back out into the fog-shrouded harbor.

Every bone in his body broken, except for one metatarsal in his right foot, the storekeeper was a long time convalescing; and when he was released from the hospital, he found that he could no longer cope with the difficulties of running his shop. Being completely brain-dead apparently had something to do with it. Ultimately, though, he did make a good deal of money in Hollywood.

But that's another story.

2

Standing on a wooded ridge overlooking Bethlehem's Lot, Tomokato scrutinized the town through a pair of binoculars.

"See any vampires, Uncle?" Shiro asked, eager to try his holy-water gun.

"They can't come out in the daytime, Shiro," Tomokato said.

"Yeah, I know. I was just hoping they'd make an

exception for us." Lifting the gun, Shiro swept it left to right, making a rattling noise with his tongue.

"I expect we'll see plenty before we're done," Tomokato said, training his glasses on a McDonald's crowning one of the two low hills in the center of the town. It was an original-style McDonald's, with two golden arches incorporated into the actual structure of the building itself, which had that large-expanses-of-plastic look which was such a big knockout back in the sixties. But the sixties were long gone, and so were the customers—the restaurant had apparently been abandoned for some time, its windows boarded over. Splintered and pocked, the plastic on its walls and arches showed every sign of having been showered with stones by a generation of youngsters who had grown up contemptuous of fast food.

Tomokato shifted the glasses to the other hill, upon which the town cemetery was located. The cat counted ten graveside services in progress; three backhoes were in the process of filling in holes.

He turned his gaze to the main road leading into the town. The chain-link gates were still closed, just as they had been when he began spying out the isolated little community—which, as far as he could tell, was completely surrounded by a fence crowned with barbed wire. Nothing stirred in the small guard post before the gates, but sharply dressed fellows with sunglasses and blow-dried hair moved slowly from rail to rail in the towers on either side of the road, carrying M-16s and Ingrams. Similar towers warded all other entrances to the town.

How to get in? Tomokato asked himself. He didn't

39

doubt that he could fight his way through one of the gates, but he couldn't afford to raise an alarm. He expected to find Count Johnson at the S.I.A. headquarters, but he hadn't spotted any building that was a likely candidate; he was going to have to do some searching, preferably as unhurriedly as possible.

"Thinking about how to get in, Uncle?" Shiro asked.

Tomokato lowered his glasses. "As a matter of fact, yes. How did you know?"

"It just popped into my nose."

Tomokato's eyes narrowed. "Nose? What are you talking about?"

"My head," the kitten answered hurriedly. "I meant my head."

Giving no further thought to this, Tomokato lifted the binoculars once more, studying the sign hung on the gate:

S.I.A. PROVING GROUND—

NO UNAUTHORIZED PERSONNEL

BEYOND THIS POINT

Proving ground, Tomokato thought. Just what was Count Johnson up to, beyond the usual vampiric doings? What were his S.I.A. henchmen testing? And why were the townspeople permitting themselves to be cut off from the surrounding world and experimented upon? Life seemed to be going on in fairly normal fashion— there was traffic on the streets, and the downtown was full of shoppers; if there was less water polo than he expected to see in a typical American town, there was more croquet. Aside from the fence and the guard towers, the only real hint of something peculiar was the number of burials-in-progress at the cemetery.

"What does *S.I.A.* stand for, Uncle?" Shiro asked.

"Sinister Intelligence Agency."

"And who do they work for?"

"The American government, I suppose."

"Count Johnson does too?"

"I assume so."

"Does the American government hire vampires very often?"

"Yes, but mostly to collect taxes." Tomokato laid the binoculars on his chest. "There must be a way in."

"There is, Uncle," Shiro replied.

"Where?"

Shiro pointed a small paw off to the east. "There's a blind spot between two towers, down in a valley. A tree's fallen across the fence, so we won't have to worry about being electrocuted."

"How did you know the fence is electrified?" Tomokato had read the warnings through his binoculars, but hadn't mentioned them to Shiro.

"I'm not sure," the kitten said, scratching his head. "A picture came into my mind—no, not a picture. It was almost more like a smell. Like I could just *smell* there was a blind spot."

Tomokato did not know what to make of this. Shiro had never displayed preternatural abilities before. But the kitten *had* been right about the wire. . . .

He also knew when you were wondering how to get in, Tomokato told himself. Perhaps it might be worthwhile to give Shiro's hunch a try.

"Show me where it is," Tomokato said.

They moved down from the ridge, working their way eastward, well hidden in the trees. When they reached the spot, it proved just as Shiro had said. Crossing the wire over the fallen trunk, they pressed through a wooded lot and stopped in a clump of bushes on the outskirts of town.

"We're not exactly going to blend in," Shiro said. "People are going to notice us before we go too far."

"Yes, this is a barbarous country," Tomokato replied. "We could wait until nightfall, I suppose. But by then the vampires will be out. Much more dangerous."

"Well," said Shiro, "Danger's our profession, right, Uncle? Between my gun and your crossbow, we'll rip 'em up four ways from Sunday. Vampires are too old-fashioned to scare me."

"Are they?"

"Unfortunately, yes."

"Unfortunately?"

"I'd prefer worthy adversaries," Shiro said. "It's more glorious that way."

"We're not doing this for the glory," Tomokato answered.

"But glory's going to stick to us whether we like it or not," Shiro said, "so we might as well be comfortable with it. We have to be honest about this. We're two fearsome studs. Someday they'll have to make a movie about us. A real gory one, like those samurai flicks back home. You know, the ones where the blood's bright orange, and it squirts out forty feet—"

"Shiro, I've shed a great deal of blood," Tomokato said. "And I've never seen it squirt out forty feet."

"Well, maybe you haven't," Shiro conceded. "But it is a splendid effect, isn't it?"

Tomokato made no reply. Still, deep in his heart, he knew the kitten spoke the truth.

Great Bl'syu followed Interstate 95 up into Maine, making tremendous progress with his sixty-foot strides. He had at first attempted to hitch a ride; disguising his hideousness with kerchief, raincoat, and black nylons, he had gotten two takers. But the first was driving a Hyundai, and Bl'syu was almost certain he'd never be able to fit into the little Korean car. Muttering "Thanks anyway," he brought his foot down on the vehicle as an afterthought, then put his thumb out again.

A trucker stopped some time after that; Bl'syu thought he just might be able to squeeze himself into the trailer. But the driver was turned on by the nylons and got fresh as he was helping Bl'syu into the back.

"You beast," the Real Old One said, crawled back out, and beat him most decisively to death with his own truck. Then the octopus-headed terror harrumphed and stripped off his disguise, resigning himself to the long walk.

He began to get hungry along about midday. Sighting a truckstop, he decided to take a break.

Reaching the parking lot, he noticed that the asphalt was littered with corpses. All were badly crushed, sporting multiple and quite gratuitous tire tracks.

The only live people in sight were watching from behind the truckstop windows. A circle of eighteen-wheelers was rumbling around and around the building, cabs quite empty unless his eyes were deceiving him.

"Oh, how *scaaary,*" he said in his best Count Floyd.

Two of the trucks peeled out of line and sped towards him. Snorting disdainfully, he kicked twice.

Five minutes later, the NASA folks down at Wallops Island discovered two new satellites of unknown origin in low earth orbit.

Bl'syu eyed the remaining trucks, which had all bunched up together, whimpering. Growling, he hopped forward. The vehicles scattered. He went over to the building and ripped the roof off.

"Oh, thank you sir!" cried the people clustered beneath. "Whoever—*what*ever you are, you saved our lives!"

"Saved your lives?" Bl'syu demanded. "From what?"

"Those trucks, sir!" they replied.

"What? You were scared of *them?* Those stupid goddamn things?"

The people toed the linoleum floor, looking embarrassed. "Well, sir, you see—"

"Vehicles going around killing people!" Bl'syu sneered, picking up a vending machine and tearing the front off it. "What a cliché." Without bothering to open the bags, he began flipping packages of potato chips into his mouth with a claw-tipped forefinger. "How commonplace can you get?"

"But, sir—"

"Sir, nothing!" Bl'syu answered, chips and cellophane flying from his rubbery lips. "Haven't you ever seen *Killdozer? The Car?* That old *Twilight Zone* show? Where's the imagination? The vision? Why not living lawn mowers? Coke machines on the rampage?"

"It's been done, sir. There's this book called *The Tommy—"*

"Shut up!" Bl'syu bellowed, swallowing a huge mouthful of snack bags, then reaching for another machine. "You're depressing me! Just shut up!"

They complied meekly, watching him devour every scrap of food in sight, including the stale popcorn and the caramel apples in the snack bar.

"No pork rinds anywhere, goddammit," he snarled.

"Sorry, sir," the people said.

"Now then," he said. "Just consider *me*. Ever see anything more terrifying?"

"Sure," they answered. "We were downright glad to see you, in fact. You saved us, didn't you?"

"Good point," Bl'syu replied, bending down and snatching them all up in his arms. "Look into my eyes."

Every soul within fifty miles heard the screams of despair which followed.

Darkness fell over Bethlehem's Lot. That was by no means uncommon; darkness was rather clumsy, and the burg did stick up out of the ground a bit.

But whatever.

Keeping to the shadows as much as possible, Tomokato and Shiro started towards the center of town. Every house they saw was shuttered up tight; small crosses hung above the windows and doors. Like strange Christmas ornaments, bulbs of garlic dotted shrubs and picket fences and hedges.

All the businesses were closed, the sidewalks deserted. The streets were empty except for patrolling S.I.A. security vans. But as the felines pressed deeper into the town, they discovered that the vans were not the only things on the prowl.

Whore-of-Babylon scarlet, the '57 Studebaker wagon was padding along on its tires after the fashion of a great dog; Tomokato was instantly reminded of the Tiger Tanks he had encountered in *Der Kampfburg*. But there was something peculiarly American in the Studebaker's gait, as well as something distinctly untanklike, which Tomokato chalked up to the Studebaker not being a tank. And in spite of the fact that he thought malevolent cars a rather unimaginative menace (his idea of scary was oceanic eldritch horrors with octopus heads), he thought this one was pretty frightening, as far as such things went. One particularly unnerving detail was a broad tonguelike appendage wagging down over the grille, drooling foam. As the Studebaker trotted past the mouth of the alley concealing Tomokato and Shiro, Tomokato distinctly heard the wagon *panting,* like a Saint Bernard sweltering under a summer sun.

And there was, of course, *no one behind the wheel,* boogety-boogety.

"Uncle-*san*," Shiro whispered, when the car had gone. "Isn't putting horrifying lines in italics just as much of a cliché as evil cars?"

"I would say so," Tomokato replied. "Although it's on the stylistic rather than conceptual level."

"Then hadn't the author better stop doing it?"

"Shiro," Tomokato said. "Considering what a dangerous situation we're in, is there any point in us reminding him that he's a hack?"

All at once Shiro was aware of soft footsteps coming up from behind. A hideous stench of decay billowed over him, and cold breath pulsed on the back of his neck, and sharp nails began to dig into his scalp—

"Nope, I take it all back, Unc," he said quickly.

The claw withdrew immediately. Footsteps receded.

"Smell anything?" Tomokato asked, looking over his shoulder.

"Like what?" Shiro asked, coming up beside him. They emerged from the alley. Presently they found themselves in a neighborhood full of fine old Victorian homes. Shiro eyed the supernatural safeguards festooning the architecture.

"Do you think those crosses work?" he asked.

"Well, there's a house without them," Tomokato said. "No garlic on the hedges, either."

A column of greenish fog was climbing straight up the side of the building in question. Reaching a second-story window, the mist condensed into the floating form of a teenage boy, very well dressed, who proceeded to tap and scrape on the shutters. As Tomokato and Shiro watched from behind a fence, a second teenage boy slowly pushed back the shutters, and the vampire drifted in at him, clasping him around the neck, pushing him back. Both vanished inside.

Tomokato and Shiro witnessed several such visitations as they continued on their way, streams of fog slipping through shutters left ajar, or sliding under unprotected doors; most startling of all was a horde of red-eyed rats suddenly merging to form a single shadowy human figure that climbed backwards up a tree, then onto the roof of a grand, turreted residence.

"I don't think I'd like to live in this town, Uncle," Shiro said, very seriously, as the thing dropped down a chinmey like a demonic Santa Claus.

47

"Didn't you say vampires were too old-fashioned to scare you?" Tomokato asked.

Shiro sniffed. "I didn't say I was scared. I just wouldn't want to live here, that's all." He paused, as though trying to think of reasons beyond the obvious one. "It's going to be a real mess soon anyway—we're going to leave it looking like a slaughterhouse. And red isn't my favorite color."

"What is?"

"Bright orange."

Shortly they spotted a police station. Two security vans were parked beside it. A group of rifle-bearing agents, still wearing their shades even though it was most flagrantly nighttime, came out of the station, got in one of the vans, and took off.

"Think that might be headquarters?" Shiro asked.

"It's worth a look," Tomokato answered.

Stepping out from behind a dumpster in a lot opposite the station, they dashed across the street. Climbing on a garbage can and unsheathing his sword, Tomokato sliced through the phone lines leading into the building, then went to the front door.

Looking through the wire-latticed glass, he saw five operatives and two policemen. Seated in front of the counter, the cops were tied to their chairs. One of the S.I.A. men produced a collapsible steel baton from under his jacket and telescoped it out.

Noiselessly Tomokato opened the door and stepped inside. None of the agents were looking his way. The cops plainly saw him, but said nothing.

"Come on, gentlemen," one of the spooks said. "We know you two were spreading rumors."

"About what?" asked the cop on the left.

"What we're testing in this town. If you'll just admit what you were up to, and tell who fed you the rumors, it'll go a lot easier on you."

"We don't know what you're talking about," the cop on the right replied. "We believe you guys. If you say you're just testing nerve gas, that's good enough for us."

"Absolutely," said his partner, looking apprehensively at the gleaming metal truncheon.

"You haven't said we're experimenting with Captain Fangs?" the spook asked.

"What, and turning everyone into vampires?" the first cop answered. "Who'd believe something like that?"

"Someone dumb enough not to mind that we're testing nerve gas on him!" cried the man with the truncheon, and raised it to strike.

Tomokato cleared his throat.

The agents whirled, whipping out their .357s.

"Is this S.I.A. headquarters?" Tomokato asked. "For Bethlehem's Lot, that is?"

"Where did you come from?" an agent snarled.

"I'd say he's from sixteenth-century Japan," one of his colleagues opined casually. "If his accent's any indication, he grew up in Omi Province, not far from Kyoto. . . ."

"Can it, Fred," the other man answered. "You think you're so damn smart."

"Of course," Fred replied. "I'm an intelligence officer."

Dead silence.

Fred laughed wildly. *"Intelligence* officer, get it?"

The other agent looked at the cat, wincing apologetically. "Don't judge us all by Fred here. A lot of us S.I.A. boys have a *real* sense of humor."

"I'm sure," Tomokato said. "Now will you all drop your weapons?"

The spooks cracked up. "Say *what?*" one grinned.

Tomokato smiled slightly, readying himself to spring.

"Look out, Uncle!" Shiro cried.

Tomokato turned. He found himself staring into the barrel of an Ingram.

The agent holding the gun was grimacing a bit, seeing as how Shiro was wrapped around his trousered leg and sinking his teeth into it; but the gun didn't waver.

"Get away from him, Shiro," the cat said, facing the other agents once more.

"Aww, Uncle-*san*," Shiro protested, voice muffled by his mouthful of spook.

"You heard me," Tomokato grated.

"Oh, all right," Shiro said.

The instant Tomokato heard him drop, the cat reversed his grip on the *katana* and thrust the sword backwards into the S.I.A. man's chest.

Dying, the agent cut loose. The others started in with their pistols.

But Tomokato had already ducked.

The man in the doorway caught ten slugs that flung him backwards over the threshold, even as bullets from his Ingram tore into two of the agents in front of the cat. Before the remaining spooks even realized what was happening, Tomokato hurtled forward, sword flashing, and two more collapsed.

He pivoted towards the third. The man snapped a shot at him, missed—then was pummeled sideways between the astonished cops, bullet-tattered suit erupting in vaporized blood. Striking the counter with tremendous force, he slid floorwards dead, a dozen exit wounds trailing scarlet smears down the wood.

Tomokato looked back at Shiro.

"Boy, I like Ingrams," Shiro said, beaming. "They may not be Avengers, but they give you a nice solid back-to-basics feeling, nothing fancy, you know?"

"Damn it, Shiro!" Tomokato said. "I wanted that last man alive—to question him!"

"But he was shooting at you, Uncle."

"You're too fascinated by guns to have a proper disdain for them," Tomokato answered.

"Could you untie us, please?" asked one of the cops.

Tomokato freed them with two lightning slashes. They flinched, sucking in sharp breaths, then jumped up as the ropes slipped off.

"Thanks a lot, buddy," one said uncertainly, searching himself for wounds.

"Maybe we can answer your questions," said the other.

"*Is* this S.I.A. headquarters?" Tomokato asked.

"No. No one knows where it is."

"Maybe the W.O.B.L. does," the first cop said.

"W.O.B.L.?" Tomokato asked.

"The Wise Old Black Lady. She's the one who told us about the vampires and Captain Fangs."

"She has all these weird powers," the second cop said. "Seems to know everything—"

"Uncle, we'd better go," Shiro announced. "I can smell some S.I.A. vans headed this way."

Indicating the dead agents, Tomokato told the policemen: "Search their pockets. See if you can find the keys for that van outside."

He went to the door. No sign of the approaching security vehicles—yet.

"Shiro, how close are they?" he asked.

"I can't smell—I mean, I can't tell," Shiro answered. "But that funny walking car is coming too. Someone heard the shots and called in."

"There are plenty of informers now, working for the spooks," one of the cops said. "Or it could have been one of the vampires . . ." There was a jingling sound. "Found the keys!" He tossed them to Tomokato.

They piled out of the station and got into the van. Unslinging his crossbow, Tomokato took the wheel, started the engine, and roared out of the parking lot.

"Which direction were they coming from, Shiro?" Tomokato asked.

"I don't know," the kitten answered.

"Where's that lady's house?" Tomokato asked the cops.

"Fifty-two Castle Rock Road," replied the one sitting next to him. "Take a hard right here."

"Are you really from sixteenth-century Japan?" the other cop asked.

"Yes. Does it worry you?"

"A little bit."

"That's only natural," Tomokato said. "It's truly disorienting to meet historical personages outside their own eras. In my younger years, I used to worry about it myself."

"What did you do?"

"I stopped."

"Turn left at that light," said the cop next to him.

But as they neared the intersection, the Studebaker wagon came dashing around the corner, lathered tongue flopping.

"*Justine,*" the cops breathed.

We're in an S.I.A. van, Tomokato thought. *Maybe it'll just go by—*

The Studebaker veered into their lane, clearly intent on a hellacious collision.

HEADON FEVER read its license tag.

So much for that argument, the cat told himself, trying to swing round the wagon.

The Studebaker swerved in response. With a tremendous jolt it plowed into them broadside. The door beside Tomokato buckled inwards, striking him like a breaking wave. Breath puffed from his lips, and everything blurred; he felt his brain jounce against the inside of his skull. Bashed off the road, the van rolled over twice, flinging its occupants about ferociously before coming to a halt.

Finding himself rolled in a ball down between the front seats, Tomokato realized he was unhurt, mostly thanks to his armor, he guessed. Unwrapping himself from around the stick shift, he climbed back into the driver's seat.

Protected by his usual preposterous good luck, Shiro was okay too. But the cops had been knocked unconscious.

Tomokato attempted to restart the van. The engine wouldn't turn over. He looked at Justine.

The Studebaker was still by the curb, front end bashed in, pouring out steam, tongue cut off. Draped over a ruined bumper, the appendage was quivering like a huge red tapeworm. A wheezing sound interspersed with a loud doglike whining came from under Justine's hood.

Climbing over the cop beside him, Tomokato flung open the passenger's side door and leaped out, Shiro scrambling behind. The cat wondered what to do about the policemen; he and Shiro certainly couldn't drag them. The place was likely to be overrun with S.I.A. in a minute.

And there was always Justine to worry about. Mangled she might be, but he couldn't be sure she was out of commission.

As he rounded the front of the van, there came a loud *bong,* and a series of popping noises. Justine's grille began to reflate, the bumper to uncrumple. The radiator steam, some of it already forty feet from the car, began to contract, shooting back under the hood. The hood flattened neatly into place; small glittering flecks and bits of red paint sifted into dents they'd flown out of, ticking against exposed metal. A new bright shiny tongue lashed out into view, and the wheezing noise stopped. Two small lights appeared on the bumper, illumining the license plate, which now read GOOD AS NEW.

Growling, Justine bounded towards Tomokato and Shiro.

They rushed up onto the porch of the nearest house. The door was locked. Tomokato drew his sword to slash through the barrier, but Justine was already leaping up the steps after them.

They dodged. The mad Studebaker crashed through

the front of the house. Splintering wood crackled and squealed.

They ran to the end of the porch. Tomokato vaulted the railing; the kitten slipped through the bars. Pausing, they looked back just long enough to see that the wagon was trying to extricate itself, but seemed to be snagged on something—a spar in a rear wheel well, perhaps.

They sprinted along the driveway into the backyard. There they almost ran into one of those crawling rivers of mist, glowing with a poisonous light all its own. It began to knit together into a body even as they skirted it.

"Come back!" called a dry, lifeless voice behind them. "I'm a cat person!"

Racing through the next yard, crossing a street, they pressed to the far side of the next block, then began to zigzag among the houses and avenues, finally plunging into a lot full of high weeds. There they stopped, reasonably certain they were not being followed. Fading steadily, sirens wailed in the distance.

"Shiro," Tomokato said, "For someone with such short legs, you run very fast. I thought I might have to carry you, but . . ."

Shiro sniffed. "You're all weighed down with that armor. And besides, you always underestimate me. I'm a very formidible little guy, Uncle-*san*."

Tomokato grunted grudging assent. "If I didn't think so, I'd never have chosen to train you."

Shiro looked a bit puzzled. "But we never *do* any training, Uncle. We just go places and have adventures."

"As far as the reader is concerned, yes," Tomokato agreed. "But what about all the time we spend getting *to* the adventures? Who knows how long we're in transit?

Perhaps we stop off at my secret volcano-crater training facility for months at a time."

Shiro snapped his fingers. "That would explain why I'm getting so much better at killing people," he said. Then his expression grew troubled again. "But why don't I remember any of it?"

"Same reason that I don't. But it would account for a lot of things, wouldn't—"

"On the other hand," a sere voice broke in above them, "some things aren't so easy to account for."

They looked up.

Hovering ten feet off the ground, dimly lit by a nearby streetlamp, was a pale-faced old woman in a hospital smock, red fires swirling in her eyes, teeth glinting faintly, the canines elongated and sharply pointed.

"Take vampires, for example," she went on, drifting slowly lower. "We're really quite strange. But in a nice sort of way, of course."

Tomokato reached for his crossbow. He realized he had left it back in the van. *What to do now?* he wondered, all the while staring up at those burning eyes.

"Perhaps the strangest thing about us is the fear we seem to inspire," she continued. "It's totally unjustified, you know. Hard to see how all those nasty legends even got started. We simply represent an alternate life-style. Or should I say alternate *after*life-style?" She put a hand over her mouth, tee-hee-heeing at her little vampire witticism.

Inexplicably, Tomokato laughed too. A pleasant haze had entered his thoughts; it occurred to him that nothing *had* to be done at all. To his dim amazement, the woman took on the form of a very attractive female cat, wearing nothing but a filmy floating kimono. The sight was very fetching indeed. He decided that perhaps he might just let her kiss him, once maybe, perhaps on the throat. And if she wanted to suck his blood and turn him into a walking corpse, he guessed he'd probably just have to let her do that too. . . .

Somewhere in the blurred depths of his mind, a voice was screaming to protest; not only because she was a vampire, but also because that kimono was positively indecent, and no *nice* vampire would ever wear something like that. Even so, when her paws settled on his shoulders, and somehow he could feel their softness even through his armor, all objections were swept aside, drowned out by a titanic medieval Japanese *Oh yeah!* which set his skull ringing, and he uttered a miaow of pure anticipation as her beautiful lips moved towards his throat. . . .

Long about sundown, Great Bl'syu, squinting at the tiny road map he had taken from the truckstop, decided that the time had come to strike off overland from Route 95.

A couple of pesky National Guard helicopters buzzed near, miniguns cooking. Dropping the road map, Bl'syu smacked the rotors from one and grabbed the Huey before it could fall, indeed, before the pilot could even take his finger off his minigun's trigger; turning the copter, Bl'syu sprayed the other with Gatling slugs. The second Huey shattered. Bl'syu crumpled the first, the whirlibird exploding in his hands.

How many more times am I going to have to go through this? he wondered. The Guard had been on his

case for the better part of the afternoon, although, if truth be told, most of them had displayed considerably less guts than those two chopper pilots.

He looked south along the highway. A huge armored convoy was parked at a safe distance. They had been following him for some time.

A cannon flamed. A 105-millimeter shell slammed home near his foot.

"If you pinheads shoot at me one more time," he bellowed, "I'll stamp your goddamn convoy flat, then resurrect you and force you to scrape your own bloody goosh out of those tanks, then make you eat it, and stick your fingers down your throat, and—"

"We get the picture," answered a speaker-amplified voice.

"And that's just for starters," Bl'syu replied.

"Well, look," said the Guard spokesman, after a pause, "you really do make a persuasive argument, so maybe we can compromise."

Bl'syu laughed. "Listen, buddy. The whole point of being a Real Old One is that you don't have to compromise. Dedication to excellence, that's what it's all about."

"Would you at least sign an affidavit that you won't inflict any further gratuitous harm on the people of Maine?"

"Define 'gratuitous,' " Bl'syu answered.

"Wouldn't it be better if we kept the wording vague? If we get too specific, it might render us both liable."

Having just been through an expensive lawsuit, Bl'syu considered the suggestion.

"Deal," he said at last.

Dismounting from his M-60, an officer hurried forward with the affidavit as the dusk thickened.

"Uncle, no!" Shiro cried, tossing away the empty Ingram. He had already unloaded the clip into the vampire; she had taken no notice at all.

He pulled the crucifix out of his kimono, but she wasn't looking at him; she was also too high up for him to touch her with it.

He unslung the holy-water squirter and tried to hose her down. The pump remained stubbornly unprimed.

Suddenly he recalled how he had primed squirt pistols back in his callow youth, before he discovered real guns—as the woman's face vanished behind Tomokato's neck, Shiro sucked on the muzzle, fetching a spurt of holy water almost instantly. Although he had never even considered the question, he was surprised to discover that the stuff tasted like Hawaiian Punch.

He turned the gun on the vampire.

Hissing, she twisted away from Tomokato, still hovering, clutching at the places where Shiro had squirted her, smoke billowing from her body.

Tomokato snapped out of the spell. He could feel blood trickling on his neck, from two spots that itched like the world's prize mosquito bites.

Screaming now, the old woman writhed horribly in front of him, seeming to float suspended on the tufted tips of the tall weeds. Acting on sheer impulse, he drew his sword and began slashing, but the blows passed through her body without inflicting any damage.

60

Crucifix, he thought.

It should've been dangling on his chest. The chain was still about his neck; he guessed the cross had swung over his shoulder when the van rolled. Reaching back, he whipped the crucifix round, fending the vampire off as she came for him once more.

Shiro started in with the holy water again. With a wail she dissolved back into a fog, which dissipated as a gust of wind came sweeping through the weeds.

"From now on, Shiro," Tomokato said, "whatever you do, don't look in their eyes."

"Sure thing, Unc," Shiro said. "But I'm not the one who got caught."

Tomokato said nothing, biting his lip. He scratched at the marks on his neck.

"Did she sink her teeth in, Uncle-*san*?"

"Not deep enough to infect me, I think. I'm not bleeding very much."

"Rats. I thought maybe we were going to do one of those cauterize-the-vampire-bite-with-the-crucifix things, real nasty."

Appalled, Tomokato demanded: "Shiro, how could you wish such on a thing on your own uncle?"

"It would be for your own good," the kitten replied. "Any enjoyment I felt would be purely incidental, and I'd do my best to stifle it."

"I'm not sure I believe you."

"I'm not sure either, Uncle. There's a war between good and evil raging in every little kitten's soul, or so they say; and sometimes it's hard even for me to tell which side's got the upper hand."

Peeved by this little routine, Tomokato answered: "You know, if you weren't so physically cute, you'd be very difficult to take."

"You think I don't know it?" Shiro replied.

"Where's your crucifix?" Tomokato asked.

Shiro held it up. "The old lady wasn't paying attention to me, so I couldn't scare her with it."

"Well, try to keep it in plain sight on your chest. And we'd better start chewing that garlic, too." Tomokato paused, listening for sirens. The vampire woman would bring the S.I.A. before long, or perhaps more of her own kind. "Let's get out of here, see if we can find the W.O.B.L.'s house."

"Do I *really* have to eat garlic, Uncle?" Shiro asked.

"It's good for you," Tomokato said, biting down on a clove he had removed from a pouch.

Yucch, thought Shiro as he took his first chew. As soon as Tomokato turned, the kitten spat the garlic out, replacing it with a wad of old used Dentyne he had been saving.

That's better.

3

Working their way back to Castle Rock Road, they reached the W.O.B.L.'s cross-festooned house after twenty minutes or so, going round to the back door. Before Tomokato could even knock, a little wizened white-haired black woman with a shawl about her shoulders ushered them swiftly in.

"About time you got here," she said, laying a copy of Thomas Sowell's *A Conflict of Visions* on a table near the door.

"How did you know we were coming?" Tomokato asked, as she led them into the living room.

"I *smelled* it," she replied, motioning them to sit down on the couch.

"You can do that too?" Shiro asked.

"As long as I'm in Bethlehem's Lot," she answered. "It's the Big Mac Burial Ground that does it."

"Big Mac Burial Ground?" Tomokato asked. "Does it have something to do with that McDonald's up on the hill?"

"No. The red man buried his dead here long before the white man arrived with his logic and technology and fast food. This was the land of the Big Mac Indians. The town was raised on the site of their tribal cemetery. But even *before* Bethlehem's Lot was built, the graveyard had been abandoned by the Big Macs."

"Did they leave to attack someone?" Shiro asked.

"You mean a Big Mac attack?" The W.O.B.L. looked as though she had just bitten into a worm. "Hit that little bastard, Tomokato."

Tomokato swatted the kitten.

The W.O.B.L. continued: "Anyway, the Big Macs gave up on the cemetary—" Suddenly she pointed a sharp old finger at Shiro. "And I don't want to hear anything about it being taken over by Quarter Pounders!"

"But how . . .?" Shiro gasped.

"I can *smell* jokes like that a mile off," she replied. "Tomokato?"

Tomokato swatted Shiro again.

"So as I said, the Big Macs stopped using the boneyard," the W.O.B.L. resumed, eyeing Shiro closely. His mouth stayed firmly shut. "They believed the Wendigo soured the earth—that the magic he put in the burial ground caused too much weird shit to happen."

Shiro's mouth began to open; Tomokato raised his hand, expecting yet another awful pun. But what came out was hardly better:

"What kind of weird shit?" Shiro asked.

"Watch your language!" Tomokato told him.

"Yeah, Shiro," said the W.O.B.L. "I'm too old to change my habits, but you don't have that excuse."

"Maybe not *that* excuse," said Shiro, "but I'm young, and I don't know any better."

Tomokato hit him yet again.

"So," the cat said, turning to the old woman, "what kind of weird sh—I mean, *things?*"

"Different people get weird different ways," the W.O.B.L. answered. "Some people levitate. Little blond girls start fires just by concentrating. A lot of folks become C.P.A.'s. Town's full of 'em. A few people get the whole package—that's what I call the Smelling."

"Will I be able to start fires?" Shiro asked, delighted by the prospect.

"Probabably, if you stay here long enough. You've got a smell on you like no one I've ever met. But you'll also probably turn into a C.P.A. I did." The old woman pointed to a framed diploma from Miskatonic University's accounting school.

"I don't mind," Shiro answered. "Just so long as I get to burn things up."

64

"We won't be staying long if I can help it," Tomokato said.

"Just as well," replied the W.O.B.L. "The firemen get enough work in this town as it is."

"Enough of this," Tomokato said. "How can I find Count Johnson?"

"His headquarters is in the basement under the Mc-Donald's."

"Why did he come to such an out-of-the-way town?" Tomokato asked.

"I only know what I've smelled," the W.O.B.L. answered. "But it goes back to the burial ground, again. It was in the summer of '57, I think—fellow named Savini buried his little girl's dead Saint Bernard Bubba in the one part of the cemetery that hasn't been built over, up on the north slope of the valley; that's the very sourest stretch—you get this lemony taste in your mouth when you just look at it.

"Anyway, this Savini fellow thought planting Bubba there would bring him back to life—and he was right, too. But Bubba came back *rabid*. Killed Savini's whole family, except for the little girl. She set Bubba on fire with the Smelling, and he ran out into the street and was hit by the mayor's Studebaker wagon, Justine.

"We thought that was the end of it; but Bubba's spirit had gone into Justine. Soon she was prowling around all on her own, running people down. We wanted to get rid of her, but the mayor wouldn't let us, and after a while she became sort of a fixture around here, like the town fool, you know, and—"

"What does all this have to do with Count Johnson?" Tomokato asked.

"I'm getting there, just you wait," said the W.O.B.L.

"Now one day in '68, Justine chased a rabbit into that McDonald's up on the hill. Killed a bunch of big shots from the McDonald's central office. From that day on, people started complaining about the hamburgers. Said they could see businessmen's faces staring at them from the special sauce on the Big Macs. Place was haunted as hell, so they closed it down.

"Was already too late, though. The McDonald's had become a psychic beacon. It was drawing all kinds of supernatural things to Bethlehem's Lot.

"Some of 'em weren't so bad, like this flock of Canada geese with stigmata that blew in here one fall. They were very upright and Christian; put up a new wing to the hospital before they headed off to see the pope when he was in Costa Rica. Worst trouble we had with 'em was when some little wiseass told 'em that their stigmata were in the wrong places. They simply refused to believe that Jesus didn't have wings and webbed feet.

"But most of the things that came were evil. Accordion players. The ghost of the guy that used to draw *Nancy* in the funny papers. Living-dead baby harp seals, clubbing folks for their pelts. And last of all, the S.I.A."

"The S.I.A.?" Tomokato asked. "What's supernatural about them? Besides their leader, that is?"

"Everything."

"I thought they were just a government intelligence agency."

"That's a cover story. They're not connected with the government at all. They were created by a paranoid horror novelist who didn't know he could bring things into existence just by thinking of them. They were the worst thing he could conceive of."

66

"Not much of an imagination, huh?" Shiro asked.

The W.O.B.L. went on: "Count Johnson stumbled onto them a while back, and decided they were the organization for him."

"But once again," Tomokato said, "what does he want with Bethlehem's Lot?"

"To test out Captain Fangs," she answered. "A virus that turns people into vampires. Starting a vampire cult takes too much time the regular way. You're real vulnerable until you've got your old-boy network built up. Captain Fangs is Johnson's shortcut. And so we woke up one morning to find the town surrounded by barbed wire, thinking Uncle Sam was quarantining us to try out some new strains of anthrax."

"I thought it was nerve gas."

"That's just what they said to calm us down—after we found out it *wasn't* anthrax."

"What about Justine?" Shiro asked. "Does she work for Johnson too?"

"All the evil things in town have joined him," she replied. "Even the harp seals. But they're off vacationing now."

"Where?"

"A Happyship Cruise."

"What about Ernie Bushmiller and the accordion players?"

"Even Johnson couldn't stomach them," the W.O.B.L. said. "He talked them into possessing a videotape of *Sgt. Pepper's Lonely Hearts Club Band,* then erased it."

"And the Smelling revealed all this to you?"

"Yes. But a lot of the stuff you smell isn't so important. In fact, most of it's pure psychic garbage, stuff no one would ever want to know, like what actually goes on in restaurant kitchens, or how long it's been since TV stars have changed their underwear. God, there's this guy on one of the nighttime soaps who's such a *pig,* and you'd never know it."

"It isn't John Forsythe, is it?" Shiro asked.

Before the W.O.B.L. could answer, there came the sound of approaching engines, then screeching brakes. Going to the door, she looked through a peephole as car doors thudded outside.

"The S.I.A.!" she said. "Bert and Ernie must've talked."

"Bert and Ernie?" Tomokato asked.

"The cops who told you about me."

"You in the house!" roared a bullhorn. "You're completely surrounded! Come out with your hands up!"

Tomokato went into the kitchen and peered out between shutters. A crowd of S.I.A. men with riot guns and M-16s poured into the back yard from the property beyond. He guessed others had taken up positions in the empty lots on either side of the house.

He went back out into the living room. The W.O.B.L. had a Winchester pump in her old black hands and two bandoliers of shotgun shells across her chest. Shiro was inspecting the Beretta double-action automatic she had given him.

"You have ten seconds!" said the voice on the bullhorn. "If you're not out here by then, we're coming in!"

The W.O.B.L. cracked open the front door and shouted: "Looking forward to it, buddy!" Then she moved back, pumping a shell into the Winchester's chamber. "Going to rush us," she chortled. "God, they're dumb. Shiro, watch the door to the kitchen!"

"You got it," the kitten replied. Crouching behind a huge stuffed chair, he jammed a clip into his pistol and pulled back the action.

"Four . . . three . . . two . . . one!" cried the man on the bullhorn. "Okay, you old bag, here we come!"

With that, an incredible hail of gunfire ripped into the house from all four sides. Tomokato and the others hurled themselves flat as the air filled with wood chips and splinters. Smashed to kindling, the front door hurtled off its hinges. The windows went white, then shattered in sparkling powder as the cross-warded shutters were buzz-sawed through. Vases exploded. Tattered shades leaped from lamps. Light bulbs popped. A small crystal chandelier burst in a brilliant glare of shining fragments. Red dust spurted from fireplace bricks; bullets spanged from andirons, tore ragged holes in the fireplace screen. Stuffing blossomed from riddled furniture. Throw pillows bounced and split, spewing bits of kapok. Pictures dropped from walls; glass face splintering, the W.O.B.L.'s diploma took five hits before it fell.

The barrage continued for a full half-minute. Then came a lull. Tomokato chanced a look through a gaping buckshot hole in the front wall.

Strewn across the lawn were the corpses of at least a dozen S.I.A. men.

Tomokato realized instantly what had happened. Charging in on the house, pouring a flood of pellets and copper-jacketed slugs through the structure, the agents on opposite sides had simply blown each other away. The cat smiled, remembering the agents offing each other back in the police station. Apparently they had a real problem with this in the S.I.A.

He liked fighting these guys.

But there were still plenty more left. Reluctantly ditching the I-don't-mind-if-I-hit-anything-just-so-long-as-my-gun's-going-bang approach, a second wave came storming in.

Shiro and the W.O.B.L. cut loose. Trailing glittering globules of blood, bodies jerked back from windows and doorways, Sam Peckinpahed from sight like unusually juicy shooting-gallery ducks. Tomokato took the spooks that managed to get inside. Soon after he sent a third severed head flying onto the front lawn, the man with the bullhorn called a cease-fire.

"All right!" he cried. "I'm tired of fooling around with you people! Either you surrender, or we send in the vampires!"

"I thought there weren't any vampires!" cried the W.O.B.L., reloading her shotgun.

"Duh . . ." came the answer.

"We're waiting," she prodded.

"We just trucked 'em in for tonight!" the S.I.A. man answered at last. "It's a one-time thing!"

"Right!" shouted the W.O.B.L. She turned to Tomokato. "Think we should make a break for it? We've killed so many of them."

"I can still see quite a few out there," Tomokato said, looking through a bullet hole.

"You could deflect their slugs. We could follow you."

"And if some came up behind us?" Tomokato asked. "Any chance you could set fire to them all?"

"With the Smelling? Nope. I had a stroke a couple years back, and now all I can do is set fire to my own head."

"Not very useful."

"You might be surprised," the W.O.B.L. said. "The neighborhood kids love it. Pay to see it, in fact. Doesn't quite offset the medical bills, but there's nothing like seeing a smile of wonder on a child's face."

"Sounds great," Shiro said.

She patted him affectionately between the ears, then told Tomokato: "If I were you, I'd start smearing garlic on your sword blade. Won't kill the bloodsuckers, but they're not so cocky when they're in pieces." To illustrate the technique, she produced a wicked-looking machete and started rubbing it down with a clove.

Tomokato followed her example with his *katana*. Shiro began removing shells from his last clip and smearing the slugs.

"Do you have your crucifix, Shiro?" Tomokato asked, glancing over at him.

"One of 'em shot it off, Uncle," Shiro answered. "I'll be all right."

"Take mine," Tomokato said, tossing it. As it sailed through the air, he glanced past Shiro. Green fog was sluicing over the sill of a window behind the kitten.

Seeing his uncle's expression, Shiro twisted to look. The crucifix bounced from his grasp. A face coalesced out of the fog and bit his other paw. The Beretta dropped. Tomokato rushed forward.

"Watch your back!" the W.O.B.L. shouted.

Before the cat could turn, two cold putrid hands locked over his face. "Mine!" a voice whispered.

There was a well-chewed clove in Tomokato's mouth. He spat it onto the palm on his muzzle. Acrid smoke spurted into his nostrils. The hands snapped back.

Machete swinging, the W.O.B.L. rushed in from the side. There was a *thunk,* and the vampire howled. Tomokato continued toward Shiro.

The kitten was firmly in the grip of the pale middle-aged man who had solidified out of the fog. Laughing uproariously, the vampire leaped backwards out of the window with him.

"Shiro!" Tomokato cried, racing up to the opening.

Dozens of fanged faces jeered at him. Taloned hands reached out; the undead swarmed to block his passage. He would have to slice his way through a solid wall of them just to get out. And there was no time for that kind of butchery—he could hear more vampires coming up behind him.

He gave back from the window, whirling, striking left and right with his garlic-smeared blade. Undead flesh parted, spewing forth the reeking artery-gravy of the damned.

Bright orange, Tomokato thought. *Hmmm.*

The vampires were pouring in through every opening in the walls, fully materialized where the entrance allowed, as a fog or torrent of rats where the hole was smaller. Between strokes, Tomokato looked for the W.O.B.L., but there was no sign of her.

He had to get out. The S.I.A. might still be waiting to

72

blast him to shreds; but he preferred bullets to being vampirized. And there was always the chance that the S.I.A. had withdrawn now that the vampires had stormed the house.

Slashing, smiting, he fled into the kitchen, leaving a grisly wake of dismembered but still-writhing blood-suckers. Carving his way to the back door, he burst out onto the patio.

Most of the vampires were already inside the house. He had no trouble laying out the few in his path as he rushed around to the front yard.

Spooks were packing Shiro and the W.O.B.L. into a van. The vehicle took off even before the agents slammed its rear doors.

There were other vans by the curb. All except one pulled out after the first. He had been right about the S.I.A. withdrawing.

Most of them, at any rate—a small crowd still stood between him and the remaining van. They spotted him pelting towards them and started up with their M-16s.

His sword flashed in a flawless qaudruple butterfly stroke; the bullets went spanging back, and for the third time he had the satisfaction of seeing S.I.A. agents stretched out stone cold dead by S.I.A. bullets.

Vampires were pouring back out of the house now, but he reached the van with seconds to spare. The keys were in the ignition. Firing her up, he roared down the street. He could see the taillights of the other vans, quite distant now, heading towards the center of town.

And the McDonald's on the hill, he guessed.

He floored the pedal, racing to catch up. But the van

began to lose power, coughing and sputtering; some of the deflected bullets had sprayed the car, and now he was paying the price. Another hundred yards, and the van conked.

Getting out, he continued on foot.

4

Shiro and the W.O.B.L. were brought before Count Johnson in a huge cellar that had been carved out under the McDonald's. Cold and damp and stinking of death, it was strewn with open coffins and thronged with vampires.

"One prisoner, two!" said Johnson in a thick Bela Lugosi accent. More than a little he resembled the Count from *Sesame Street.* Shiro doubted he would ever be able to enjoy the show again.

"It's a giant muppet," said the W.O.B.L. "I bet Jim Henson's not happy about this at all."

Johnson nodded. "He tried to sue me for trademark infringement. It came down to whether or not I predated his character. But I just happened to have this portrait by Holbein—"

"Hans Holbein painted your portrait?"

"No. It was a picture of Thomas More. Frankly, I don't know why Henson dropped the suit." Johnson laughed. "I was born in Perth Amboy, New Jersey, in 1952, though I can't prove it. At first I modeled myself on Rowlf, from *The Jimmy Dean Show,* you know? But I couldn't master the piano, so I took up vampirism instead." He smiled. "So. You are the W.O.B.L."

"For now," she replied. "The position alternates between me and Pearl Bailey."

"Does she have supernatural powers too?"

"No, but I can't sing, so it all evens itself out. I never get invited to the White House."

"Could you introduce me to her?"

"Sure. Just let me loose, and I'll go phone her."

"Of course," Johnson answered. "Perhaps later." He pointed to Shiro. "Who is this?"

Struggling in his captor's arms, Shiro lifted his chin haughtily. "My name's Miaowara Shiro," he gritted.

"Did you come here with your uncle, by any chance?" Johnson asked, amused.

"Yes. And he's going to kill you!"

"End my career, you mean," Johnson answered. "I've been dead for quite some time, you know. But let me tell you, little one, it's been tried. I drained my first vampire hunter back in Nineveh, and I've drained a lot more since then. One hundred. Two hundred. Three hundred . . ."

"Nineveh?" asked the W.O.B.L. "Didn't you say you were born in '52, in Perth Amboy?"

Johnson shrugged. "I told you I couldn't prove it. I guess there's a reason why. But anyway, what about young Shiro there? Apparently fresh out the litter. Yet if one wanted to be strictly logical about this, he's about five hundred years old. Frankly, I'm just as confused as you are. But I'm not about to let that stop me."

"Why are you such a son of a bitch?"

"Depends on which theory of evil you wish to accept. If you're a Manichaean, a cosmic dualist who believes

75

that matter is the principle of evil, you might say that I was seduced by the physical universe—that I became obsessed with corporeal survival to the extent that I felt compelled to embrace living death."

"But I'm an Augustinian!" said the W.O.B.L. defiantly.

"Then you'd say that my evil arose from my own will, which, being contingent, was always drawing back towards the nothingness from which the Man Upstairs created it."

"What about from an Existentialist perspective?" Shiro asked.

"Perhaps I just wanted to keep on existing. And existing. And existing."

"But what's *your* opinion?" the W.O.B.L. demanded.

"Me, I think philosophy's crap," Count Johnson replied. "I like blood."

"What shall we do with them, My Lord?" the vampire holding Shiro asked.

"Suck their veins dry, of course," the Count answered. "One pint, two pints, three pints, four . . ."

"Now, My Lord?"

"No. Let's string them from the ceiling, let them think about it for a while. Now how many ropes will we need? One? Two?"

"Two, My Lord, only two."

"Very well, Hasbrouck. Hoist them up—let all that lovely juice go straight to their jugulars."

Johnson's underlings hastened to obey. Before long Shiro and the old woman were dangling slaughterhouse style above the floor, a host of vampires staring hungrily at them, licking their lips.

"I think this just might be the end of the road," said the W.O.B.L.

"Don't worry," Shiro answered. "I'm here."

Nearing the base of the hill on which the McDonald's stood, Tomokato scaled the gate of a large automobile junkyard as a fleet of security vans approached. They passed by, but he decided not to climb back outside, guessing that a gravel road leading in among the wrecks might be a shortcut to the hill.

As he set off, he noticed moonlight gleaming on something hanging from the rearview mirror of an ancient white Impala with its windshield knocked out. Going closer, he saw that the object, rotating slowly in the breeze, was a small cross made of some shiny metal. He unwrapped the beads from the mirror, then hung the cross around his neck.

He was about forty feet farther in when he heard a sniffing noise. Pausing by the office, he looked back at the gate. Like the rest of the fence, it was chain link backed by sheets of corrugated steel; he could not see what was on the other side, but the shadow of something massive played along the ground beneath, moving back and forth, as though some huge animal were shifting its weight from paw to paw.

There was a low growl, and the gate crashed down. Grinning hellishly, headlight to headlight, Justine stalked in over it.

Tomokato thought of fleeing. He looked about, catching sight of a car compactor; that gave him an idea.

A tree overarched the road, and the ground about him was littered with sticks. Picking one up, he waited.

Justine paused momentarily, as though she suspected something, then resumed her advance at an even pace, gravel cracking beneath her tires, CATLOVER blazoned on her license plate. Tomokato allowed her to get very close before playing his hand.

"Look, girl!" he cried, waving the stick.

Justine's grilled maw dropped wide open, and she began to pant excitedly, sitting up.

"Stick, Justine, stick!" Tomokato shouted, and tossed it into the car crusher.

Eagerly Justine rushed after it, bounding into the compactor. Dashing up to the control board, Tomokato threw the switch.

Evidently there wasn't much space inside the crusher —Justine began to howl as soon as the hydraulics kicked on. A terrible metallic screeching began; Tomokato guessed it was her flanks scraping the walls as she tried to struggle back out. Her howls grew more desperate, ringing with pain and betrayal.

Tomokato stepped back from the control. The howling reached a tremendous crescendo; then there was only the sound of metal crumpling. With a final gruesome spurt of oil, moon-silvered above the top of the crusher, the compression was complete.

"*Sayonara,* Justine," Tomokato said, and continued on his way.

He felt a pang of remorse at having taken advantage of her that way; she had gone so merrily to her destruction. But his determination to fulfill his duty soon pushed all self-reproach from his mind. He could allow nothing to stay him from his path—not even guilt over having compacted a doggy-possessed '57 Studebaker.

Reaching the edge of the junkyard, he clambered over the fence, finding himself at the foot of the hill. That side of the slope was mostly wooded; as he made his way upwards, he sharpened branches into stakes with his sword, slid them into his belt, then smeared fresh garlic on the blade.

At the top he halted beside the overgrown hedge that surrounded the McDonald's lot, and looked out through a gap at the rundown fast-food palace. Three S.I.A. men stood before the entrance, holding rifles.

"I'm telling you," Tomokato heard one say, "he used to make all these really *lousy* horror movies."

"Oh, for Christ's sake," another shot back, "He's been nominated for Academy Awards. He was in *Reds*!"

"Only good thing in it," the third man put in.

"So what if he's a big deal now?" the first man said. "He *wasn't* back in the early sixties. There's this flick where he's kissing this girl, but she's been dead a long time, only he doesn't know it, and her face just melts all over his mouth."

"Go on," said the second man.

"May I drop down dead if it isn't true," said the first man, an instant before he struck the concrete walk with one of Tomokato's *shuriken* in his chest.

The cat broke cover, running towards them.

"Stand back!" he cried. "I'm a doctor!"

Stunned, the remaining two complied. Tomokato knelt and examined the corpse. Presently one of the spooks tapped him on the shoulder.

"Just what kind of doctor are you?" the man asked.

Tomokato straightened. "Brain surgeon," he said, and slashed them both through the foreheads with a single

79

stroke. Blood rivered down their faces, black in the moonlight. They crumpled.

They'll never even know he was right about Jack Nicholson, Tomokato thought. He strode up to the door and went inside.

The air was thick with a sweetish, rotten smell; long strands of cobweb hung from the ceiling, whose acoustic tiles were still dotted with ancient cheeseburgers, flipped up there by sixties hooligans, no doubt. Old wrappers littered the floor, along with small animals that had crawled in to die.

Off to the left was a large, shapeless, phosphorescent mass. After a few moments Tomokato distinguished limbs and heads; it was a tangle of ectoplasmic figures. All appeared to be middle-aged men—the ghosts of the guys from the McDonald's central office, or so he guessed.

Slowly they began to slither out from under each other. Rising to their feet, they stared at him with sunken eyes.

"What do you want?" one whispered. "Why did you kill the guards?"

"Why do you think?" Tomokato asked.

"Have you come for Count Johnson?"

Tomokato nodded.

"Good," the ghost answered. "We haven't had a day's peace since he showed up. First the S.I.A. dug out that big cellar. Then they brought in the other vampires. Then it was roller-disco parties, wet T-shirt contests, bingo—have you ever been around vampires playing bingo?"

Tomokato shook his head.

80

"Wipe the mother out," the ghost went on. "Him and his whole damn crowd." He pointed an ectoplasmic finger. "See that doorway at the back of the restaurant? That leads to their lair."

Tomokato bowed. "Thank you, honorable deceased person." Leaping over the service counter, he went through the door.

Emerging from the forest onto Castle Rock Road, Great Bl'syu marched toward the main gate of Bethlehem's Lot. A bunch of little fellows in sunglasses had assembled behind the fence, the crowd bristling with assault rifles and LAWS tubes; searchlights glared from the watchtowers.

"Halt!" a man cried. "Halt in the name of the S.I.A.!"

"S.I.A.?" Bl'syu thundered, not stopping.

"Sinister Intelligence Agency!" came the response.

That gave Bl'syu pause. "You mean, like the SD or the OGPU?"

"Well no, nothing like that," the agent replied, sounding a little embarrassed. "The man who created us really didn't have much of an imagination, and—"

"Yeah, I know," Bl'syu answered, resuming his advance. "Well, I'm the cure for that!"

The spooks cringed back. "Are *you* from the OGPU?"

"Nah. Not even old H.P. was *that* creative. But I'll do, buddy. I'll do." By then, Bl'syu was nearly at the gates.

Panicked, the S.I.A. began to fire. Bullets tore chunks of hardened sea-bottom crud from Bl'syu's scales before bouncing off.

"Come on," he roared, treading the gates underfoot. "Try the LAWS rockets."

81

The spooks were retreating frenziedly, but a couple paused and shouldered launchers. Rockets screamed towards Bl'syu's face.

"BOO!" he bellowed.

Totally emasculated, the rockets dropped to the road, bouncing soggily on the surface, mushy as week-old bananas.

Two APCs rolled around a corner up ahead, forming a roadblock. Plucking up their courage, the agents gathered behind them to make a stand.

"Okay, if you want it that way!" Bl'syu roared.

But he never got the chance to show them just how foolishly they were behaving. Out of the sky blazed a huge elongated object, trailing sparks and smoke; it landed atop the roadblock in a mushrooming burst of fire, obliterating the APCs and the spooks.

Bl'syu moved closer, squinting at the wreckage. It was difficult to tell with all the damage, but the visitor from space seemed to be one of the eighteen-wheelers he had kicked, back at the truckstop.

Before long the other came plummeting down too, crashing a hundred yards away. It was still alive when he reached it; seeing him, it tried to crawl off.

"There, there," he said gently.

And kicked it back into orbit.

Tomokato descended a circular staircase hewn from solid rock; green-flaring tapers were mounted at intervals on the curving wall. At the bottom a corridor led back beneath the restaurant, toward an oaken door covered with iron studs.

82

In front of the entrance, a vampire in a chef's outfit was ensconced in a wicker chair, reading a blood-pudding cookbook. Tomokato hastily thrust his cross down inside his breastplate, and spritzed his mouth and paws with Binaca to cover the garlic smell.

The chef looked up from his book.

"I was told to report to the Count," Tomokato announced.

"Just drafted, eh?" the chef asked, rising. "Let me see your fangs."

Tomokato bared his canines. Or were they his felines?

Well, felines *or* canines, the chef never inspected them. His eyes went directly to the stakes at Tomokato's belt.

Tomokato, you fool, the cat thought, pushing the man's eyes right back at him.

"What are those for?" the chef demanded.

"This," Tomokato replied, whipped one out, and thrust it up under the chef's breastbone.

"That's what I thought," the chef gasped, and sagged back down into the wicker chair, a huge dark blot widening around the stake.

Tomokato slid a second stake up one mailed sleeve; discarding the rest, he went to the door and eased it open.

Beyond was a huge cellar, in which a great conclave of Johnson's vampiric followers had gathered. Tomokato guessed there were more than a hundred of the undead, listening to a speech in heavily accented English; Tomokato could not see the speaker, but thought he must be the Count.

On the far side of the crowd, two figures were suspended head-down from the ceiling. One was Shiro, the other the W.O.B.L. Obviously they had not yet been "drafted."

Bert and Ernie, on the other hand, hadn't been so lucky. Standing at the back of the crowd, the two cops turned as the door creaked slowly shut.

Tomokato moved nonchalantly towards them, showing his fangs. Apparently satisfied by the sight of them, Bert and Ernie turned back around.

Tomokato came up behind them. He knew he could slash his way to the front of the assembly, maybe even kill Johnson with the stake. But a horde of vampires would still remain. And the garlic on his sword blade would certainly be worn off by then. There would be only the cross to protect him. At best, he would be backed into a corner, holding off the undead until he dropped from exhaustion. He doubted he would even have time to free Shiro and the W.O.B.L.

Bert and Ernie looked at him again. He smiled, revealing his fangs a second time. That seemed to satisfy them once more; but plainly he had aroused some suspicion. Had they caught a whiff of garlic? He kept the stuff well wrapped in its pouch, and it seemed unlikely they were smelling the juice on his sword—the sheath was very tight. Even so, he sprayed pouch, hilt, and scabbard with Binaca, shoving the small bottle back into hiding an instant before the cops gave him yet another once-over. He gave them yet another smile. They sniffed mightily, glanced at each other as if they couldn't quite make up their minds, then turned.

Tomokato began to listen to Johnson's speech.

"The virus has been fully tested," the Count was saying. "One time. Two times. Three times. Four . . ."

Tomokato heard a faint roll of thunder.

"We'll spray the whole town tonight," Johnson continued. "And there are enough of us now to make sure even the resistant townsfolk are infected; those who do not join us tomorrow will be ours the night after. And then we shall begin our march to victory. Every state in the union will soon fall to us . . ."

He counted rapidly to fifty; thunder rolled again.

"Then, every nation on earth . . ."

He counted his way through that list too; more thunder.

"And when we're done, the whole Earth will experience Better Living Death Through Vampirism. Our cult will be the means by which the black magic of logic and technology and dental hygiene will be expunged once and for all. Humanity will become a race of immortal twelve-year-olds. We'll read nothing but *Famous Monsters of Filmland,* watch nothing but George Romero movies—none of that tasteful Val Lewton crap for us! Everyone will be blessedly free of the poison of rationality. We'll look at the moon and tell ourselves that big invisible guys are rolling it across the sky! We'll watch TV and think that there are actually little people inside! We'll eat our own mudpies, have as many imaginary playmates as we like, and fly when we flap our arms!"

"You sound like a villain in a Stephen King novel, My Lord!" a voice from the crowd cried rapturously.

"Actually, I sound more like one of his *heroes,* but so what?"

85

"Where will we get blood when everyone's a vampire, My Lord?" another voice called.

"We'll drink tomato juice and *pretend* it's blood!" Johnson answered. "After all, we don't have to be rational about it!"

"But why don't we just drink tomato juice now? It would save us a lot of trouble."

"Because we're vampires, and we're already irrational!"

"Oh Master!" the second follower cried adoringly, and the rest of the crowd roared approval of the vampire lord's argument.

Having listened to quite enough of this, Tomokato returned to pondering his predicament. But wrack his brain as he might, he arrived at no solutions.

Up at the far end of the cellar, the Count Johnson show dragged on and on; by the time Tomokato began paying attention again, the Count had gotten around to characterizing the opposition.

"Look at these two hanging here!" he cried, obviously meaning Shiro and the W.O.B.L. "Consider this so-called kitten! Look at the little fiend! Look at the subhuman features, the sheer bestiality of that fur! Do you know what the little animal was using on us? A holy-water gun! *Full auto!* Thus the living warp their children, giving them such toys!! Behold, the devilish instrument!"

Tomokato could not see, but guessed Johnson was holding the Uzi up.

"And do you know what his *uncle* was using to persecute us? Have you ever heard of an assault cross-bow?"

A groan of horror went through the crowd.

The crossbow, Tomokato thought. *Yes!*

Very politely, he began working his way forward. If he could just lay his paws on the weapon . . .

He was about halfway through when he heard Bert's voice behind him. The vampire cops were following.

"Listen, Ernie," Bert was saying, apparently believing that Tomokato couldn't hear him over the harmonica medley that Johnson had lapsed into. "I think *all* cats have fangs, not just dead ones."

"Aaah, I don't know, Bert," Ernie replied. "My cat Josh had fangs when *he* died . . ."

"Your reasoning's fallacious, and you know it, Ernie. That's an unwarranted generalization."

"So I'm not so hot on induction. So what? How does *anyone* know when they've got enough of a sample to generalize? Even Francis Bacon never managed to come up with a quantified inductive calculus, and I'm just a vampire anyway, and I'm supposed to be illogical, so why don't you just get off my case?"

"But Ernie," Bert persisted, "I'm sure I smelled garlic on him. And you know damn well my nose works better than yours."

"What a talent. I'm *so* impressed . . ."

Tomokato neared the front of the crowd. Shiro and the W.O.B.L. had spotted him already; despair was written on their faces. Clearly they thought he was one of the undead. But they would learn the truth soon enough.

Johnson's medley ended with a rousing rendition of "Turkey in the Straw."

"And so," he cried after a round of applause, "To celebrate our coming triumph, let us now drain the kitten and the hog. After them, the world—"

87

"Count Johnson!" Bert cried. *"The cat!"*

Sweeping his sword free, Tomokato pivoted. The keening edge bit Bert's hands off before the vampire could grab him.

Other bloodsuckers tried their luck. Whirling low, Tomokato cut their legs out from under them. Vaulting a crumpling meter maid, he burst out of the crowd.

"Way to go, Uncle-*san*!" Shiro shrieked with amazed delight.

But Count Johnson was almost on the kitten, with an upraised blade.

Pulling the stake out of his sleeve, Tomokato hurled it southpaw. Johnson twisted; the stake missed his heart, but sank in deep with a dull *thwuk.*

"Get him!" he cried, grabbing at the stake with both hands, blood gushing over his fingers. He scrambled off into the crowd.

Tomokato looked for the crossbow. It was leaning against a wall. Dashing forward, dropping his sword, he snatched the weapon and cocked it.

Johnson's followers surged near. Spinning, Tomokato sprayed out a burst of quarrels. Five vampires toppled, bolts buried to the fletching.

Cries of fear rose from the rest. Tomokato waded forward, slaughtering them. Back washed the tide of the walking dead. But even the Barnett's huge clip was not inexhaustible.

The second drum was taped to the side of the stock. Tomokato pulled it loose and slid it home. Seeing him reloading, the vampires charged once more, snarling.

Raking back the action, he unleashed a fresh and furious cardiac attack. The foremost *nosferatu* dropped clawing at his feet, the head of a quarrel protruding through its back; the rest didn't even get close. When the second drum emptied, the whole throng was down.

"Tomokato!" cried Count Johnson.

The cat whirled to see the vampire king still very much undead, holding a knife to Shiro's throat. Johnson was now wearing a heavy flak jacket.

Tomokato dropped the crossbow and advanced towards him slowly, over the fallen vampires. He drew the cross out of his breastplate. Johnson flinched at the sight of it, but forced a smile to his greenish lips.

"One step closer, and he's dead!" the Count said.

"Don't worry about me, Uncle!" Shiro cried. "He'll kill me no matter what!"

Tomokato felt a tremendous flush of pride at his nephew's bravery. Still, he halted.

"Do your duty, Uncle!" Shiro pleaded in anguish. "I'm dead anyway!"

"Not necessarily," Johnson said. "I'll make a bargain with you, Tomokato. I'd rather have you than him anyway, for the moment at least—I'm willing to save him till we're done."

"What are you proposing?" Tomokato asked.

"A test. Your faith against mine."

Tomokato was puzzled. "My faith?"

"Your Christianity. I'll step back from your nephew, drop the knife. You drop the cross and meet me. Faith to faith."

"Run that past me again."

"Okay, it's like this," Johnson answered. "That cross is just a symbol. Its power derives solely from your belief. But if you really believe, you don't need it, right?"

Tomokato considered this. "Very well. Get away from him."

"You swear you'll drop the cross?"

"I swear."

"Uncle!" Shiro cried, horrified.

Grinning, fangs gleaming, Count Johnson stepped back several yards.

"Farther," Tomokato said.

Johnson obliged, letting the knife fall. "Now—fulfill your part of the bargain."

Tomokato ran forward, placing himself between Shiro and the vampire.

"Drop the cross," Johnson said. "You gave your word."

"Under duress," Tomokato said, advancing. "I'm not bound by it."

"Well then," said Johnson, moving to meet him, "I have you now. That cross won't help you. As I said, it's just a symbol. Your faith in *Him* gives it its power. But if you won't face me without it, you obviously don't have any faith, do you? And that cross becomes a mere trinket, doesn't it?"

They halted, facing each other, the vampire towering above Tomokato, gloating down at him, the cat averting his eyes from the full intensity of Johnson's flaming stare, holding the cross practically in the nosferatu's face.

"Here," Johnson said. "Let me show you."

He snatched at the cross with a taloned hand.

Tomokato held on tightly. "There's something I neglected to mention," he said. "I'm a Buddhist, not a Christian. And all I know is that you were trying to get me to drop this."

Smoke burst through Johnson's fingers. He recoiled with a shriek.

Following, Tomokato pressed the cross into Johnson's forehead. There it stuck in sizzling flesh, fuming as though it were a hot brand. Johnson went to his knees, trying to pull it free, burning his hands, trying again . . .

Tomokato ran to the nearest corpse. Yanking a quarrel out, he rushed back to Johnson.

The vampire gaped up at him, hands dropping to his sides. Pouring out black tears, his eyes were pinched slits of agony. The cross had eaten through his forehead; only the very bottom was still visible, the rest sunken in his brain. The beads hung down across Johnson's face, dangling from his chin.

"Only a symbol, eh?" Tomokato asked.

Johnson shrugged. "Hell, I was raised Methodist."

"Enough theology," Tomokato grunted, and plunged the quarrel straight down beside Johnson's neck, inside the collar of the flak jacket; slamming it all the way in with the heel of his paw, he pierced the vampire's heart from above.

Gasping, Johnson sagged forward. A long, bright orange spurt arced out of the flak jacket. Tomokato could hardly believe how far it squirted.

"Just splendid!" Shiro cried. "Forty feet at least! Just like in those movies!"

Sprawled on the earthen floor, Johnson began a very garish, smelly, and convincing M. Valdemar imitation, great dark puddles widening around him as he decomposed into a mass of detestable putrescence.

"Well, now that that's over with," the W.O.B.L. said, "how about getting me down?"

The ropes were attached to wall-set cleats. Tomokato gently lowered the W.O.B.L. and Shiro, then untied them. Rising, the old woman looked at Johnson's corpse.

"How the mighty have fallen," she said. "And stunk up the place." She pulled out a can of Glade. Spraying, she turned to the cat: "You sure played the Count for a fool. Thank God you are a Buddhist."

"Johnson pretended he wasn't scared of you, Uncle," Shiro said. "He told us he'd killed hundreds of vampire hunters. But he didn't frighten me one bit. I knew you'd save us."

"Even when you saw me in the crowd?" Tomokato asked. "You didn't think I'd been turned into one of *them?*"

"Nope, not even then. What if I *hadn't* looked scared? The vampires would've known you were still alive."

"I see."

"It takes more than vampires to worry me," Shiro continued. "When it comes right down to it, they turned out to be no big deal. Too old-fashioned, just like I always thought. No problem for a couple of studs like us. After all, we tangled with Great K'Chu and lived to tell of it."

"Great K'Chu?" asked the W.O.B.L.

"One of the Real Old Ones," Tomokato explained.

"And Uncle-*san* did him in, no sweat," Shiro said.

"What was this K'Chu like?" the W.O.B.L. asked.

As if in response, there came a tremendous grating;

the concrete ceiling moved to one side as though it were some kind of titanic sliding panel, the talons of a huge scaled claw hooked beneath it. Kneeling beside the pit he had opened, Great Bl'syu glared down at Tomokato.

"Like that," Tomokato told the W.O.B.L.

"You dirty cat!" the Real Old One thundered, tentacles squirming and knotting. "You killed my brother!"

He reached for Tomokato.

The cat slashed at the clawed hand. The blow bounced off. Bl'syu had nothing to fear from garlic juice, it seemed. Tomokato dodged away.

Shiro rushed to his side. "Look what I have, Uncle!"

He was holding the talisman that had killed K'Chu.

"Where'd you get—?" Tomokato began, as the claw lunged again.

"Stole it, Uncle!" Shiro broke in, striking with all his might. But the talisman did no more damage than Tomokato's sword. Leaping backwards, the kitten barely saved himself.

"Make for the door!" the W.O.B.L. shouted.

Hurdling corpses and coffins, they raced for the other end of the cellar. But with a deafening laugh, Bl'syu jumped down in front of them, cutting them off.

Tomokato snatched the talisman from Shiro and hurled it at the monster. Bl'syu caught it and popped it in his mouth.

"It was my *brother* that couldn't take Hubbard relics," Bl'syu chortled. "Me, I'm a Scientologist." He gulped the talisman down. "Ahh."

Tomokato brandished his cross at him.

"I'm not a vampire," Bl'syu said. "If you want to take

94

me out with Christian stuff, you have to shoot St. Athanasius straight through my head." He thought a moment. *"And* St. Anselm."

Tomokato lowered the cross, sensing that Bl'syu was telling the truth.

"Now then," Bl'syu rumbled, "to business."

Two beams of yellow-green energy hummed from his eyes, enveloping Tomokato and his companions, sinking into their flesh.

"Boy, I hate to do that," Bl'syu added, rubbing his temples.

Tomokato tried to move, but found he was frozen in place. Shiro and the W.O.B.L. seemed paralyzed too.

Bl'syu reached for them with both hands. "I'm going to show you what the universe is *really* like, guys," he said, reaching for them with both hands. "Prepare yourselves for the Ultimate Downer."

"Shiro!" shouted the W.O.B.L. "Use the Smelling! Burn him!"

"I don't know how!" Shiro replied as the claws encircled them.

"Just think of him on fire! Concentrate!"

"I've waited so long for this!" Bl'syu gloated, fingers closing slowly.

Shiro let out a shriek.

Bl'syu's hands jerked back, igniting with a *whoosh.* The Real Old One roared with pain.

Tomokato felt the paralysis drop from his limbs. He looked at Shiro.

The kitten's young face was contorted in a mask of awesome concentration. Suddenly his whole body seemed to waver, rippling behind a violent convection. Tomokato felt a pulse of fierce heat, and looking back towards Bl'syu, saw the demon-god behind the ripples now, only the convection was fifty feet high, sixty, seventy; there was a sound like a thunderclap, and with a tremendous red flare, Bl'syu's whole body went up, and he was bashed back out of the pit as though uppercut by a giant invisible fist.

"Good one!" the W.O.B.L. cried.

An inhuman torch, Bl'syu struggled back to his feet.

"You know," he cried, "things like this really burn me up!"

Shrieking, Shiro gave him another pulse, blasting the flesh from Bl'syu's bones with such ferocious speed that the monstrous skeleton did not even have time to rock backwards in the conflagration.

For a moment the skeleton continued upright, feeling about itself as if to ascertain that yes, indeed, it was completely denuded. Then, with a snap of its fingers, it keeled over, clattering to the ground.

"Maybe the universe isn't such a bad place after all," the W.O.B.L. said.

Tomokato turned to Shiro. The kitten grinned at him.

"Was that nifty or what?" Shiro asked.

"You should be ashamed of yourself," Tomokato answered.

"For what?"

"Stealing that talisman."

"I thought it might come in handy."

"But it didn't, did it? And even if it *had* worked, it *still* would've been wrong to take it."

Shiro looked floorward. "Oh, I suppose so, Uncle."

They went up from the cellar. Beyond Bl'syu's skeleton, a number of flattened S.I.A. security vans could be seen in the McDonald's lot, leaking a tomato-pasty substance that might have been squished spook.

"They must've made a last stand here," the W.O.B.L. said. "Bl'syu killed every agent in town, I can smell it."

"Good," Tomokato said. "But what should we do about Captain Fangs? Do you know where it's being stored?"

"Back down in the basement," she replied. "Don't worry about it. I'll notify the proper authorities."

"Can the proper authorities be trusted with it?"

"Of course not. But I sure as hell don't want it sitting in *my* refrigerator."

"You know," Shiro said, "This must be an okay town when you don't have to worry about vampires and spies. I wouldn't mind living here—it's sure nice having all these powers."

"I could put you up," said the W.O.B.L. "Things haven't been the same since my cat died."

"Sorry, but Shiro's coming with me," Tomokato said. "Believe me, it's for your own good."

The W.O.B.L. sighed. "All right," she said. "But would you do us all a favor before you leave?"

"What?"

"Would you let him torch the McDonald's and end this psychic beacon business once and for all? Who knows what sort of weird sh—I mean, weird stuff is going to descend on this town next? With our luck, it'll probably be the Ray Conniff singers."

Tomokato considered her request, finally deciding he might just as well let the kitten have a last fling with his powers. It was, after all, in a good cause.

"Go to it, Shiro," he said.

And Shiro complied with the pyromaniacal relish of five year olds everywhere.

Samurai Cat and the Temple of Dog Doom

Tomokato's quest for vengeance next took him to India, in pursuit of the notorious Thuggee guru Alberth Shankar. Once head of the Lucknow Teacher's Union, Shankar had, upon losing his position, gravitated to the Cult of Collie, the Indian goddess of death, blood, and bad breath in dogs; primarily to show his solidarity with the forces of evil (and also, if truth be told, to give Tomokato a reason to kill him), Shankar personally commanded a contingent of stranglers during the attack on Nobunaga.

Tomokato and Shiro began their search in Lucknow in the spring of 1935. This date is problematic for some historians, who hold that the practice of Thuggee had been eradicated by Sleeman nearly a hundred years before, and that the account which follows must be pure fiction, perhaps another demented dream sequence. But these very same bozos are physically quite unattractive, with big fat butts, so we can safely

99

disregard their quibbles, and proceed with our narrative.

>—from *Cat Out of Hell, A Biography of Miaowara Tomokato* by William Shirer and A.J.P. Godzilla

1

The air was turgid with moisture; the shafts of sunlight that broke through the foliage of the towering trees were burning spears. The jungle birds, which had been quite raucous earlier in the day, were silent now. Eyes drawn to an orange mass lying at the foot of a hardwood giant, Tomokato was startled by the realization that it was a huge tiger, fast asleep.

Mounted on an elephant, he and Shiro were riding northwards along a red-mud road. They had purchased the beast in the bazaar at Lucknow, using Shiro's Gold Card. Tomokato's Visa had failed to pass muster when the elephant trader ran a check on it.

The memory still rankled; Shiro had been needling Tomokato about his financial affairs ever since they left the city. Wearing a pith helmet, Shiro was seated in front of the cat, a Mossberg pump shotgun across his thighs, loaded with deerslugs.

"It's not enough just to save, Uncle," the kitten was saying. "You have to *invest*. You're not just living off your interest anymore. You're eating into your capital. And one day, you're going to send in that Visa payment, and the check's going to bounce sky-high."

Mark E. Rogers

"That's easy for you to say," Tomokato replied. "You've got the royalties on all those arms patents. All I had to work with was my salary from Nobunaga."

"Come on, Unc," Shiro said. "It took money to develop those patents. I used my allowance, bought some rice futures, made two real good calls, and bingo! I had my start-up money. Sometimes you have to take risks. You should let me manage your money." He chuckled. "I know this Israeli. Used to work at Dimona. Designs the niftiest little suitcase nukes you ever heard of. I'm going to pour everything I've got into his operation. You could get in on the ground floor, Unc. We've already got a tentative deal worked out with some French separatists in Quebec, and—"

"Terrorists?" Tomokato cried, disgusted. "Shiro, not only will I *not* allow you to handle my money, I'm going to tell your parents what you've been up to."

Shiro swatted a mosquito. "Just fooling, Unc. I don't like terrorists either."

"Why not?"

"I'm not quite sure," Shiro admitted. He pointed. "Look! The mountains!"

The road had come out into a broad clearing; the treetops on the far side stood out darkly against the white peaks of the Nepalese Himalayas.

"Relief at last!" Shiro said. "I can't wait to get out of this blasted jungle."

"It'll be several days still," Tomokato answered. "Those mountains aren't as close as you think."

"I hate deceptive appearances," said Shiro. "They're worse than kissing junk in the movies."

"That bad, eh?"

102

Shiro nodded his pith-helmeted head. "They make my little life hell."

Four days later, they reached the foothills; the forest gave way to boulders and brush. The road turned to the east, bordering the higher ground.

Twenty miles or so ahead, a Himalayan spur struck due southwards. Tomokato had been told that the road would wind its way up into the mountains, leading directly to Epkot Palace.

He had first learned of the palace from the British colonel in charge of the Lucknow Imperial Intelligence Bureau, known to the locals as the *Thagi Daftar* or "Thug Office."

"Epkot?" the cat had asked, remembering the stronghold of the Holy Pterns on Bazoom.

"Experimental Paradisal Kommunity of Thugs," the colonel had replied. "At least that's the rumor. We suspect Shankar's cult has established itself there, under the protection of Babesh Ruth, the Sultan of Swat. Ruth is supposedly a Muslim, but we believe he converted to the Collie cult after watching too many episodes of *Lassie.* He apparently believes he will marry June Lockhart in a future life.

"Unfortunately, we can prove none of this. Every agent we've sent into Swat has disappeared, some before even reaching the palace. The roads are very dangerous."

Indeed, ever since crossing the boundary from Oudh into Swat, Tomokato had been expecting some sort of brush with Shankar's stranglers. The thugs insinuated themselves into groups of travelers, usually arguing that with all the thugs abroad, there was safety in numbers; entertaining their potential victims with innumerable shaggy-dog stories, they would wait until they saw their moment, then strangle the wretches with *fhido*s, or ritual dog collars. The corpses were then mutilated with the sharpened claws of *bhowsar-fhuttsi*s, mummified dog feet, and buried in ring-shaped trenches called *dhonut*s, dug with the wicked thug pickax known as the Tooth of the Dog Goddess, or Dhawgi-Devi-Fanga.

"How could anyone actually worship death, Uncle?" Shiro asked.

"Perhaps you could tell me," Tomokato replied.

"I don't worship death," Shiro said. "Death is very bad."

"Oh?" Tomokato asked, thinking, *Perhaps I've taught him something about morality after all.*

"Yeah," Shiro went on. "It keeps you from killing people."

"Shiro, how many times—" Tomokato broke off, hearing a far-off sputtering.

Pouring out black smoke, a twin-engine plane soared overhead. Passing above the foothills, it swept towards a looming snow-clad mountain.

Tomokato and Shiro lifted their field glasses. Just before the plane crashed into a cliff, something dropped out of the cargo hatch. Falling hundreds of yards towards the white slope beneath the cliff, the object began to swell; it was a few moments before Tomokato recognized it as an inflatable rubber raft. There were three people in it.

Great Buddha in Heaven, he thought, *I hope they're not expecting to survive just because they're in a rubber raft.*

The raft bounced to the slope in a burst of sparkling snow. To Tomokato's amazement, the passengers came through just fine.

"You know, Shiro," the cat said, "if they put that in a movie, I wouldn't believe it."

"They did, Unc," Shiro replied. "And you wouldn't. Just wait. It gets worse."

"How . . .?" Tomokato began, even as the raft, sliding down to the tree line, began to maneuver nimbly through a stand of towering pines.

"And worse," Shiro said, just as the raft, having made it somehow out of the pines, dropped over the edge of a black precipice. Down and down it plunged. It was a full ten minutes before it disappeared behind the crest of a foothill.

"They can't possibly make it through that—" Tomokato began.

"And worse," Shiro broke in.

Rocketing through a water gap, the raft shot back into view on some gratuitously placed rapids, its occupants still very much alive.

Tomokato halted the elephant on the stone bridge spanning the river, watching the raft approach. It was soon out of the white water.

Adjusting his glasses, the cat began to notice a certain familiarity about one of the people on board. Not far from the bridge, the raft ran aground on a ledge protruding from the river's western side.

"Come on, Shiro," Tomokato said, easing the elephant to its knees and dismounting. He and his nephew proceeded along the bank towards the raft.

Accompanied by a little Chinese kid in a baseball hat

and a blond woman in a slinky, sequined evening gown, a rumpled-looking fellow wearing a leather jacket and a fedora came to meet the two felines, a long white towel over one shoulder.

"Wisconsin Platt!" Tomokato said, bowing.

Stamping with sudden rage, the Chinese kid stabbed a finger toward the cat. "You call him *Doctor* Pwatt!" the youngster snapped.

"Blank Round, that's enough of that," Platt said, then bowed to the cat. "Miaowara Tomokato! What a surprise!"

Tomokato indicated Shiro. "This is my nephew, Miaowara Shiro."

Shiro nodded politely, then squinted at Blank Round.

Blank Round pointed his finger at the kitten. "You no talk Doctor Pwatt at all!"

Shiro tugged on Tomokato's mailsleeve. "Can I kill him?"

Tomokato looked to Platt.

Platt shook his head. "Well, Blank Round you've met," he continued.

"What about me?" the blonde asked eagerly.

"Floozie, Miaowara Tomokato," Platt said. "Tomokato, Floozie Scott."

"Is that really my last name?" Floozie asked.

Platt nodded.

"You're a great big cat, aren't you?" Floozie asked Tomokato.

"Yes," Tomokato replied.

"I'm a supremely irritating idiot, whatever that is."

Tomokato smiled. "Where did you acquire such charming companions, Wisconsin?"

"I toll you, pussy!" Blank Round shrieked. "You call him—"

Shiro chambered a round in his Mossberg. Blank Round's mouth clapped shut.

"You were saying?" Platt asked Tomokato.

"Why are Floozie and Blank Round with you?"

"I think I sinned against the Holy Spirit," Platt replied. "What are *you* doing in this neck of the woods?"

"I'm on the trail of a man named Alberth Shankar."

"The notorious Thuggee guru and ex–teacher's union president?"

"The same," Tomokato answered.

"What a coincidence. I might be crossing swords with him myself."

"You're bound for Epkot Palace?"

"Yep. Shankar's been collecting some holy relics, and since his purposes are totally nefarious, I thought I'd help myself to them. They're sacred stones, called the Shiva Rhocksa."

"Sacred stones?" Tomokato asked. "Do they do anything?"

"Kind of. I think they glow."

"They glow?" Tomokato asked, thinking this quite a comedown after the Holy Spad and its terrifying Divine-Ideal special effects.

"Okay, so it's not much. But I've kind of fallen on hard times."

"How so?"

"The Mormons hired me a year ago, to see if I couldn't find these cuneiform tablets that supposedly prove that the Lost Ten Tribes really *did* wind up as the first American Indians. I got a bundle in advance. But I managed to blow it all playing go fish with Haile Selassie, and I never found the tablets. As you might expect, the Mormons got real pissed. They sent these two grinning maniacs named Donny and Marie to get the advance back, or grease me, and so . . . well, it's the usual story. If I can put a couple of those sacred stones on the market, I might be able to get the state of Utah off my back." He paused. "By the way. What did you think of that raft ride? Pretty exciting, huh?"

It was some time before Tomokato spoke, and only then with the greatest discomfort. "I'm sorry, Wisconsin, but it was totally ridiculous."

"What do you mean?" Platt asked, with a crestfallen expression. "You do things that are every bit as unbelievable, all the time."

"Very true, my friend," Tomokato said sadly. "But I'm *supposed* to be funny."

The elephant accommodated them all; towards noon, they stopped in a small village. Floozie wandered off looking for the "little ladies room." Shiro bought a *kukri,* or Gurkha knife, in a shop that appeared to be the original inspiration for Pier One stores; Tomokato picked up some canned cat food. Platt plied several of the locals with questions about Epkot Palace, then spotted Blank Round, dressed in a widow's garments, being carried kicking and screaming towards a small bonfire by a group of kids playing *suttee.* Platt rushed to Blank's rescue.

"Why are you saving this little swine?" they demanded.

"Interesting question," Platt replied, but freed him anyway. He and Blank Round went back to the elephant.

"I love your dress," Shiro told Blank Round.

Blank pulled the sari off, glaring at him.

Floozie came running up to Platt. "I forgot how to go to the bathroom!"

"No," Platt said. *"You?"*

"Oh well," she laughed gaily, "I guess I'll just have to *pop!"*

Tomokato appeared, chopsticking a last few bits of food out of a tin.

"How is it, Unc?" Shiro asked.

Tomokato tossed the empty in a receptacle marked KEEP INDIA CLEAN, then handed him a couple of full ones.

"Not bad," the cat said. "A bit too heavy on the curry, perhaps, but . . ."

They climbed back on the elephant. Tomokato was about to goad the beast forward when several men on horseback rode near.

All had fiercely curled moustaches, and were quite elegantly dressed in white *dhotis* and pantaloons. Silk turbans were on their heads, and sandals with curled toes shod their feet.

"Pardon, *sahibs,* please," said one, a hugely corpulent fellow, "but are you taking the mountain road, towards Epkot Palace?"

"We are," Tomokato said.

"How fortuitous," the other answered. "For we are bound the same way, and would be happy to share your company tonight. The jungles of Swat are very dangerous. There are *dacoits* and stranglers abroad, and travelers should seek safety in numbers."

Platt leaned forward, whispering in Tomokato's ear: "What if they're thugs?"

Tomokato looked over his shoulder. "If they attack, we'll take one alive, see if we can learn anything about Shankar."

"Sahib?" asked the fat man.

"We'd be happy to have your company," Tomokato said. "What is your name?"

"Thugsi Aliath," the fat man replied.

"And your friends?"

"As it so happens, they're all named Thugsi Aliath too. What of *your* companions?"

Tomokato went down the list, ending with Platt.

"You call him *Doctor* Pwatt!" Blank Round warned the Indians.

The fat man's eyes blazed at the youngster. Then he smiled unctuously. "Young *sahib* should be more polite. Local legend says that horrid little rude foreign gits often wake up strangled, and ritually mutilated, and buried in donut-shaped trenches."

"Is that threat?" Blank Round demanded.

"Certainly not, young *sahib*. Friendly advice. We are not thugs. We are so obviously thugs that we cannot possibly be. Orient is inscrutable, is it not, ha-ha?"

"I'm Oriental, and I'm not inscrutable at all," Shiro said.

"I'd wink knowingly at you, as though we were sharing a private joke," Chunky Thugsi said, "but that would imply I understood your secret motive in telling such a fib. Which in turn would imply your ultimate scrutability, confirming only that you couch your fibs in the strictest truth. This I cannot admit. Thus I will not wink, kitten *sahib,* but leave you in suspense."

"I didn't follow that," Shiro said.

"I say again, kitten *sahib,* I shall not wink," the fat man answered, winking.

"Shall we be off?" Tomokato asked.

The group started from the village.

A short distance along the road, a large crowd of fellows wearing nothing but dog collars and breechclouts emerged from behind an outcropping and began to follow, carrying small pickaxes and humming, in unison, "Whistle While You Work."

"Don't mind them," said Chunky Thugsi. "They're with me." Riding along beside the elephant, he grinned up at Tomokato. "Do you like shaggy-dog stories, please?"

They made camp near nightfall. The guys in the didies built a large fire, and the company gathered round it. After supper, the Thugsi Aliaths spun out one ridiculous story after another. Most of them were quite wretched, but Blank Round had a wonderful time; so did Floozie, once Platt explained the punch lines to her. Tomokato and Shiro laughed politely, all the while staying very much on guard. Every time Tomokato looked over his shoulder, the fellows with the pickaxes squatting behind him seemed to have squatted a little bit closer.

"So Alexander the poisoner comes to the gates of the Christian heaven," Thugsi Aliath Number One was saying. "There he meets Ivan the ax murderer, and they proceed to dispute whether sins committed neatly are still sins. Alexander says cleanliness is next to godliness, and that he did not spill blood; Ivan admits the splatteriness of his crimes, but insists that Alexander will be just as damned as he in the final judgment.

"The Christian St. Peter appears. 'Ivan,' he says, 'You will not inherit the Kingdom of Heaven.'

"'I told you you would burn,'" says Alexander the poisoner. 'Messy sins are damning.'

"Whereupon St. Peter replies: 'Ah, but Alexander, so's your neat sin.'"

Blank Round slapped his knee. "I get, I get," he laughed. *First Circle, Cancer Ward.* I get."

"Would you believe it?" Platt asked Tomokato. "Blank Round has a Ph.D. in literature."

Tomokato had no difficulty believing it at all.

"I've got a Ph.D. in English too," Floozie said, "but *I* don't get it."

"That because you shithead," said Blank Round.

"I'm rubber, you're glue," said Floozie. She paused to work through the implications of this. "I can't be a shithead."

Chunky Thugsi started another shaggy dogger. Tomokato looked over his shoulder once more.

The didy guys had squatted in still closer, the dog collars no longer around their necks.

Several noticed Tomokato staring at them, and did their damnedest to put on harmless-looking expressions, which was rather difficult in light of the veins bulging on their sweaty foreheads and their sunken slitted eyes and all the saliva cascading over their chins.

"So Motor the Singing Worm was gone," said Chunky Thugsi. "Barney did not know what to do. His career in show business was finished. He began to drink. He spent all his money. Certain the worm would never return, he decided to take his life, and he went to the great bridge of Brooklyn to hurl himself off . . ."

Tomokato cocked his head to one side, the squatting sounds drawing ever nearer. His paw wandered to the hilt of his sword.

"But Barney realized he did not want to die on an empty stomach," Chunky Thugsi continued. "And so he went to a fruit vendor whose cart stood by the bridge. . . ."

More squatting, closer yet. Tomokato eased the *katana* a few inches from the scabbard.

"Barney bought three apples," said Chunky Thugsi.

Looking to his right, Tomokato saw Platt casually slipping the wet towel from around his neck.

Chunky continued: "He ate the first—"

To Tomokato's left, Shiro yawned and set his Mossberg up on his hip.

"He ate the second—"

Shiro's free paw wandered to the pump.

"And he was about to eat the third when—"

Tomokato heard a series of dull flapping sounds, like leather straps being pulled taut. Chunky's voice rose to a shriek:

"OUT BORED MOTOR!"

That was the signal. From all over the camp, the thugs converged.

But not on Tomokato or Shiro or Platt.

As the cat whirled round, longsword flashing free, he was amazed to see the stranglers all running frenziedly in the direction of Blank Round and Floozie.

113

"I'm first!" one screamed.

"No *me!*" cried another.

"You take the bimbo, I want the brat!" a third bellowed.

"This isn't fair!" a fourth lamented.

Suddenly there was a loud *pwut!,* as if a gargantuan water balloon had burst. The thugs, every man jack of them, including Chunky, uttered a collective "Ugghhh" and dropped down dead from sheer disgust.

"Well," said Platt, "Floozie *said* she was just going to pop."

Donning galoshes, he and the felines went over to the corpses.

Blank Round was dead too. He appeared to have been killed instantly by the Floozie-blast itself. Tomokato studied Platt's face, reading it for signs of grief.

"Are you all right, Wisconsin?" he asked.

Platt shrugged. "Yeah. I suppose I should feel bad, but it just seems so appropriate, somehow."

In the morning, they reached the foothills of the mountain spur and began to wind their way into the uplands. The road eventually led to a gorge spanned by a long, rickety-looking rope bridge.

"We'll have to leave the elephant here," Tomokato said.

Eyeing the bridge, the elephant sighed with relief. They all got down and started across. The bridge swayed beneath them, creaking; footing was treacherous. Slats gave way; cords on the suspension hawsers parted with annoying regularity.

The trio were dead in the middle when two columns of thugs appeared, approaching the bridge from either side.

"Shame on you, *sahibs*," one cried. "We were most grossed out to discover the state in which you left our colleagues. True warriors do not rely on popped floozies to kill their foes."

The man marched boldly onto the bridge, his followers following.

"They don't try to strangle guys who have shotguns, either," Shiro said, and blew a hole in the thug through which you could clearly see the holes in the second and third and fourth thugs.

"Gosh, I love deerslugs," the kitten added.

But the remaining numbskulls kept on coming, the thugs across the way advancing as well; the carnage was just about to start in earnest when Tomokato noticed a light bulb glowing hovering above Shiro's head.

"Shiro, you have an idea," the cat said.

"Thanks, Unc," Shiro replied. "How come, if the bridge is in such terrible condition, it can support all those guys?"

With that, the author totally lost his nerve. Wood splintered; except for the part Tomokato and his companions stood on, the whole bottom of the span dropped out, pitching the thugs a thousand feet to their deaths.

But there were even more thugs waiting in the wings; chastened, the author utilized them in a much more logical fashion. It took the better part of an hour, but after they ran up a flag of truce and made a few side trips to the local Rickel's, they had the bottom of the bridge completely reconstructed.

"Whew," said Shiro, as the thugs moved to the attack once more. "If that's what's going to pass for believability in this story, we might as well stay asinine."

"Well then," said Platt, "why don't we tangle ourselves in some of the ropes, and I'll hack one of the main hawsers with my machete, and the bridge will break, and—"

"No," said Tomokato. "I have an even more asinine idea."

Leaping to the right, he sliced through the bridge, then leaped to the left and sliced again. The thugs were almost to the slashes when the segments beneath them swung downwards as though they were on hinges, leaving the tiny middle section still suspended above the gorge, Tomokato, Shiro, and Platt standing upon it, serene as a holy trinity of Road Runners.

"Have Lucas and Spielberg put *that* in a movie yet?" Tomokato asked Shiro, watching the second hundred stranglers tumbling towards the corpse convention at the bottom.

"Give 'em time, Unc," the kitten replied. "But how do we get across?"

"Perhaps we could wait till a submarine goes by, then cling to the periscope," Platt suggested.

"What if it submerges?" Tomokato asked.

Platt snapped his fingers. "Damn."

116

2

In the end though, they did have to settle for a submarine.

3

As the day waned, they sighted Epkot Palace. Blood red in the afternoon sunlight, it crowned one of the taller foothills, the gold-sheathed domes of its many minarets ablaze.

"So," Tomokato asked, "how do we get in?"

"I'm a world-renowned archaeologist," Platt said. "I vote we march right up to the gate and tell them I want to do some grave robbing. Thugs or no, I bet they'll be honored. At the very least, they'll probably play around with us a little, try to maintain the fiction that they're really aboveboard. Who knows? We might even get dinner."

Tomokato weighed the point. "I like Indian food."

Platt went on: "We ask a few questions, and if we're still alive after lights out, we do some sneaking around, see if it really is Thug Central. What do you say?"

"We might as well give it a try," Tomokato answered, and they went up to the entrance.

Two turbaned guards with Lee-Enfield rifles stood at the threshold. They summoned a tall thin man wearing what someday would be known as a Nehru jacket.

"I am Abdul Abulbul," he said.

"Emir?" Platt asked.

"No, palace steward," Abulbul replied. "To my Lord Babesh Ruth, Sultan of Swat. What may I do for you, *sahibs*?"

Platt introduced himself.

"The world-famous archaeologist!" Abulbul exclaimed. "What a surprise. I shall quick tell the sultan. We have many choice tombs for you to violate; but first, I think, you must join us at tonight's *durbar*. There is just enough time for us to prepare dishes in your honor. Come, come. I will show you to your chambers."

Going under the portcullis, they crossed the courtyard beyond. Passing through an ornate archway, they entered a corridor lined with pillars carved into voluptuous female shapes, all with the same face—June Lockhart's.

"Your master is a Muslim, is he not?" Platt asked Abulbul.

"Such is so."

"Why then does he not observe the Prophet's injunction against images?"

"Ah, er . . . the Prophet, blessings and peace be upon him . . . made an exception in the case of June Lockhart."

"I was unaware of that," Platt said. "Although I *have* heard that worshipers of the goddess Collie frequently develop a fixation on June."

"Er . . . I have heard that too. Understandable, is it not?"

"I have also heard that they do not believe that she could ever have been in such a lousy series as *Lost in Space*."

119

"They do well not to believe," said Abulbul, a sudden edge in his voice. "For it is a vicious thing to say, and there is no proof."

"But I have seen the shows myself," Platt said.

"With all due respect, *sahib,* this I cannot believe."

"Furthermore, she allowed her own daughter, flesh of her flesh, to appear in *Battlestar Galactica.*"

"I have also heard such rumors," Abulbul gritted. "Them also I do not believe."

"But it's true," Platt said.

Abulbul halted, glaring at him.

"The *whole . . . first . . . season,"* Platt continued.

Abulbul started forward once more, walking very fast. Coming to the foot of a broad marble staircase, he pointed to the top. "Guest quarters up there. Find your own goddamn room."

He stamped off.

"Guess this must be the place," Platt told Tomokato.

They went upstairs. Finding themselves a chamber with a triple-tiered bunkbed, they stashed their luggage.

"You're sure you wouldn't like a separate room?" Tomokato asked Platt.

"As Chunky said, there's safety in numbers," Platt replied. "And there aren't only the Thugs to worry about. Donny and Marie might still be on my trail."

"You sound genuinely frightened of them."

"If you ever saw those sharklike smiles . . . listened to them mutilating *'Proud Mary'* or *'I Heard It Through the Grapevine' . . ."* Platt broke off, shivering.

"Well, maybe you'll be able to steal the Shiva *Rhocksa* and pay the Mormons off," Tomokato said.

"I hope so. I really feel like they got a bum deal. If only I could've found those tablets."

"You're convinced that they exist?" Tomokato asked, surprised. "That the American Indians really *are* the Ten Lost Tribes?"

"Yes on one, no on two. After they overran Israel, the Assyrians apparently packed the tribes they captured on a slow boat to America. They were Mormons too, you see; the reason they attacked in the first place was that they couldn't figure out what so many Israelites were doing in the Holy Land. But I know for a fact that the ship stopped in Britain."

"So the *Brits* are actually the Ten Lost Tribes?" Shiro asked. "Just like the British Israelites always believed?"

"No, the ship only put in for provisions," Platt continued. "Ultimately, it wound up in northern Scandinavia."

"And the *Lapps* are Ten Lost Tribes?" Tomokato asked.

"Exactly."

"Boy, you learn something new every day," Shiro said.

"Thank you for enriching our minds, Wisconsin," Tomokato said.

"Science marches on," Platt replied.

Three hours later, they were summoned to the *durbar*. The setting was a huge taper-lit banquet hall. Musicians plunked away at an all-sitar version of the theme from *Lassie* over in one corner. Visiting dignitaries mingled and exchanged pleasantries in front of the salad *durbar*.

Presently Abulbul announced:

121

"Babesh Ruth, the Sultan of Swat."

A potbellied fellow in a Karnak the Magnificent–style turban and a New York Yankees uniform appeared, followed by rifle-toting guards. The guests approached the sultan; Abulbul introduced them, finally coming to Platt, Tomokato, and Shiro.

"My steward informs me that you questioned him closely on points of Muslim law," Ruth told Platt.

"I did not mean to offend," Platt said.

"There, you see, Abulbul?" Ruth said. "Personally, I am pleased when foreigners show an interest in our ways. It is stimulating to exchange points of view."

"And toy with your victims before the kill?" Platt asked, doing his best Froggy the Gremlin.

"And toy with my victims before the kill," the sultan answered, apparently without the slightest idea of what he had just said.

Abulbul whispered hurriedly in his ear. Ruth's jaw dropped.

"—As we all toy with our victims," the sultan continued, trying to regain his composure. He indicated Tomokato and Shiro. "Undoubtedly, these two have some experience in that."

"I merely *eat* mice," Tomokato said. "I never torture them."

"Neither do I," Shiro said. "Uncle-*san* made me stop."

"They are most unsatisfactorily small," said Ruth. "Ah well then. To dinner."

The guests arranged themselves on sumptuous pillows around a long, low table. A vast array of tempting Indian dishes had been set.

Abulbul clapped his hands. The food before Tomokato and his companions was whisked away.

"But . . ." the cat said.

"We have no wish to disgust you with our wretched Third World cuisine," Abulbul said. "And so we shall serve you according to your Western tastes."

"I'm not Western," Tomokato protested, as a platter of Big Macs was laid in front of him.

Abulbul looked mildly puzzled. "The Golden Arches have not taken root in Japan? Is not the largest McDonald's in the world located in Tokyo?"

Tomokato opened one of the Big Macs. To his amazement, he saw what appeared to be a miniature businessman's face staring up at him from the special sauce.

"You burned us out," the face whispered in a tiny voice.

Tomokato closed the sandwich and laid it back on the platter.

"*Sushi* then, perhaps?" said Abulbul, thrusting a dish of glistening translucent raw fish on a bed of overcooked rice under Tomokato's nose.

Tomokato smiled politely. Abulbul laid the dish in Tomokato's lap. The cat looked over at Platt. The archaeologist was turning a horrible shade of yellow-green as servants confronted him with one variety of Grand Guignol Western eats after another, pig's feet, beef brains, tongue, sweetbreads, raw oysters, jellied eels, blood puddings, five kinds of liver, tripe, chitlins, anchovies, headcheese, Luxury Loaf, fried pork rinds, Pac-Man Pasta, and a huge tureen with chopped okra bits floating in a thick, sparkling fluid that looked for all the world like a gallon of mucus.

123

"Eat hearty, my foreign friends!" called the sultan from the head of the table. "Just like home, is it not?"

Tomokato heard loud snarfings and chewings to his left. Turning, he saw Shiro making inroads on vast, bloated haggis.

"Mmmm," the kitten said, between chews. "This is great. Do we have to kill anyone in Scotland anytime soon?"

Struggling against the nausea heaving within him, Tomokato slowly shook his head.

"Hey Wisconsin," Shiro called. "Pass me the gefilte fish."

Ultimately Tomokato waited till his stomach settled, then opted for the dish least loathsome to him, the *sushi*. Like any cat, he was not averse to the idea of fish. But as a civilized person, he preferred it properly breaded and deep-fried, so it didn't *taste* like fish. Lord Nobunaga had always had it that way, though Tomokato had never shared his enthusiasm for ketchup.

When the food was cleared away at last, a troupe of zaftig and suggestively dressed nautch dancers did some highly immodest things. Platt made more conversation with the sultan, asking if the potentate had ever heard of the *Shiva Rhocksa*.

"I have," Babesh Ruth replied. "They are just legendary, of course." He pulled a large cylindrical green stone, marked with three notches and polished smooth, out of his intricately embroidered silk sleeve. "But if they *were* real, they would look like this."

"Ah," said Platt.

"The tales say that if all five are united in the presence

124

of two-thirds of the significant lost treasures in the world, they will glow."

"Just glow?"

"And confer ultimate power on he who wields them."

"I hadn't heard that," Platt said.

"Now you have," said Ruth. "It does render the legend more interesting, does it not?"

"Oh, I don't know. Conferring ultimate power is rather typical of McGuffins."

"What is McGuffin, please?"

"It's what the spies are after, but the audience doesn't care."

"None of us are spies," said Ruth, setting the stone on the table in front of him.

"Then that's no McGuffin," Platt answered.

Once the *durbar* was finished, Tomokato and his companions retired to their chamber.

"They'll attack later tonight," Platt said. "Give us a few hours, hope we're making nonny—"

"Making nonny?" Tomokato asked.

Platt looked a bit embarrassed. "You know."

Tomokato thought a bit. "Ah so. Like going to La-La Land?"

"You got it."

"Whatever," Tomokato said. "We must not be here when the assassins strike."

"Granted. Once the servants douse the lights outside, we'll slip out and have a look round."

"My thoughts exactly," Tomokato answered.

"I notice you didn't ask for my opinion," Shiro huffed.

"Lips that touch haggis will never advise me," Tomokato answered.

And so they waited. The cat looked into the hallway from time to time. Eventually a serving girl appeared, extinguishing the tapers. Tomokato eased the door shut.

"Lights out?" Platt asked.

Turning, Tomokato nodded. He noticed a hint of motion beyond Platt; a section of the richly carven stone wall was swinging silently forward. Three didy guys snuck from the secret passage, *fhido*s stretched tight in their hands.

"Shhhh," the first thug was saying, looking back over his shoulder. "Be vew-wy, vew-wy, quiet . . ."

Tomokato drew his sword. Platt snapped his towel from around his neck. Shiro pumped his Mossberg. The thug's face whipped towards them.

"Ah," he said, the other two bunching up behind him. "Perhaps we should come back when you're asleep."

Tomokato and the others stood squinting at them. The thugs backed carefully into the secret passage. The wall swung slowly shut behind them.

The cat went over to the bunks, quickly arranged the bedclothes and pillows to look as though each bed were occupied. Then he stationed himself beside the hidden door.

"No shooting, Shiro," he said.

Shiro slung the Mossberg over his shoulder and unsheathed his *kukri*. Then the kitten and Platt placed themselves across the door from Tomokato.

"All right," Tomokato whispered. "One, two, three . . ."

They began to snore mightily.

The wall opened again. The thugs crept back out. Totally lacking in peripheral vision, they never saw Tomokato. Also ill-equipped in the x-ray vision department, they didn't spot Shiro and Platt behind the door either.*

There were ten stranglers this time. As they made for the bunks, Tomokato fell into line behind them, Platt and Shiro following. With hideous deftness, the cat stabbed the man in front of him in the base of the skull, sidestepped the body, let Platt ease it to the floor, then repeated the process with the next man. By the time the lead thug reached the bunks, Tomokato was second in line.

The strangler turned around with a huge grin on his face, as if to say, *Look at those idiots sleeping there.* Tomokato smiled back at him, nodding. The thug turned once more toward the bunks, stretched forth his *fhido*— then whirled in one of the best double takes Tomokato had ever seen.

Tomokato shrugged.

The thug's mouth flew open.

Tomokato thrust his sword up into it before the man could scream. The man's turban jumped from his skull; three inches of protruding katana gave a grisly new meaning to the expression *pointy head.*

Tomokato yanked his sword out. The thug crumpled. Shiro admired the corpse.

"Whoa! Juicy one, Unc," he said.

"What now?" Platt asked. "Out into the hall?"

_____

*Don't you feel superior? I do.

127

Tomokato pointed to the secret passage. "That looks more promising, I think."

Platt nodded, taking a taper from a wall socket. Needing none, Tomokato led the way into the darkness.

They found themselves in a long, low corridor. Thick masses of cobweb hung from the ceiling. Huge hairy red spiders clambered among the threads. Large black beetles scuttled over the floor, singing "Norwegian Wood" in thin, tinny voices.

"I thought John was dead," Shiro said, eyeing a particularly unpleasant specimen climbing up his leg. He brushed it off. Platt examined it.

"That's Yoko," he announced.

The bug problem grew steadily worse the farther they advanced. Fist-sized scarabs appeared, rolling foot-wide balls of Keynesianism and New Age philosophy. Cockroaches cocked and roached. Millipedes played elaborate practical jokes. Centipedes played less elaborate ones, equipped as they were with fewer legs.

Hearing machine-gun fire from one intersection, Tomokato halted; Tommy guns blazing, James Whitmore and James Arness backed across the juncture, pursued by ants the size of Buicks.

"Are you *sure* we're still under L.A.?" Jim asked Jim between bursts of gunfire, just before they vanished from sight on the other side of the passage.

Tomokato waited until the ants crossed, then proceeded into the junction—only to encounter a little fat Italian guy and a consummate straight man.

"Who were they?" the former asked his partner.

"Them," the straight man replied.

"Yeah, but who *were* they?" the first asked.

"Them," the other repeated.

"Them?"

"That's right."

The Italian howled in frustration. Even after a hundred yards or so, Tomokato could still hear them going at it hammer and tongs.

Yet soon a heavy whooshing drowned the echoes of their routine; a vast moth came flapping along the corridor. Tomokato struck it down with his sword. Two little princesses hopped off the carcass and ran to his feet, kicking them.

"Big damn bastard!" they cried. "You kill our moth!"

He picked them up. "I'm sorry."

"What kind of Nipponese person are you?" they demanded.

"It was coming right at me—"

"Traitor, traitor!" they broke in. "Wait till Toho hear about this!"

He brushed them from his paws. They landed safely atop George and Ringo.

"Let's go," Tomokato said, starting forward once more. But a sixth sense warned him to look behind; Shiro, with a fiendish expression on his little face, was just about to step on the tiny tarts.

"Shiro," Tomokato said.

"Aww, *Unc,*" Shiro said, lowering his foot.

"What's the matter?" Platt said, bumping into the kitten.

Shiro staggered forward.

Ker-unchhh.

"Forget it," Tomokato replied.

They descended a long, slippery staircase. At the

129

bottom there were fewer insects; that was probably because of all the didy guys running about with butterfly nets, looking like employees from a nuthouse staffed solely by Mahatma Gandhis. One wall was lined with stuffed Hefty lawn bags, their surfaces squirming and bulging.

Noticing the newcomers, the thugs paused in their efforts.

"Look, Salim," one said. "What sort of bugs are those?"

Salim answered in the weighty tones of a born expert: "Those are Cat Bugs, Ravi. Except for the foreigner."

"What sort is he?"

"Looks Waspy."

"They appear much too big for our nets," Ravi said. "Ask them what they want."

"What do you want?" Salim asked.

"I'll ask the questions here," Tomokato said.

"You who are too big for our nets, ask away."

"What are you doing with all the bugs?"

"We sell them to the Soviets," Salim replied. "They put them in other people's embassies."

"Why?"

Salim shook his head. "They appear to think they are listening devices. We tell them, no, no, they are just insects, they will tell the Soviets nothing, even if they stick wires in them. The Soviets say if that doesn't work, they will beat the truth out of them. It is a very good source of hard currency for us—"

Without warning, two guards stepped from an adjoining arch.

"Spot inspection!" they announced.

The didy guys snapped to.

"Salim!" came Abulbul's voice. "Are the bugs bagged?"

Salim gulped. "Not all. We were interrupted by this Cat Bug here."

Abulbul stepped out from between the guards. His eyes widened when he saw the cat.

"That is no Cat Bug!" he cried. "They are all spies!"

"Quick, men!" said Salim to his coworkers, "Let us go conceal the McGuffins!" They all disappeared into didy hidey-holes, leaving Abulbul and his guards to face Tomokato and his companions.

"Kill them!" Abulbul cried.

The guards rushed in front of him and lowered their Lee-Enfields, fumbling with the bolts. Shiro unlimbered his Mossberg and packed them off to their next incarnations.

Abulbul tried to grab one of the falling rifles. Shiro pumped in another round and blew a big wet one in the steward's Nehru jacket. Platt rushed forward as the steward collapsed.

"Can you tell us how to find Shankar?" he asked.

"Why should I talk?" Abulbul gasped, and coughed up a huge gout of blood.

"You've already spilled your guts," Platt replied.

Abulbul examined an intestine, wrinkling his nose. *"This* was inside *me?"*

"This too," said Shiro, holding up a pancreas. "Disgusting, isn't it?"

Abulbul nodded.

"Well, what about it?" Platt asked.

"You will find Shankar Guru in the *Housatha Dhawgi Devi*," Abulbul said. "The Temple of Dog Doom. Go straight up this corridor, take two rights. You'll find yourselves on a ledge above a sea of molten lava. Go along the ledge to a doorway on the far side. Beyond lies the temple. Shankar Guru will just be starting the Saturday service."

"Saturday service?" Platt asked.

"It's such a bummer getting up Sunday mornings, especially after a *durbar*."

"I understand."

Abulbul hawked up another ruby freshet. "Going bye-bye now." His head sagged to the floor.

Tomokato and the others shoved him into one of the hidey-holes.

"I'm not sure I trust the directions," the cat told Platt as they got under way once more. "You really didn't give him too much of a reason to betray his cause."

"You know it, and I know it," Platt said. "Perhaps even *he* knew it." The archaeologist tossed off a laugh that fairly brimmed over with the full-blooded spirit of adventure. "Who cares?"

4

Going some distance and rounding a corner, they saw an archway limned in sulphurous yellow. Through it they reached the ledge Abulbul had spoken of. It was perhaps five feet wide, jutting from the face of a vast subterranean cliff. Five hundred yards beneath, molten rock seethed, covered in places by a shiny black crust; above, the ceiling was lost in darkness.

Platt led the way. Looking past him, Tomokato could barely see the opposite wall of the cavern. But as they progressed, he began to discern huge Sanskrit letters carved into the stone.

"Can you decipher that?" he asked Platt.

Platt donned a pair of glasses and read:

> "IF YOU CLIMBED OUT ON THAT LEDGE,
> YOU ARE REALLY DUMB.
> INTRUDERS GET WHAT THEY DESERVE.
> YOU GONNA GET YOU SOME!"

"Anything else?" Tomokato asked.

"Yes," Platt answered. "Burma-Shave."

Finally they reached the other side. There a wooden door awaited them, reinforced with studded iron bands. Platt banged the knocker. A little hatch opened.

"Password?" a thug asked.

"A show from the 1960s," Platt replied.

The thug smiled fondly. "Allen Ludden," he said. "Good family fare. Intellectually stimulating. So much so that I did not become the sucker that I might otherwise be. Tough luck, *sahib.*"

He slid the hatch shut again.

There was a distant clank, and a sound like rushing water. Tomokato had no idea where it was coming from. The stone began to vibrate beneath his feet; suddenly he realized that the ledge was retracting into the cliff wall.

He looked over the edge. Hot wind swept his face, stinking of brimstone.

Platt joined him at the brink, holding onto his hat. "Abulbul sure did us dirty," he said. "Are you going to say you told me so?"

"I really should, but I'm far too noble," Tomokato answered. "Shiro, see if you can't blast a hole through that door."

Shiro pumped nine slugs into it. Not one went through. Tomokato examined the wood.

"Must be ten inches thick," he said.

By then, the ledge had withdrawn a full foot into the wall.

"Go back the way we came?" Platt asked.

"We won't make it," Tomokato answered. He craned his head back. Above, the cliff was completely sheer. Getting down on his paws and knees, he peered under the ledge. There was nothing down there to cling to either.

Leaning back, he eyed the adjoining wall. It was the same story, except perhaps for the door; he thought he might be able to dig his claws into the wood. But that was definitely a last resort.

"Maybe we could jam the mechanism," Platt said, producing a hunting knife. Tomokato unsheathed a *tanto*. They tried to force them into the joint between ledge and wall.

The crack was not wide enough.

"You know," said Platt, "This really is a wonderful piece of engineering."

"I'd like to meet the engineer," said Shiro.

Only three feet of ledge remained.

Platt went back to the door, banged the knocker again. The hatch opened.

134

"Password?" the thug asked.

"Er . . . ah, you see . . ." Platt fumbled. "I noticed you opened the hatch again, even though we obviously proved, by not knowing the password the first time, that we shouldn't be admitted. . . ."

"Is there an argument buried somewhere in all that?" the thug demanded.

"Why yes," Platt answered. "Seeing as how you had no justification for beginning this conversation, much less continuing it, why look for a justification for opening the door?"

"Because your argument itself constitutes a kind of justification," the thug answered. "After all, you take it for granted that I have no reason to do what you want. Besides, I don't have to explain my motives to you, Imperialist Stooge of the Iron Heel of the Archaeologist State."

The hatch shut again.

Only two feet of ledge left.

"Wisconsin, let me past you," Tomokato said.

Gingerly they changed places. Tomokato hooked his talons in the door. By the time he was done, the ledge had slid out from under him; his legs hung straight down.

"Wisconsin, grab me," he said.

Platt edged along the remaining strip of ledge and reached across, snagging his fingers over the rim of Tomokato's back plate. Within moments, he had no choice but to suspend his full weight from the cat. Grimacing at the sudden strain, Tomokato dug his claws even deeper.

"Shiro?" the cat called.

135

The kitten jumped. Luckily, he didn't add much to the burden his uncle was already bearing.

Tomokato looked to the side. The ledge had vanished, its surface perfectly flush with the cliff face.

Just above him was the door knocker. A stratagem leaped to mind.

Setting his foot on one of the steel bands reinforcing the door, he shifted some of his weight onto it and hauled himself slowly, agonizingly upwards. When his face was just barely level with the hatch, he unhooked a paw and rapped twice with the knocker.

The hatch didn't open.

A burst of hot air ripped upwards along the rock wall. The living chain formed by Tomokato and his companions snapped outward like a whip. As they banged back against the door, the cat's talons pulled loose. He fell six inches—

Before locking his other paw on the knocker.

"I'd say this is pretty hairy," Platt said appreciatively.

"Have you ever been in a worse situation?" Shiro asked.

"Not that I survived," the archaeologist answered.

Tomokato set his foot on the band again, raked his free claw back into the wood.

"Buddha, grant me strength," he gritted, dragging the weight of two and a third bodies once more, muscles popping, joints cracking, ligaments screaming, tendons twanging as only tortured tendons can. Body echoing with the hideous music of the climbing damned, he reached the hatch. Without warning, it opened.

"Can that racket!" the thug demanded.

"Password?" Tomokato asked.

"Swordfish," the thug answered. "Now open this door!"

"I can't. You'll have to do it."

"Oh all right," the thug answered sourly. Tomokato heard locks clicking. Then the door swung inwards.

Tomokato trailed Platt and Shiro in behind him, then dropped to the floor, panting. Platt got to his feet, Shiro unwrapping himself from the archaeologist's left leg.

"When are you going to give up trying to fool me?" the thug asked.

Platt's towel lashed out. "About now," he answered.

"How do you clean that towel?" Shiro asked.

"Like this," Platt said, and snapped the cloth again. Every last drop of gore came flying out of it, splattering the wall.

"Ve-ry sharp," Shiro laughed.

Tomokato cocked an ear. Far-off voices chanted hollowly.

"What are they saying?" Shiro asked.

"It sounds like *hollowly, hollowly, hollowly,*" Tomokato replied.

"We must be close to the temple," Platt said.

After chucking the thug's body in the lava and locking the door, they followed the sounds to an immense colonnade. The pillars were carved into the shape of human thigh bones, the ceiling into ribs and vertebrae; stairs at the end led up into the mouth of a vast yawning stone skull.

Slipping stealthily from pillar to pillar, the trio approached the skull. Inside its maw was a towering archway; climbing the steps, Tomokato and the others saw a kneeling multitude of didy guys, all facing the colossal, buxom, multiarmed statue of the Dhawgi Devi that loomed at the far end of the temple. They were no longer chanting hollowly; but if I were to mention what they were chanting, it would still be basically the same joke, so you'll just have to use your imagination.

Two narrow circular staircases flanked the doorway. Platt and Shiro followed Tomokato into the one on the left.

They came up in a rough-hewn gallery fifty feet above the temple floor. Squat, close-set columns lined the edge. Tomokato led some distance along the gallery, then peered from between two of the pillars, looking out over the ceremony.

Dressed in robes and a horned headdress that looked like rejects from *Inframan,* Shankar, a tall, powerfully built man, stood in front of the statue of Collie, directing the chanting with a sequined baton.

"More feeling, thugs!" he cried. "Now! 'Wake Up Devi'!"

Whereupon the didy guys responded, to the tune of *Frère Jacques:*

> "WAKE UP DEVI.
>
> WAKE UP DEVI.
>
> GODDESS, WAKE UP.
>
> UP, UP, UP.
>
> GONNA KILL A VICTIM.
>
> GONNA KILL A VICTIM.
>
> WAKE UP, PUP!
>
> WAKE UP, PUP!"

139

Shankar's acolytes led a young man out from behind
the statue and bound him to a pillar. Then one of the
assistants threw a great switch.

A tremendous section of floor opened. Red smoke
belched upwards. Stretching wall to wall, the lurid crack
yawned like the mouth of Hell itself. From his vantage,
Tomokato could look straight down into the abyss. A
river of lava crawled sluggishly at the bottom.

It occurred to him that he was seeing rather more lava
than he had expected; volcanic activity was uncommon
or nonexistent in India, as far as he knew. He wondered:
Was he ill informed? Was the author? Or was the author
satirizing someone who was? Tomokato decided not to
let it worry him.

Shankar handed his baton to an acolyte, then went
over to the captive. The chanting hushed to a mere
expectant whisper. The prisoner struggled against his
bonds, staring in horror as Shankar raised one hand high
above his head.

"And now," the Guru cried exultantly, *"The Brain
Trick!"*

With a shout he thrust his fingers into the victim's
brow, his whole hand sinking from view. Blood jetted up
his arm. Just for dramatic effect, he left his hand in a few
moments, then pulled the man's brain out dripping. Two
acolytes rushed up on either side of the victim, pointing
to his forehead.

"And see, faithful ones?" they cried. "No hole!"

Yet stranger even than the lack of a wound was the fact
that the victim was still alive. He no longer struggled,
but asked in a loud, clear voice:

"How's this for a scene: The Han Solo character falls

off the shield. Sliding to the bottom of the slope, his companion Sumac the Fake Hobbit looks round to see him rolling down the incline, steadily accumulating snow until he is transformed into a giant white roll with feet sticking out from one side, like something from a subpar Warner Brothers cartoon, only less believable. . . ."

"See! See!" Shankar cried. "Totally brain-dead, but still talking!"

"Are you listening, Wisconsin?" Tomokato asked. "There is still time for you to change the road you're on."

"Sounded pretty exciting to me," Platt replied.

Tomokato turned and slapped him one across the chops.

Platt shook his head, rubbing his cheeks. He blinked a couple of times. "Thanks, I needed that," he said.

"Now, thugs!" Shankar bellowed. "'Wake Up Devi'! Fortiss*iss*imo!"

The chanting rose to a roar. Shankar tossed the brain toward the idol of Collie. Each of the statue's many hands gripped a gigantic curving steel tulwar; to Tomokato's amazement, a stone arm lunged forward, catching the organ on sword's point. Surprisingly lady-like for a dog-headed death-goddess, Collie daintily brought the horrible tidbit to her lips.

Whereupon Tomokato and Platt both thought of groaners involving brain food, but had the decency not to utter them.

After a lightning display of multiple sword sheathing that left the cat quite thoroughly impressed, Collie strode forth from her pedestal, making for the victim.

141

The acolytes untied him and stood back. Collie took up the victim, who was still babbling loudly.

"Oh Collie *Ma,*" Shankar cried, "take our offering of flesh, and according to the ritual that Thou Thyself ordained, toss him in the lava for no other purpose than to be sadistic."

Holding the victim up with one pinky extended, Collie looked more than anything like a duchess at tea that had accidentally picked up a particularly offensive and moldy biscuit; lightly, gracefully, she sashayed toward the fissure.

Suddenly Tomokato's attention was drawn by the appearance of a lone, white-clad figure in the gallery opposite.

"A Hollywood Ninja," he said.

"How do you know he's from Hollywood, Unc?" Shiro asked.

"Here we are, a mile underground in a gloomy temple—"

"And he's dressed all in white," Shiro broke in.

Reaching the brink of the fissure, Collie dropped the victim. But suspended from a rope, the Ninja swung out over the crack and snatched the victim in midair, hurtling directly towards the cat.

Putting her hands on her hips, Collie stamped pettishly. Tomokato and the others stepped back. The Ninja swung in between the pillars.

"Come back here with our brainless person!" thundered Shankar's voice. The worshipers were in an uproar. The victim still under his arm, the Ninja showed himself to the outraged thugs.

"You must be kidding," he laughed. "My masters in

Lotus Land will pay me a fortune for this guy, so ha-ha on you!"

Tomokato tapped him on the arm. "You put your skills to evil use."

The Ninja sneered over his shoulder at him. "Save it till we meet again, kitty!"

And with that, he swung towards the far gallery once more.

Collie was waiting for him this time. Grabbing the rope, she dangled him and the potential scriptwriter over the lava for a moment, examining them. Then she flicked them off.

Brain-dead plunged straight into the glowing river, vanishing beneath the molten surface with a burst of flame. The Ninja, on the other hand, settled gracefully on the liquid rock, tiptoed quite Zenly over to the side of the chasm, leaped thirty feet in the air, and slipped through a crevice as though he had been sucked in, feet first.

"Bummer," said Shankar. "Oh well. At least we didn't lose the sacrifice. Would've been the third one this month. Nice work, Devi."

Collie looked down at him with a terrible Joan Crawford-at-Christina glare. Instantly Shankar seemed to be as aware of the comment's implicit condescension as Collie was.

"Collie *Ma*," he began desperately, "it was great work. It was *stupendous* work, truly worthy of the goddess that you are, your best killing yet . . ."

Collie bent close to him, still glaring.

"Or, well . . . I mean . . . it *would* have been your best, if all the others were not equally so grand." He

143

knelt, clasping his hands. "Forgive me, Devi. I am but a worm. A pustule. A herpes simplex virus. A fan of George Michael, Debbie Gibson and Milli Vanilli—"

Collie straightened. He had abased himself enough. Shankar heaved a huge sigh of relief, swiping sweat from his brow.

Collie returned to her pedestal. Unsheathing her swords, she assumed her former pose and went still once more.

Shankar rose, facing the multitude. "Talk about a religious experience, huh?" He laughed, none too convincingly. "Ah well. Show's over."

"All thanks to Collie, for it was dynamite," the congregation responded.

He threw the switch to close the chasm in the floor. Then he and his acolytes disappeared behind the statue, the worshipers heading for the main exit.

Once the temple emptied, Tomokato and his companions crept downstairs. Approaching the idol of Collie, they watched warily for any sign of movement.

"You think she'll try to stop us?" Shiro asked.

"They had to wake her with chanting," Platt replied.

"If she's a goddess, why didn't she wake up on her own?"

"It might be that she believes in giving her followers the dignity of efficacious action," Platt answered. "It's also possible that her powers are restricted by factors outside our knowledge, such as the actions of other Hindu deities. Perhaps she's constrained by her own nature—i.e., she simply lacks the power to intrude into our plane of existence on her own, and must be conjured. . . ."

"Okay already," Shiro said.

But Platt forged ahead: "Maybe she's only a mental construct of her worshipers, taking on temporary reality through the sheer fervor of their belief. Perhaps this whole operation is being run by tramps who created a fake Collie to scare everyone out, then discovered there were benefits to running a cult, but can't run the fake for more than a few minutes without it breaking down. Finally, maybe she's just dim."

"And she just forgets to move?" Shiro asked. "The same way Floozie forgot how to go to the bathroom?"

By then they were very near the statue. Tomokato looked up at the goddess's face, remembering that *Mommie Dearest* stare.

"Somehow, I don't think that's the reason," he said. They paused apprehensively, wondering if one of those mighty swords, or all at once, would suddenly come swooping down on them.

"I say we opt for the tramp explanation," Shiro said in a hushed voice.

"Right," Platt replied.

Collie remained motionless. Drawing a collective deep breath, they went behind the statue, entering a corridor hewn from solid rock. Ceiling-hung butter lamps exuded a dim, guttering light. Bas-reliefs along the sides depicted in grisly detail the dos and don'ts of human sacrifice.

Ultimately the trio reached a dead end. The wall that blocked the passage was adorned with a huge carving of Tommy Rettig's face. Tommy was winking at them.

They turned to find that another wall had risen silently behind them. This barrier was graven with Collie's face, her mouth open, tongue wagging.

"Bad breath in dogs!" a voice intoned from somewhere. A fetid blast of black vapor puffed from Collie's maw, rolling over them. The stench knocked them straight to their knees. Simultaneously, the ceiling opened in a terrifying cascade of Kibbles and Bits.

Shiro was instantly covered. Tomokato was buried to the neck, Platt to mid chest.

Still gagging at the Black Breath of Collie, struggling against the surrounding dog food, Tomokato fought to his feet, remaining waist-deep in the stuff.

A feeble heaving off to his right revealed Shiro's location. Tomokato waded towards it, but Platt got there first, reaching down into the canine chow. Kibbles raining from his kimono, Shiro burst up into view, gasping for breath, dangling from Platt's hand.

Tomokato looked up at the rim of the trap. It was ringed with thugs. They began to leap into the enclosure.

The cat's sword hissed into action. A hurtling didy dude parted like a bandsawed plank. Platt's towel sent another flying into a wall. Shiro's Mossberg blew two clear back to where they came from, the corpses trailing an entirely new variety of bits over the Kibbles.

Tomokato and Platt tried to get up on top of the loose, shifting dog food, but it was no good. They had no choice but to stand and have it out with the thugs dropping all around them. The bodies piled up real fast.

Shiro fired till he was out of ammo. Then a dead thug toppled over him, pinning him fast.

His uncle and the archaeologist fared little better. Before long they were totally immobilized by the sheer volume of corpses. Only their heads protruded from the grisly surface.

Shankar and Babesh Ruth appeared on a wall above.

"Why, Tomokato!" Shankar said, clapping his hands delightedly, "whatever are you doing in such an awful situation?"

"You recognize me?" Tomokato asked.

"You're a cat, you're Japanese, and you're buried in your own victims. Who else could you be?"

Shankar signaled. Two thugs knelt beside Tomokato and Platt, holding clubs.

"Knock them out so that we can just switch to the next scene," Shankar ordered.

Platt went under after the first blow. Tomokato remained conscious.

"He is resisting the transitional device, Shankar Guru," the thugs reported.

"That is because you hit the other one," Shankar replied acidly. "Now take off his helmet and strike!"

"We are not wearing his helmet, Shankar Guru," they replied.

Swearing, Shankar leaped down and did the job himself. Then he pulled a Webley-Fosberry automatic revolver from his sash and let the two chuckleheads have four apiece.

"It is impossible to get good thugs these days," he spat, and slid the smoking pistol back into place.

When Tomokato regained consciousness, he found himself chained to a wall; before him an immense room stretched as far as the eye could see, filled with all manner of items, exotic-looking statues, bizarre weapons, parchment scrolls, huge hasped books, rare automobiles, Mars Invades cards, and lots and lots of postage stamps.

"As you can see, Dr. Platt, we have gathered an abundance of lost treasures," came Shankar's voice, from off to the right. Tomokato turned his head slowly. Beside him hung Shiro, and beside Shiro, Platt. Shankar and Babesh Ruth stood in front of the archaeologist; at least a dozen guards lounged nearby on a very long couch, smoking Turkish cigarettes.

"Let me point out a few of our more remarkable finds," Shankar continued. "Do you see that Roman lance? It is none other than the spear of Longinus. There's the Holy Grail, and that's the True Cross, all twenty of it. We'd show you the Shroud of Turin, but we think it might be a fake."

He lifted a volume from a bookstand. "The only remaining copy of the Second Book of Aristotle's *Poetics,* his commentary on slapstick comedy. He's particularly fond of the Three Stooges—with Curly of course."

He hefted a stack of film canisters. "An original, unbutchered print of *The Magnificent Ambersons.* Let me tell you, the part where Tim Holt dances with the cartoon mouse is just as enchanting as Welles always said it was. And Joseph Cotten's nude scene is daring even by today's standards."

He walked over to a barnacle-encrusted airplane, cupped his hands and shouted up to the cockpit: "Hello, Amelia!"

No answer.

Shrugging, he tugged on a hanging cord. Bells chimed. From off to the right, a shuffling horde of American Indians approached, eyes empty, mouths slack; all wore huge warbonnets, sausage curls dangling from under the headgear.

"The Ten Lost Tribes," Shankar announced.

"Good Lord," Platt said. "Where did you find them?"

"Lapland."

Platt sighed with relief.

"What have you done with them?" Tomokato demanded. "They look like zombies."

"For all intents and purposes they are," Babesh Ruth said. "And they were highly instrumental in their own subjection. Remember, when I mentioned that the Shiva *Rhocksa* confer ultimate power in the presence of two-thirds of the lost treasures? Once the Ten Tribes were shipped here, that condition was fulfilled. The *Rhocksa* tapped into the Tribes' own mystic energies to enslave them."

"But even the *Rhocksa* require the ultimate conduit for their powers to be expressed," Shankar added.

"Such as the High Priest of Collie?" Platt asked.

"Such as the King of Rock 'n' Roll," Shankar replied. Going to a rhinestone-and-leather coffin standing up on end, he flung open the lid. A scent like roses wafted forth.

"Elvis!" Shiro gasped.

"Do the folks in Graceland know about this?" Platt demanded.

"Why is his name misspelled on the tombstone?" Shankar answered cryptically.

Apparently incorrupt, the King stood serenely in the midst of the gold-lamé quilting, mouth slightly ajar, as though he were just about to awaken and launch into "Love Me Tender." His hands were crossed over his chest, each holding a brightly glowing Shiva *Rhock;* two more were stuffed under his armpits, while a third had been jammed down solidly into the congealed Brylcreem of his pompadour.

"But doesn't he have to be alive to use the *Rhocksa*?" Platt asked.

"The mere touch of his flesh activates them," Shankar said. "And nothing accomplished through their power can be negated, unless his corpse is destroyed by Anti-Elvis."

"Anti-Elvis?" Platt asked. "You mean *the* Anti-Elvis, like in that Mojo Nixon song?"

"No. *Anti* as in antimatter. An opposite physical substance whose touch will result in mutual annihilation. But enough foreshadowing." Shankar smiled. "You came here for the *Rhocksa,* did you not?"

Platt said nothing.

"Well, you should at least be allowed to experience their power. You will become one of us, Dr. Platt. A son of Collie *Ma.* Not willingly, perhaps. But none of us has free will, after all. All is karma."

Platt sneered. "Is that one of your dogmas?"

Shankar nodded. "A Dog Ma dogma, to be exact. I

150

suppose from your perspective, it might even be a dog of a Dog Ma dogma."

"And if you added to it," Platt said, "that would be a dog of a Dog Ma dogma augment."

"And if you then took a piece of that," Shankar continued. "It would be a dog of a Dog Ma dogma augment fragment. And if you hid that in the cellar—"

"The cellar would be the dog of a Dog Ma dogma augment fragment basement," Platt broke in. "And if it belonged to a cartoon pooch, it would be Augie Doggy's dog of a Dog Ma dogma augment fragment basement."

"And if two pilots fought there," Shankar went on, "it would be a dogfight in Augie Doggy's dog of a Dog Ma dogma augment fragment basement. And to think that I was expecting you to trot out that old one about 'your karma ran over my dogma.'"

"Which one is that?" Platt asked.

"You are a funny fellow," Shankar said. "It will be a shame to turn you into a zombie. But you really must be forced to pull out the living brains of your two companions in the upcoming ceremony."

"Must I?"

Shankar smiled hideously. "Believe me, it is a much underrated experience." He touched the sacred stone on Elvis's head. All five suddenly blazed much brighter. "Mind-control time, *Rhocksa*!"

Tremendous bolts of zombie-colored energy crackled from the stones, converging and disappearing up Platt's left nostril. Platt stiffened, standing straight upright against the wall.

"Wisconsin?" Shiro asked. "How do you feel? Wisconsin?"

151

"Answer him, Dr. Platt," Shankar said.

Platt turned towards Shiro, eyes glazed. "Like I'd like to reach right into your skull and squeeze your brain just like it was a little Nerf ball."

"Would you even like to eat it yourself?" Shankar asked.

"Num-num-num," Platt said, rubbing his stomach, the chains on his wrists clinking. "Mmmm-boy. But it is dedicated to the *Dhawgi Devi,* so I will have to eat something else."

Shankar leered at Tomokato. "Do you still doubt the power of the stones?" he asked.

"I never doubted the power of the stones," Tomokato answered.

"Oh," said Shankar.

The captives were returned to the temple. Acolytes bound Tomokato and Shiro to the sacrificial pillar, then laid the felines' weapons (and Platt's towel) nearby.

"A tantalizing sight, eh?" Babesh Ruth asked the cat. "We just want you to remember that you've been disarmed."

Seminude temple bimbos removed Platt's shirt and finger-painted a psychedelic Sanskrit version of the Motor joke all over his chest and back. Zombie or no, Platt seemed to enjoy it. Afterwards, he stared at the colorful scrawls on his flesh.

"Looks like Judy Carne," Shiro told Tomokato.

Platt strode mechanically over to the pillar. "I heard that," the archaeologist said, and slapped Shiro across the nose. "You'll soon see that I'm no laugh-in matter."

"Wisconsin, get a hold of yourself," Tomokato said.

152

"Some spark of humanity is still within you. You still have your sense of humor."

"You're grasping at straws," Shankar said, approaching. "You know as well as I do that that pun showed precisely the opposite. He will commit any atrocity, tell any joke in the service of Collie. The *Dhawgi Devi* is most sadistically enamored of lousy humor. She became Mel Brooks's muse some time ago. Have you ever seen *Spaceballs*?"

"Funniest movie ever made," Platt said. "Particularly all the stuff with Dick Van Patten."

Never in his life had Tomokato felt the slightest urge to scream with horror; but those words on the lips of his friend were vile beyond belief. Not until that moment did the cat realize the true evil of Shankar's religion.

The congregation was summoned back to the temple; the worshipers arrived in a surly mood, grumbling about having "gone once this week." Noticing their disposition, Shankar had the temple girls do some bumps and grinds to get them into a more religious state of mind, then warmed them up further with a mind-boggling shaggy dogger that climaxed with a play on the entire first act of *King Lear,* though a not very good one. When they finally got more receptive, Shankar drew their attention to Elvis.

"As you may have noted, the King will be with us during the ceremony," the High Priest said.

" 'Hound Dog'!" a worshiper shouted.

" 'Blue Christmas'!" cried another.

" 'Burning Love'!" yelled a third.

Shankar put his hands up. "He will not be taking requests, as he is quite dead."

153

"Impossible!" someone cried. "He was seen at a Mall in Delhi, just the other day! The King lives!"

"In our hearts, perhaps," Shankar said. "But the truths of religion cannot always be taken literally. And on the literal level, this Elvis is a stiff." To prove his point, he pinched Elvis's cheek. Even though the flesh had been miraculously preserved, its consistency was about that of old chewing gum; the pinched bit stayed up like a piece of squoze putty.

"Oh man," the crowd moaned. "At least smooth it out again."

"Quick, Babesh, the mallet," Shankar said.

As Ruth pounded away at the protrusion with a rubber hammer, Shankar continued: "But the King is useful to us even in his defunctitude. Behold what the Shiva *Rhocksa* have done to this unbeliever." He led Platt front and center. "Take a bow."

Platt bowed.

"Before your very eyes, he will tear out the brains of his comrades," Shankar went on. "He has been transformed from an infidel into a perfect slave of Collie *Ma*. And he was just a normal man, not a mystical presence interacting with the stones. Total power is within our grasp! I tell you, my beloveds, we are truly onto something here!"

"Does this mean we get a raise?" they demanded.

"Symbolically, yes. Literally, no."

"What about eschatologically?"

"We will give you a raise at the end of time, certainly."

The crowd seemed satisfied with that.

"Now," said Shankar. " 'Wake Up *Devi*'!"

The thugs began to chant. An acolyte threw the switch to open the chasm in the floor. Shankar laid his hands on Platt's shoulders.

"Your true belief will set you on the path to sure brain removal," he said. "Fear not. You shall not flub it. Now, Dr. Platt. What do you say?"

"Arf, arf!"

"And who do you like the very best?"

"Dhawgi *Devi*!"

"Atta boy. Now *FETCH!*"

Right arm extended, Platt marched robotically towards Tomokato.

"Wisconsin!" Tomokato gritted. "Wisconsin, listen to me!"

Platt moved steadily forward.

"Fight the spell!" Tomokato cried. "You're still in there somewhere! Use your will!"

Platt's clawlike hand drew closer and closer.

"You don't want to kill us!" Tomokato said. "You hate what they're doing to you—"

Platt's fingertips touched Tomokato's forehead. "Wanna bet?" the archaeologist asked.

His nails dug into flesh. Blood poured over Tomokato's snout. But an instant before Platt reached anything important, a voice rang out:

"Everyone freeze!"

Platt looked round. Over the archaeologist's left shoulder, Tomokato saw two figures, a dark-haired man and woman, up in the gallery. Both had Heckler and Koch MP-5s.

"Shoot them!" Shankar cried to his guards.

But their Lee-Enfields were no match for the H and K's. The guards had more holes than a pair of screen doors by the time they struck the floor.

Still, Shankar had accomplished something; Tomokato saw Babesh Ruth slip from sight behind the idol of Collie.

The newcomers lowered a rope. While the woman climbed down, the man kept his gun trained on Shankar; then she covered the high priest as her companion descended.

Across the chasm, the congregation howled and screamed, proclaiming their willingness to charge the machine guns if only they could find some way over. The newcomers sprayed a burst across the fissure. Corpses tumbled over the edge.

"Silence!" the strangers cried.

The throng quieted.

"Who are you?" Shankar demanded.

"I'm a little bit country," the woman said.

"I'm a little bit rock 'n' roll," said the man. "We go by many names. In Canada, they call us Those Two Goddamn American Singers. In Mexico, we are known as Los Cucarachas de Utah. In Vegas and Tahoe, we are billed as Donny and Marie."

Simultaneously, the two flashed blinding smiles.

"What about in the East?" Shankar demanded.

"To the East we go not," Donny replied.

"This *is* the East," Shankar said.

"Well, we'll be leaving soon."

"Now, Dr. Platt," Marie said, leveling her MP-5 at the archaeologist. "You were paid a generous advance, but you never delivered the tablets."

156

Platt said nothing, staring at them.

"Tablets?" Shankar asked.

"Assyrian cuneiform," Donny said. "Proving that the Ten Lost Tribes actually *were* the first American Indians."

"Well, I don't know about the tablets," Shankar said, "but we can show you all the proof you need. As it just so happens, the Ten Lost Tribes are in one of our back rooms."

"Bring 'em out," Donny commanded.

"All of them?"

Donny fired a burst past Shankar's head.

"Go get them," Shankar told a flunky.

Tomokato noticed Shankar backing slowly towards Elvis's coffin. The guru began to smile; the cat guessed it was because Babesh Ruth had reappeared on the other side of the idol, behind Marie.

A dagger in his upraised hand, Ruth advanced stealthily, step by step, foot by foot, inch by inch—until, apparently very much to his surprise, Zeno's paradox stopped him dead in his tracks, well short of Marie.

Shankar swore with frustration. "Babesh, you fool!" he cried.

Donny and Marie looked round. Babesh hurled the knife. Marie put a couple of bullets in him before the dagger hit her hilt-first in the head, knocking her over.

Shankar ran to Elvis's coffin, placed his hand on one of the stones. "*Rhocksa,* mind control!" he cried.

But they did not respond immediately; they were too far from the treasures in the store room.

Donny turned, H and K spitting slugs. Shankar took one in the leg; another grazed his cheek.

157

Energy burst from the stones. Dazzled by the flash, Donny squinted, lifting his chin, his fire going wild, off toward the sacrificial pillar. The mind-control beam struck his teeth and glanced away, dissipating; one of his bullets tore into the ropes binding Shiro and Tomokato.

As the ropes dropped away, the cat and his nephew rushed for their weapons. On the other side of the lava, the congregation went absolutely nuts.

Tomokato picked up his swords, shucking the scabbards. Shiro snatched his Mossberg, reloading feverishly.

Tomokato looked over at Platt. The archaeologist closed in on Donny, who was shaking his head and rubbing his eyes as though he had lost his sight. Platt knocked the H and K from his hands, grabbed him by the lapels. The two whirled round. Donny broke the archaeologist's hold, then caught a powerful uppercut beneath the chin. Donny staggered backwards, past Tomokato and Shiro, who turned to see him topple into Elvis's coffin.

The casket went over. Nearby, Shankar was just getting to his feet when it exploded, flattening him again. When the flash faded, the coffin was nothing but splinters, and the Shiva *Rhocksa* were rolling in all directions across the floor.

"I get it," Shiro said, awestruck. "Donny must've been . . ."

Tomokato nodded. "Anti-Elvis."

They looked at Platt. Already back to his old self, the archaeologist rushed over to pick up his towel.

"I'm glad I didn't pull your brains out," he said.

"Me too," said the cat and his nephew, with some feeling.

Behind Platt, Marie had recovered from the dagger bash; using the selfsame knife, she was doing some embroidery on its hapless owner, who was still stuck in place. Once her good arm got tired, she picked up her fallen H and K and added some additional decorative motifs, several clips worth, more than enough to solve the paradox. Ruth crumpled, very little of his original color scheme remaining.

Shiro nudged his uncle, pointing. Across the chasm, the congregation was parting; up rolled a Soviet-made KrAZ-214 truck, lowering a TMM mechanized bridge. Waving pickaxes, gripping *fhido*s, the thugs poured onto the span.

Shiro held them back briefly with the shotgun; Tomokato was just about to charge when a tall Plains Israelite in full headdress and war paint appeared beside him, cradling a Henry repeating rifle.

"Excuse me," said the warrior, "Zedekiah Ben Bullet-Proof at your service. Could we be of assistance?"

Tomokato looked round. The full Ten Tribes stood there, liberated from the mind-control spell, just as Platt had been. Never one to turn down such a gracious offer, Tomokato nodded.

The chieftain grinned, roaring: "Scalp the goyim!"

Answering with ferocious whoops, his braves scoured the bridge clean with a shower of arrows, then followed him across.

"Gosh, Unc," Shiro said. "Looks like you're not going to get in on any of the climactic mayhem."

"That reminds me," Tomokato said. *"Shankar."*

The guru was still alive, standing by the base of the idol. As Tomokato approached, Shankar pulled his Webley and aimed it at Platt, who had just finished scooping up the last of the *Rhocksa,* making a bag for them with his towel.

"Stop right there, cat," Shankar cried.

Tomokato halted. "Shiro?"

"Out of ammo, Unc."

Tomokato looked over at Marie. Hand to her forehead, she stood swaying, apparently dizzied by her exertions on Ruth.

"Dr. Platt," Shankar said. "The stones."

"They're no good to you now," Platt said. "You lost Elvis."

"There's always Buddy Holly," Shankar replied.

"His body isn't lost," Platt countered.

"It will be after we steal it. Give me the stones."

"If you kill me, Tomokato will finish you. He'll deflect your bullets."

"Then I *won't* kill you," Shankar answered.

And shot him in the shoulder.

Platt howled in agony.

"Give me the stones," Shankar said.

"Sooner or later, he'll run out of shoulders," Tomokato said. "What then?"

"Look," Platt said, grimacing, "I've been thinking about this. I need my shoulders. And seeing as how my interest in the stones is purely economic . . ."

Crouching, he rolled the bag across the floor towards Shankar. It went a few yards before the stones spilled out, scattering.

160

Desperately shoving his Webley back into his sash, Shankar tried to pick them up. He got two, thrust them inside his robes; then, seeing Tomokato and Platt converging on him, he retreated to the statue, hitting a button. A recording of "Wake Up *Devi*" reverberated from the temple's PA system.

"From compact disk!" Shankar shrieked exultantly. "Even the gods can't tell it from live! And to complete the ceremony . . ."

He reached up and pulled out his own brain.

Totally taken aback by this move, Tomokato lowered his blade, jaw hanging slack.

"Tomo*ka*to," Platt said beside him.

Out of the corner of his eye, Tomokato saw the archaeologist jerking his thumb upwards, towards the statue. Tomokato looked.

Collie was looking back.

Tomokato and Platt backpedaled as fast as they could. Collie stepped down from her pedestal, lazily swinging her many swords, each of them fully five times as long as Tomokato's. Looking through the massive arch formed by her legs, Tomokato saw Shankar smugly stuffing his brain back into his skull.

"I get to because I'm high priest," the guru explained. He began gathering up the sacred stones still on the floor.

Each footstep booming, Collie started toward Tomokato and Platt.

"Get behind me, Wisconsin," Tomokato said, just before Collie launched a windmilling cascade of mighty sword strokes. Never before had Tomokato been grateful for his fencing master's insistence on practice against whirling helicopter rotors; bones rattling, teeth clacking

in his head, he felt as if he were parrying every prop in the 101st Airborne. But he was wielding what were perhaps the finest *katana* and *wakizashi* ever forged by Masamune of Tamba, while Collie was armed with shitty Indian steel; and despite the weight and fury of her blows, he rapidly took her tulwars to pieces. Fragments sprayed into the temple walls and ceiling. Powdered stone rained down.

Collie halted her assault, eyeing what was left of her weapons. She tossed the hiltshards away. Twelve vast *katanas* appeared magically in her paws.

Tomokato's mind raced. How could he possibly cope with her now?

He saw that Shankar had followed the goddess; gloating, the guru waved one of the *Rhocksa* triumphantly at him.

"When she starts again, get Shankar," Tomokato said over his shoulder to Platt. "Try to toss me one of the stones."

A new storm of swordblows rained down at Tomokato. He risked few parries, choosing instead to dodge and retreat. Platt slipped out from behind him. Collie appeared not to notice, intent as she was on the cat. As Tomokato backed steadily towards the fissure, Platt circled behind the goddess.

Shankar saw him coming. Whipping out his revolver once more, he shot him in the good shoulder, then put a second bullet in the other just for good measure. Platt staggered, swaying. Shankar drew a bead on his forehead. Grimacing with pain, the archaeologist was sure he was done for.

Two figures rushed towards Shankar from left and right. Holding her emptied H and K by its extended collapsible stock, Marie swung a terrific blow at the back of his head, Shiro simultaneously whacking him across the spine with his Mossberg.

Like an Ice Capades clown in the midst of some ostensibly funny routine, Shankar reeled forward, spinning, whirling out from behind Collie. He dropped at Tomokato's feet just as the cat found himself with his back to the fissure.

By then, the Ten Lost Tribes had just finished with the thugs. A volley of arrows swept across the gulf, striking Collie in the face. They did no damage, but distracted her momentarily, giving Tomokato just enough time to drop his swords and snatch the *Rhock* from Shankar's hand.

"One more move," he told Collie, "and it goes in the lava."

She remained frozen in place, staring at him. With one *Rhocksa* destroyed, Tomokato knew the rest would be useless; the power of her cult would vanish.

On the other side of the gap, Zedekiah watched tensely, signaling his followers to lower their bows.

Standing at the very brink, Tomokato looked over the side, studying the precipice below. Then, sensing movement, he whipped his face back round; Collie had sheathed her swords, and for a moment it seemed she was about to reach for him. He made as if to throw the stone. She went totally still.

"Why not just take it from me with your divine powers?" he asked.

"Maybe I'm constrained by factors outside your knowledge. . . ." she began in a huge hollow voice, sounding rather startlingly like—you guessed it—a thirty-foot-tall Joan Crawford. Swiftly she ran through a list of theological possibilities very similar to Platt's.

"I can, however, completely rule out tramps and dimness," she concluded. "Alberth, do you have any ideas?"

"Devi," Shankar groaned, "I was just smacked in the back of the head with a machine gun."

"Why would that keep me from doing it?" Collie asked.

"I don't know, Devi," Shankar answered. "Why, given our situation, would I do something as dumb as *this?*"

He lifted his pistol.

That really didn't change anything as far as Tomokato was concerned. It was only when he saw the hammer going back that he stamped on the guru's hand.

Yowling, Shankar let go of the gun. It bounced into the fissure. Tomokato kicked him in the face, but spitting blood, Shankar fought to his knees, grabbing for the stone.

Having no choice now, Collie made her move. Tomokato glimpsed a massive arm sweeping towards him. He looked towards her briefly—

And Shankar knocked the *Rhock* from his paw.

For a moment the guru stood bobbling it. Then it bounced clean away from him, over the side.

Collie stamped. "You little shit!" she bellowed. "That was incredibly dumb!"

Shankar looked at her as though he couldn't quite

understand her objection, blinking. "What did I tell you, Devi?"

Standing off to the side with Platt and Marie, Shiro watched as Collie bent towards his uncle and Shankar. To his horror, Tomokato turned and jumped into the chasm. The kitten shrieked; eyes suddenly bursting with tears, he started forward.

Marie pulled him back. "There's nothing you can do," she said.

"Let go of me, you Mormon person," he said, yanking free. If nothing else, he would bash the *Dhawgi Devi* with his shotgun. He would surely die. But at least he would go out uselessly, like a samurai.

Yet even that was denied him.

"You blew it all!" Collie thundered at Shankar. "Everything wasted! The whole cult shot!"

"Oh Collie Ma!" Shankar pleaded. "I told you I was hit on the head! Cut me some slack in your infinite mercy!"

"Mercy? I'm the goddess of Death!" She scooped him up, holding him tight in one of her mighty paws. "I'm out of here."

And with that, she clamped another paw over her nose; leaping high in the air, she tucked her knees up to her chest, wrapped her remaining arms about her legs, shouted "WATERMELON!" and sailed downwards into the lava.

Ten seconds later there was a tremendous echoing splash. Glowing globules of molten stone arced into view above the fissure.

Wiping his eyes, sidestepping splattered lava, Shiro

went to the edge. Collie had landed on her back. About the consistency of thick mud, the lava was slowly swallowing her.

One of her paws was upraised. Shankar flamed in its grasp, still wriggling as she sank.

Platt and Marie appeared beside Shiro.

"That's pretty unpleasant," Platt said.

Shiro wiped a tear from his eye. "It's not unpleasant enough."

As if in answer to the kitten's criticism, the twenty sticks of dynamite that Shankar always kept under his robes suddenly exploded; the guru's head rocketed up past Shiro and the others, trailing flames, and struck the ceiling of the temple, bursting like a burning, overripe melon stuffed with five times the amount of bright scarlet blood and brains that a melon would ordinarily be stuffed with.

"Better," said Shiro. "If only Uncle could have seen it."

"But I did, Shiro!" cried a familiar voice, from the other side of the chasm. Shiro looked up, beaming with joy when he saw Tomokato standing with Zedekiah.

"If you'll look down, you'll see a ledge," Tomokato said. "I landed on it when I jumped."

"But how did you get over there?" Platt cried.

Tomokato shrugged. "Submarine."

Marie sidled up to Platt. "So you were on the trail of the Ten Tribes all along," she said.

"No," Platt answered. "To be honest, I was after the Shiva *Rhocksa.*"

"And the Ten Tribes just happened to be here?" she laughed. "You're a riot." She batted her eyelashes at

167

him. "You know, I really go for guys with shoulder wounds."

"Shouldn't you be in mourning for your brother?" he asked.

"Nah. He was a twerp. I was always much cuter anyway."

Tomokato and Zedekiah came across the bridge.

"Well, Zedekiah," Platt said, "where will the Ten Tribes go now? Back to Lapland?"

"No," the chieftain replied. "We were thinking of Israel."

"They might not let you in."

"What about the Law of Return?"

"You might not be Jewish enough for some people."

"You could come to Utah," Marie offered. "That's where God lives now anyway."

"He whose four-letter name we will not pronounce?"

"Robert Redford? Sure."

Zedekiah looked about as though he were expecting a lightning bolt. "You pronounced his name."

"Only the thirteen-letter version."

He counted on his fingers. "How many without the vowels?"

"It's cool, really," she assured him.

Tomokato went to pick up his swords. Shiro followed him.

"Uncle-*san*," the kitten said, "What about a mining-car chase?"

"The story's over, Shiro."

"But people might be expecting one."

"Having a mining-car chase after the big supernatural manifestation would just be anticlimactic."

"Oh." Shiro was silent for a few moments. "You know, Uncle, I really thought you were dead. It felt so bad."

"Does that surprise you?"

"No. But do you think I should try to have the same feeling when *anyone* gets killed?"

"Are you actually acquiring a reverence for life?"

"What do you think?"

"That you'll have to grow up some time."

Shiro nodded. "Can't put off the inevitable, huh?"

"No, you can't."

"Ah well," Shiro sighed. "No point rushing things either." He smiled angelically at Tomokato, resting his Mossberg on his shoulder. "Who's next?"

169

The Invasion
of the Kitty Snatchers

The unfortunate honor of being next fell to the infamous international terrorist Carlos LaFong. LaFong had made his name in the mid 1980s, taking on the entire New York Police Department and several FBI SWAT teams in a daring and successful attempt to hijack spring fashions for Muammar Kaddafi; soon after supplying the colonel with several ravishing dresses, he had participated in a truly Sikh plot to transport the Punjab region bodily out of the Indian subcontinent. That failed, but it got a lot of people killed anyway, and he landed a great deal of work as a result; in cooperation with the Japanese Red Army, he shot up a lot of noncombatants in the airline terminal at Azuchi Castle before wounding Nobunaga with a car bomb.

Once again contacting the Hardware Man, Tomokato learned the latest information on LaFong: the terrorist had apparently taken an extended leave from the business. Rumor had it that he was about to embark on a cruise from New York to the Bahamas. Discovering that the

Mark E. Rogers

Happyship Line was offering a fifty percent terrorist discount on one particular off-season jaunt, Tomokato reserved a stateroom and headed for the Big Apple with his nephew.
    —from *Cat Out of Hell, A Biography*
       of Miaowara Tomokato by William Shirer
       and A. J. P. Godzilla

1

Now *this* is a boat," Shiro said, following his uncle up the boarding ramp of the Happyship *Gross Indulgence*. It was an hour before departure.

"Hurry, Shiro," Tomokato said. "We must get to our quarters as soon as possible."

"Do you really think LaFong will recognize you?"

"I don't know," Tomokato answered. "But I don't want to give him the opportunity."

They flashed their tickets at the top, got directions, and hastened to their stateroom. Shiro started bouncing on the bunk at the first opportunity.

"Shoot me, Unc!" he said.

"What?" Tomokato asked, turning from the porthole.

"Shoot me."

Tomokato pointed at the kitten.

"What caliber?" Shiro asked.

"What?"

"If I don't know what caliber, I don't know how far to bounce."

172

Tomokato thought it over. "Parabellum."

"That's millimeter," Shiro objected.

Tomokato shot him anyway. "Bang," he said disinterestedly.

"Yah!" said Shiro, flinging himself against the bulkhead with astonishing force. He seemed to hang suspended against it for an impossible instant; then he peeled forward, landing on the bunk on his face.

"Vrrt vrrt vrrt," he said, out of the corner of his mouth. Tomokato knew from experience that this was the sound of blood pumping from an imaginary exit wound.

Shiro leaped back up, good as new. "Shoot me again, Unc."

Tomokato gave him another one, this time in the head.

They remained inside until the ship was well out to sea. In the event that LaFong realized he was in danger, Tomokato had no intention of leaving him anywhere to run.

"Where we going, Unc?" Shiro asked as they went back out on deck.

"Purser's office," Tomokato replied. "Perhaps they'll give us LaFong's cabin number."

"What makes you think he'll be using his real name?" Shiro asked. "He's wanted in sixty countries. *And* Canada."

"How would he qualify for the terrorist discount?" Tomokato replied.

"He could use some other terrorist's name."

"He'd still have the same problem."

173

"He could *prove* he was a terrorist. Hijack the ship."

"Then why would he *need* the discount?"

"You got me," Shiro admitted. "Actually, I'm surprised that they get many terrorists on Happyship Cruises as it is."

"Why would you expect vicious killers to have good taste?"

"Well, *I* do," Shiro sniffed.

They came to the purser's office.

"What's his name?" the purser asked.

"Carlos LaFong," Tomokato answered.

"How's that spelled?"

Tomokato shrugged. "LaFong. Capital *l*, small *a*, capital *f*, small *o*, small *n*, small *g*. Carlos LaFong."

The purser smiled the tight, nasty smile of a bureaucrat with the upper hand. "We don't have any Carlos LaFong, capital *l*, small *a*, capital *f*, small *o*, small *n*, small *g*, and if we did, I wouldn't tell you. We don't give people's cabin numbers to just any medieval Japanese puss-puss who comes strolling up, even if he does know how to spell a name such as Carlos LaFong's."

Tomokato decided on a different tack: "Would I be connected if I used the courtesy phone?"

"Not if I had anything to do with it."

"Do you?"

Without answering, the purser walked over to a corner and stuck his face in it, humming a tune from *Il trovatore.* Tomokato and Shiro went back out.

"The minor characters in these stories are getting very ugly and strange," Shiro said.

"The author was treated very badly by a minor character when he was young," Tomokato replied.

"Is that why he kills off so many spear carriers?"

"So I've heard."

They discovered a phone some distance up the passageway from the office.

"What are you going to tell LaFong?" Shiro asked.

"That the Popular Front for the Liberation of Palestine is having a wine-and-cheese party. I'll give him our cabin number. And if he shows up . . ."

Shiro laughed wickedly. "He'll sample the bitter wine of vengeance."

"Not to mention the still-more-bitter cheese of death," Tomokato added.

He rang the operator, who promptly connected him with LaFong's berth. But there was no answer.

"Very well then," Tomokato said, hanging up. "We should stroll around the ship, familiarize ourselves with it. Perhaps we'll encounter him."

Going out on the starboard side, they made their way aft in a leisurely fashion. After a time Tomokato stopped a steward heading in the opposite direction.

"Have many terrorists taken advantage of the discount?" he asked.

"Nah, it's been a total bust. All we got is a few Tamil Tigers and that LaFong guy."

"Isn't he a leading light in the terrorist world?"

"Yeah, but he's giving it up. Says it's really a bummer thinking of yourself as a bloodthirsty sadistic scumbag."

"You've talked to him, then?"

"Sure."

"What's his cabin number?"

"3306. But I just saw him back on the fantail. You know, by the pool." The steward groaned, trying to readjust the weight of the huge steamer trunk on his back. "Actually, would you mind if I delivered this? It's full of bowling balls, and—"

Tomokato stepped out of his way. "By all means."

The felines hurried to the fantail. The pool was full of swimmers; white-uniformed waiters brought trays of colorful tropical drinks to guests reclining on deck chairs. Tomokato and Shiro saw no sign of LaFong. But they did get a wonderful surprise.

"Tomokato!" cried Shimura, lounging at poolside.

Standing nearby, Hanako was keeping an eye on Huki, Duki, Luki, and Agamemnon, who appeared to be reenacting the battle of Sekigahara in the shallow end of the pool, rather to the consternation of the kiddies nearby. Hearing Tomokato's name, Hanako turned and smiled, waving. Shimura rose from his deck chair.

Shiro bowed to his father. "Papa-*san*!" the kitten cried.

Shimura bowed in response. "And how are you, killer?"

Shiro flashed him a smile and ran to his mother, hugging her.

Tomokato and Shimura exchanged bows, then embraced.

"And how's life with my son?" Shimura asked.

Tomokato picked his words carefully: "Truly . . . *interesting.*"

"How so?"

"I am constantly astonished by progress in the martial arts," Tomokato said, turning to watch Shiro being pulled into the pool by his brothers. "It is quite frightening at times."

176

"He takes after us," Shimura said.

"But his lack of *moral* progress is more frightening still," Tomokato continued.

"He takes after Shimura," Hanako said, slipping an arm around her husband. Shimura sniffed, pretending to be annoyed.

"You know it's true," Tomokato said. "You were always beating me up."

Shimura laughed. "That *would* be the first thing you'd remember. No mention of all that banditry, or my ninja days . . ."

"I was getting to that. You're just lucky that your younger brother set you back on the path of righteousness."

"You mean becoming a hired killer for Nobunaga?"

Tomokato was unfazed. "Nobunaga did many good things for Japan. He made the trains run on time, or would have if we'd had trains."

"He was the least of many evils, true," Shimura admitted. "So, what are you doing on the *Gross Indulgence*? You wouldn't be after Carlos LaFong, would you?"

"Once again, your information is impeccable. You haven't seen him around here, have you?"

"We just arrived."

"So what are *you* doing on a Happyship Cruise?" Tomokato asked.

"Poets get to take lots of vacations," Shimura replied.

"Otherwise they go quite mad," Hanako said.

"I just finished a poem on the second Mongol invasion," Shimura continued. "It involves a muppet calling

177

the Divine Wind down on a group of southwest American Indians fighting for the khan."

Remembering the horrible Augie Doggy interplay between Platt and Shankar, Tomokato said, in not-entirely-mock disgust: "Let me guess. It's called *Kamikaze Fozzie and the Anasazi.*"

"Hey, come on," Shimura said. "Poetic license."

"It really is Shimura's finest work yet," Hanako said. "He's done some very interesting things with placing the words on the page, just like E. E. Cummings, only with ideograms."

Shimura looked sidelong at Tomokato, smiling slyly. It was always very difficult to tell when to take him seriously. "Critics'll eat it up," he said.

Tomokato was about to voice his opinion of critics when a column of spray erupted some distance astern; it looked almost as though someone had discharged a single fifty-caliber round into the ocean.

"What do you see?" Shimura asked.

"Something just struck the water back there."

More columns shot up; light tan against the blue sky, strange objects were raining from the heavens.

"Incoming!" yelled one of the kittens from the pool.

Tomokato looked up to see what appeared to be a large butternut squash shooting down towards him. He dodged. It smashed into the deck where he had been standing.

"Look at 'em all!" Shimura cried. From out of nowhere, he and his family, Shiro included, produced gaily painted steel umbrellas. Tomokato dived beneath Hanako's as the kittens scrambled up the pool steps, squashes dropping all around them. Once they splashed down, the vegetables seemed to explode under the water; pulpy-looking mush floated to the surface, smoking.

"Just like *The Day of the Triffids,*" Huki announced, as he and his brothers drew near. "Seawater destroys 'em."

"Definitely extraterrestrial," Duki pronounced.

Pandemonium reigned on the fantail. Passengers and waiters were scurrying madly for cover, trying to avoid the falling squashes, legs splattered with pulp and seeds. Tomokato saw several take direct hits, one dropping into the steaming squash soup that had been the swimming pool; others remained on their feet, looking a bit stunned but otherwise little worse for wear, aside from being decorated with alien goo.

"All right, kids," Shimura said, a squash bonging powerfully on his metal bumbershoot. "Back to the cabin."

The clan dashed from the fantail. Pausing under an overhanging deck, they scraped off as much of the squash guck as they could before entering the super-structure.

Acrid-smelling yellow smoke rolled over the ship. Tomokato looked out to sea. Wind parted the vapor clouds for an instant. He could see the water being peppered with falling squash clean out to the horizon. The ocean was boiling, huge rafts of corroding pulp collecting on the surface.

He and the others went inside. Shimura's cabin was nearby, with a porthole looking out over the starboard rail.

"This is no ordinary rain of extraterrestrial squash," Shimura said solemnly.

"Why do you say that?" Tomokato asked, having lived

through several such incidents in Japan, where they are quite common, as any schoolchild knows.

"Normally, the vegetables reach lethal velocities," Shimura said. "Yet we saw several people struck, and none were killed. What does that tell you?"

"That this is no ordinary rain of extraterrestrial squash?" Tomokato asked.

"Precisely."

"We *still* tracked some of it in," said Hanako, eyeing some slime that had come off Agamemnon's feet.

"I expect the Happyship Line will forgive us," Shimura said, "seeing as the stuff's splashed all over the boat."

Tomokato peered out of a porthole. The vapor was clearing. The hail of squashes had stopped. Long streams of pulp swung from the walkway above, white seeds spiraling down along them; thick gobbets dripped onto the rail and the deck.

"It's going to be quite a cleanup," he said.

"Not too bad," Shimura said. "They'll wash most of it overboard with the firehoses."

"Just think, children," Hanako said. "You had to go halfway across the world to see your first hail-of-squash."

"Japan isn't what it used to be," Shimura said. He nudged Tomokato with his elbow. "Remember the time it rained Szechuan beef?"

"Those were the days," Tomokato said.

He spent the next several hours catching up with Hanako and Shimura. They ordered cabin service; dinner arrived late, since some of the galley help had been drafted for the cleanup efforts. But the meal was fine, and Tomokato had such an excellent time that he nearly forgot why he had come on the voyage in the first place.

"LaFong can wait until tomorrow," Shimura told him. "After all, where can he go?"

By then, it was well into the evening; Tomokato wound up staying nearly till two. Having heard Shiro recounting his adventures, the other kittens were all wide awake and wired, very much of the opinion that he should spend the night with them. But thinking they were all far *too* wired, Hanako gently suggested that Tomokato should take her son with him. Shiro did not seem to mind; after all, his guns were back in the other cabin, including his "security gun," the little full-auto Mauser Broomhandle that he always slept with.

Tomokato's stateroom was on the port side of the main deck. Leaving Shimura's cabin, the cat and Shiro made for a passage that would take them to the far side of the superstructure.

Three men came out of a stairwell up ahead.

One was LaFong.

The terrorist turned briskly. Tomokato did not think LaFong had seen him.

The men with LaFong followed close behind, each with a hand thrust into a coat pocket. The trio increased their speed, vanishing from sight at the adjoining corridor.

"That was him, wasn't it?" Shiro asked.

Tomokato nodded. "Come on."

They rounded the corner. Going down the passage-way, they came out by the port rail just in time to hear one of LaFong's companions say, in French, "No one leaves the QLF."

There came the *thap!* of a silenced pistol. Before LaFong's legs could buckle, the executioner's partner flipped the corpse over the side. The two men turned.

Their eyes widened.

"Shiro," gasped the man with the gun, and aimed it at the kitten.

Tomokato drew his sword and sliced the man's hand off. As the severed member spun through the air, cadaver reflex discharged a shot. On its way to the executioner's vitals, the bullet shattered two fountain pens in his breast pocket. Spewing ink like some bizarre negative advertisement for ballpoints, he catapulted over the railing.

"Neatly done, Unc," said Shiro.

"Come on now," the other man said in French-accented Japanese, holding his hands high. "You're not going to tell me he did that deliberately!"

"Do you have a gun?" Shiro asked him.

"Oui."

"Why don't you pull it and find out for yourself?"

The man shrugged. "I must admit, I am very curious," he said, and went for the rod.

The very spirit of fair play, Tomokato let him get it out, then amputated his gun hand too—but at a slightly different angle, just to show his complete mastery of technique; this time the bullet went through the man, bounced off the railing behind, exited back through his chest, ricocheted off the bulkhead behind Tomokato, and landed spent on the guy's tongue.

The victim spat the bullet out. "I am utterly in awe," he said.

"As you certainly should be," said Tomokato. "Now would you kindly climb over the railing and dispose of your body?"

"Delighted," the man replied. "Hell of a trick." He obliged gratefully.

Tomokato looked round to see that a large crowd of witnesses had gathered. But instead of raising an alarm, they gave him thirty seconds of sustained applause before dispersing. One man flipped him a coin over his shoulder.

"That first killer recognized you," Tomokato told his nephew, pocketing the quarter.

"I'm just as puzzled as you are, Unc," Shiro said, avoiding his uncle's gaze.

"Tell me the truth, Shiro," Tomokato said.

"All right," Shiro replied. "I met 'im back in Chicago, when I was working for Moran. Competitors. They used to run liquor down from Canada. I put a bullet in one of 'em during a hijack."

"But what do they have to do with LaFong?"

"How should I know? *We* get from one historical period to another. Why couldn't they?"

"That wasn't the question, and you know it."

"Yeah, but it *is* the more interesting question, isn't it? How *do* we manage the time travel, Uncle?"

"You're trying to distract me."

"How can you tell?"

183

"Because *you* time-travel with me all the time. It's the *readers* that don't know how we do it."

"And just as well, too," Shiro went on. "If they had the slightest idea how easy it was—"

"They'd simply abuse it," Tomokato agreed sadly, setting him down.

"Ah, evil," Shiro said. "Such a bottomless mystery. And an even more interesting question than time travel, don't you think?"

"Yes, but one we won't solve tonight. Come, Shiro. Let's get some sleep."

They went back into the superstructure.

"You think you distracted me, don't you?" Tomokato asked.

"About what?"

"Don't try it again," the cat warned.

"What?" Shiro asked. "And have you catch me again? You bet I won't, Uncle-*san*. You're much too clever for me. I don't know why I even tried it to begin with. I never even had a prayer."

"Shiro, you're doing it now—"

"Look, Uncle!" Shiro interrupted, pointing into an open stateroom. "The Marx brothers!"

Tomokato tugged his arm, refusing to look.

"*With* Gummo!" the kitten added.

At that, despite his iron resolve, Tomokato could not help taking a gander.

"So *that's* what Gummo looks like," he said, thoroughly distracted at last.

2

Having kept such late hours, he and Shiro did not rise until practically eleven; the restaurants on the promenade were no longer serving breakfast, so the cat and his nephew had to settle for lunch.

During the meal, Tomokato noticed that their waiter was acting oddly; the man's eyes were very wide and vacuous, and he smiled perpetually, like a Moonie in constant contemplation of Reverend Sun. Instead of a rose, he tried to persuade them to take a little plant rising out of some wet white sugar in a coffee cup. Tomokato refused gently.

"It's free," the waiter replied. "On the house."

"But why would I want it at all?" Tomokato asked.

"It grows very quickly," the waiter replied.

"Yes, but—"

"You don't even need the sugar, though that helps," the waiter continued.

"I'm delighted to hear it," Tomokato said. "But—"

"You can actually see it get bigger, minute by minute. You've heard of towns where the big thing is watching the grass grow? Now you can capture the very same thrill, right in your very own stateroom."

He set the coffee cup on the table, sliding it towards Tomokato.

"You can even put it under your bunk," he said, leaning slowly forward. Tomokato noticed for the first time that the waiter's pockets were stuffed with sugar packets.

"Even?" Tomokato asked.

The man nodded slowly. "Even."

Tomokato started to push the plant back towards the waiter, but the man left immediately. As the fellow headed for the back of the restaurant, Tomokato noticed him taking sugar packets out of the dishes on unoccupied tables.

"Peculiar sort," Tomokato said.

"I'd say his mainframe's off-line," Shiro replied.

Presently the waiter returned with another plant.

"For the tot," he explained.

"Tot?" Shiro snarled.

The waiter departed once more, but the cat noticed him looking at them over his shoulder. The man waved languidly, called "Even" in a soft voice, and went on his way, looting other tables for their sugar.

Tomokato rose to leave.

"You know, I think you really *can* see it grow," Shiro said, reaching for the plant the waiter had brought him.

"Leave it," Tomokato said.

"But I bet I *could* really put it under my bunk," Shiro protested.

"Is that a reason?"

"Not a good one, maybe," Shiro said, getting up. "But it *is* a reason."

They left the restaurant. On their way to Shimura's cabin, they were descending the main stairway from the promenade when Huki, Duki, Luki, and Agamemnon came running up to them, looking quite terrified.

"Our parents are coming," said Luki breathlessly.

"Are you playing hide-and-seek?" Tomokato asked.

186

"No," said Luki. "We have to get away. They're not . . . they aren't . . ."

"Aren't what?" Tomokato asked.

"Our parents," Duki broke in breathlessly.

"But Luki just said—"

"They'll be here any second!" Agamemnon cried.

"Stall 'em, Unc!" said Duki, charging up the steps.

"Don't let them get us!" said Luki, following Duki.

"Come on, Shiro!" said Huki.

Shiro shrugged at Tomokato. "Sounds like a great game, whatever it is," he said, and pelted after his brothers.

Trying to dodge out of the kittens' path, a steward dropped his huge tray; down rattled an avalanche of coffee cups, soggy sugar and little plants spilling out of them. With a blank expression that utterly belied his frantic movements, the steward set about trying to get the plants back in their receptacles.

"Tomokato!" came Shimura's voice. Tomokato turned. Paws behind their backs, his brother and sister-in-law stood below him on the steps, smiling like a couple of brain-damaged seraphim.

"You haven't seen our sons, have you?" said Hanako.

Tomokato started to reply; but the look on their faces, so uncharacteristic of them, held him in check.

"We have presents for them," said Shimura in a curious monotone; he and his wife brought their paws out from behind their backs.

"What makes you think they'd want little plants in coffee cups?" Tomokato said.

"You can practically see them grow," said Shimura.

187

"And you can put them under your bunk," said Hanako.

"Excellent," Tomokato answered, for lack of another response.

"Now then," Shimura said. "Have you seen the kittens?"

"No," said Tomokato.

"What about Shiro?" Hanako asked. "Is he back in your cabin?"

Tomokato shook his head. "He said something about poking around the lower decks."

Hanako and Shimura looked at each other as if some mysterious communication were passing between them. Then Shimura told Tomokato:

"Please disregard any appearance of telepathy."

"Ah well," said Tomokato. "I'm feeling a bit seasick. I think I'll go back to my berth and lie down."

Shimura proferred him a plant. Tomokato tried to demur.

"I insist," Shimura said. "Better than Dramamine."

"Certainly," said Tomokato, accepting it. "Hope you find the kittens. If I meet them, I'll tell them you're looking for them."

He headed down the stairs. But when he reached the bottom, he had a curious feeling that he was being watched; looking back, he saw Shimura and Hanako beaming at him.

"You'll feel better soon," said Hanako.

"Much better," said Shimura.

They both turned and proceeded to hop upwards three steps at a time, looking uncannily like kangaroos.

Tomokato thrust the plant into the nearest trash can. Immediately a pale hand pushed from under the metal flap and gave the plant back to him. In a singsong voice, the person inside said: "How ungrateful; you must keep it; it is on the house."

Tomokato found another can. Again the coffee cup was thrust back at him, but this time he didn't accept it, retreating slowly.

The hand took the cup back inside the can, then reemerged, pointing a long stern finger at him. Two old women with blue hair immediately came out of the ladies room and shook their heads at him.

He strode briskly for his cabin, and was about halfway there when an elevator opened on his right; out marched a steward with a cloth-covered box. Tomokato paused. He could not see what was in the container, but he thought he heard leaves rustling.

He looked into the elevator. It held only one passenger now, a man standing ramrod-straight against the back wall.

LaFong.

Tomokato was completely mystified. He had seen the terrorist executed. And even if LaFong had somehow survived the bullet, how had he gotten back aboard the ship?

The doors began to close. Tomokato shoved his paw between them, and they sprang back. LaFong barely looked at him.

Up till then Tomokato had not known whether the terrorist would recognize him. But LaFong did not appear to have the slightest idea that he was in danger.

Tomokato stepped inside. LaFong had the button pressed for E deck, the lowest level. The doors sighed shut, and the elevator began to descend.

Paw on the emergency stop switch, Tomokato faced him.

"Carlos LaFong," he said.

"Capital *l*, small *a*, Capital *f*, small *o*, small *n*, small *g*," LaFong replied. "What can I do for you?"

Tomokato clicked the switch. The elevator came to a halt between decks, deep in the belly of the ship.

"Die," the cat said.

"Are you from the QLF?" LaFong asked with a kind of spacier-than-spacy tranquillity, as though he had taken a truckload of Valium.

"QLF?" Tomokato demanded.

"Quebec Liberation Front," LaFong answered.

Tomokato squinted. Hadn't Shiro mentioned French-Canadian separatists, back in India?

The question was driven from his mind as LaFong reached under his sports jacket. Tomokato's point was in his chest an instant later.

A Tokarev automatic dropping from his hand, LaFong remained on his feet until Tomokato pulled his sword free, then dropped like a marionette with its strings cut, a dark stain opening over his heart.

But it was not red.

It was green.

Tomokato looked at his blade. It was smeared with the same color. He sniffed the liquid on the steel. It smelled rather like skunk cabbage.

What had he just killed?

He wiped the sword off on LaFong's clothing, then went back to the control panel and took the elevator all the way down, theorizing that he was least likely to encounter witnesses on the lowest deck.

When the doors opened, he stepped out into a dark passage filled with heat, humidity, and a sour oily smell. Pipes ran along the ceiling, steam leaking from their joints.

There was a stairwell nearby. As Tomokato made towards it, he noticed two laundry carts some distance beyond the entrance; they were covered with sheets, but he saw what appeared to be a hand sticking out of one. Curiosity aroused, he went to the cart and lifted the sheet.

Inside were Harpo, Chico, and Gummo Marx, staring with glazed eyes. They were barely breathing. Harpo's hand was frozen in mid honk on the bulb of his horn.

Shocked, Tomokato went to the other cart. Raising the cloth, he uncovered Zeppo, Groucho—

—and W. C. Fields.

Tomokato gasped. He hadn't even known Fields was on the boat.

He heard footsteps ahead; several men were about to round a corner, their shadows bobbing towards him along the wall. He dashed noiselessly into the stairwell.

Soon he was back on A deck. Approaching his cabin, he saw a woman pulling violently on an officer's arm; the fellow wouldn't budge.

"They already got Samantha," she cried. "And if you don't help me, they'll get Jimmy too."

"There, there," he replied, shaking free of her and lifting his cap. There was a teacup balanced on his head; how he had managed to fit it under his hat, Tomokato hadn't the foggiest.

"Perhaps you'd like a nice plant," the officer said.

The woman fled shrieking.

Tomokato walked swiftly past the officer, who tried to hand him the cup. "On the house," the man whispered behind him.

Reaching the stateroom, Tomokato found it open. A maid was inside. He eyed her cart. The back shelf was covered with coffee cups. As she went about her business, he watched the little plants. Sure enough, he could see tendrils uncurling, tiny leaves opening.

The maid finished making up the bunks and deposited two chocolates on the desk; Tomokato shooed her out, then looked beneath the bunks.

There was a plant under each.

He removed the coffee cups. Going to the toilet, he flushed the plants down.

There came a rap on the door. He went to answer it. In piled Huki, Duki, Luki, and Agamemnon, with Shiro.

"You have to hide us, Uncle-*san*," Luki said.

"From who?" Tomokato asked, closing the door.

"Mom and Dad," said Huki.

"Shiro, what's going on?" Tomokato demanded, eyeing him carefully. The kitten seemed quite genuinely spooked.

"They *aren't* our parents," Shiro said. "I want my gun!" He rushed to his luggage and pulled out the Mauser.

"Got any for us?" Duki asked.

"Help yourself," Shiro replied.

They scrambled for the suitcase. Huki got a Skorpion submachine gun, Duki an Erma MP-40. Luki fought with Agamemnon for a Steyr AUG bullpup, but had to settle for an Owen gun.

192

"Don't worry, Luki," Tomokato said. "That Owen's a fine weapon."

"Yeah, but it looks real dumb with the clip on top—" Luki broke off. Someone else was at the door.

"No shooting now," Tomokato said.

"Will *you* kill 'em?" Agamemnon asked desperately.

"And if they really are your parents?" Tomokato answered.

"You talked to them, Uncle. *They're not our parents.* You know it."

"No I don't," Tomokato answered.

Another knock.

"Just get in the closet," the cat commanded.

The kittens scuttled from sight.

Tomokato went to the door. Shimura and Hanako stood outside, the plants they were holding noticeably larger.

"Are the kittens in there?" Shimura asked.

"No," Tomokato said.

"Might we come in?" Hanako asked.

Tomokato hesitated a few moments. "Of course." He stepped aside.

"You wouldn't be hiding them, would you?" Shimura said. He and Hanako moved slowly about the room.

"I resent that question," Tomokato said, eyes racing back and forth between the two of them. It was quite impossible to watch both at the same time.

Finally Hanako sat on the bed, holding her coffee cups in her lap. Tomokato's attention shifted to his brother as Shimura went toward the closet.

"They wouldn't be in there, would they?" Shimura asked.

"You know, brother," Tomokato said, "you're acting quite strangely."

Shimura halted, smiling at him. "Strangely?" he asked. "What could you possibly mean by that?"

"What about hopping up stairs like a kangaroo?"

"You should try it," Shimura recommended.

"It's an exercise plan," Hanako said blandly.

"What plan is that?" Tomokato asked.

"It's called Wallaby Weight-Off," Shimura said. "It's very big back on Altair Four."

"Altair?"

"Omi Province has been renamed," Shimura replied, without missing a beat. "You should come home more often. Everyone's hopping, hopping, hopping."

As if to emphasize his point, he began bouncing towards the closet, looking unnervingly like Bobby Van in *Small Town Girl.* Tomokato put himself between him and the sliding door.

"They're not in there," he said.

"Then you won't mind if I take a look, will you?" Shimura asked.

"I very much mind," Tomokato answered. "You are questioning my word. My honor. I cannot take such a slur lightly, even from my own brother."

Their eyes locked. Shimura had no difficulty holding Tomokato's stare. But Tomokato had the uncanny feeling that no one at all was looking back at him. If the eyes were the windows of the soul, then he was peering into an empty gourd.

Or a butternut squash? he asked himself.

"Come, Shimura," said Hanako. "Perhaps we should be off."

194

"If I have offended you, I apologize," Shimura told Tomokato, bowing.

Tomokato bowed stiffly in response, noting that Shimura and Hanako still held two plants apiece. He guessed they had not secreted any in the cabin.

Once they left, he closed the door, leaning up against it. Pondering what he had observed, he waited a few moments in silence.

"Can we come out now?" Shiro called.

"Yes," Tomokato said.

The closet opened. The kittens rushed out.

"Altair Four," Shiro spat. "Do you *still* think they're our parents, Uncle-*san*?"

"I don't know what I think," Tomokato said, going to the porthole. "But something very peculiar *is* happening on this ship. I killed Carlos LaFong today."

"But he was murdered *yesterday*," Shiro said.

Tomokato nodded. A man strode past outside; the cat swore.

"And there he goes again!" he cried.

"Who, Uncle?" Shiro asked.

"LaFong!" Tomokato bolted for the door. "Stay here, all of you! And keep the door locked."

But by the time he came out of the superstructure, LaFong had disappeared.

Tomokato looked all over A deck, then searched B and C. No sign of his prey. Finally he went up to the promenade, just in time to see LaFong going through an arch leading to one of the ship's pools.

The ocean had gotten somewhat rougher; waves in the pool would have endangered swimmers, and so it had been drained to about one-third full. An officer stood by the side of it, looking down at the water sloshing back and forth. LaFong went up to him. They stepped away from the edge.

Aside from the cat, there was no one else on the deck. Tomokato passed by them. Strain as he might, he could hear no conversation passing between LaFong and the other man.

The cat went to a rail and leaned against it, watching them. He scratched the side of his snout.

Immediately they came over to him.

"We saw you give the signal," said the officer.

"Are you in difficulty?" LaFong asked. "Come, you must speak. There is no mental contact between species. You have assumed the wrong form."

"I was wondering what the problem was," Tomokato said.

"No matter," LaFong said. Suddenly a hint of suspicion crossed his face. He turned to stare at the officer. Then both looked at Tomokato.

"What are you doing up here?" LaFong asked.

"Didn't you bring your original to the designated place?" the officer asked.

"Of course," Tomokato said.

"But how then did you discover where the designated place was?" LaFong pressed. "You must have made contact. But if you made contact, you would have learned speech was necessary before you met us."

Tomokato nodded, trying to follow the logic. "Because one cannot make mental contact between the species," he answered.

"Yes," said the officer. "But once again, how did you learn the designated place?"

Tomokato groped for an answer. "My original was not the only cat on this ship."

It was a good reply; but he did not give it fast enough. The two stared at each other once more. Tomokato knew they were onto him. He drew his sword.

"Where's the designated place?" he demanded. "Where's *your* original, LaFong?"

They backed away from him. LaFong pulled a gun. Tomokato batted it from his grip.

Suddenly the two ran in opposite directions. Tomokato followed LaFong. About to be caught, LaFong veered to the side, throwing himself headlong into the pool. Tomokato rushed to the edge just in time to see him strike the water.

Closing over LaFong, the liquid began to boil furiously, spewing out yellow smoke; masses of thick floating tan scum rolled to the top.

Just like the squashes, Tomokato thought.

A humanoid shape rose from the waist-deep water. It turned towards Tomokato, hands to its throat, flesh melting like wax. Its hair was gone, its face featureless except for the widening cavity of a gaping mouth; dripping strings hung like stalactites over the hole, which resembled nothing so much as Mammoth Cave on its runniest, most nauseating day ever.

"Just look what you made me do," the thing gurgled, hands dropping away from its throat.

"I'm very sorry," Tomokato said. "Where's the designated place?"

"I will *not* betray the Cause to an animal supremacist," the thing said. "Moreover, I will sing the anthem of my kind right at you." Reaching into a pocket, the thing produced a little flag with a squash on a field of stars, and began to wave it as it sang. The corrosion of the replica's vocal cords had proceeded to the point where Tomokato could no longer make out words, but he thought he recognized the tune: it was either "On Wisconsin" or "Do the Freddy."

But the grisly performance did not last long. A flood of green fluid burst from the thing's mouth, and the body simply seemed to collapse upon itself, not sinking into the water, but pouring out of its clothing and spreading out over the surface, like cheese on French onion soup, LaFong's jacket floating in the midst of it.

Seawater destroys them, Tomokato told himself. *It is just like The Day of the Triffids. Thank Buddha for literary rip-offs.*

He wondered how many of the people aboard had been taken over. The crewmembers and other help seemed to have been singled out; that would, of course, make things much easier for the replicas. He asked himself if it would serve any purpose to go to the captain with his story.

You have to try, he decided, and made his way into the upper reaches of the superstructure. As he approached the bridge, he saw the captain standing at the top of the steps; Tomokato recognized him from a photo in the restaurant. With the captain were two officers. The three were just staring at each other. One was the man who had been with the replica of LaFong.

They became aware of the cat. All three gave him the same vanilla smile, and lifted their hats: there was a coffee cup under each one.

Only one real option remained to the cat now. He had

to put out an SOS. Guessing the radio room would be behind the bridge, he sprinted up the stairs.

The three replicas moved out of his way, offering no resistance. The radio room's hatch was open. Two communications officers sat inside on revolving chairs, slowly turning themselves around and around on tiptoe. They were wearing their headphones, but the wires were cut; languidly, they waved to the cat. Behind them, their equipment was completely covered in soggy white sugar dotted with little green plants.

Tomokato retreated from the entrance. The captain and his companions came nearer.

"It's quite useless to fight us," they said in unison.

"That's what you evil types always say," Tomokato answered. "But it's never true."

"Oh yeah?" they demanded. "Who have you beat?"

Tomokato went through the list. "And last but not least, I destroyed the collected forces of darkness on Ragnarok."

They were silent for a few moments. Something that might have been doubt registered in their eyes.

"Ah, horsefeathers," they answered at last. "You'd better stop believing your own PR. Because you're already dead meat."

A gun cracked behind Tomokato. He felt the impact against his back, but no pain. He turned.

A fourth officer stood there, a smoking pistol in his hand. The weapon was small caliber, a .25 at most; the slugs had flattened on Tomokato's armor.

The man aimed at Tomokato's face. Tomokato plucked out a *shuriken* and flung it deep into the fellow's Adam's apple. The man staggered about, bumped into the railing, and threw himself over it after the fashion of all heavies who have the slightest chance to do a high fall.

Tomokato turned. He would make the captain or one of his companions talk.

But somehow the captain and the others had gotten onto the roof of the bridge, and were looking down at him. He could not reach them.

"How did you get up there?" Tomokato demanded, enraged.

"Movie magic," they replied.

"This isn't a movie."

"Ah well. To err is human, eh?" They laughed mirthlessly. "Do you always talk to squashes?"

Tomokato swore and dashed down the steps. He had to get back to the kittens.

"There's nowhere to run," the officers called.

At the bottom Tomokato passed three young black women in sequined dresses, all wearing crimson-gash lipstick and mile-high beehive hairdos.

"Nowhere to hide," they chimed in.

The cat forced more speed into his strides, praying that his nephews had kept the stateroom locked. Arriving outside, he tried the handle, thanked Buddha when it didn't turn.

"Open up," he cried, knocking.

There was no response. Did the kittens think he had been duplicated?

He knocked again. "Really, it's me—" He bit back the words, realizing how absurd they were. A replica would've said the same thing.

Still no answer from inside. Weren't his nephews even curious? He took out his key and unlocked the door.

200

Even before he entered, he knew that something had gone horribly wrong.

Shiro was lying on his berth, staring at the ceiling, body rigid. Tomokato called his name. The kitten didn't stir. And his brothers were nowhere to be seen—

Except for Huki. Eyes wide open, mouth slack, he was sliding up the bulkhead opposite the door. Hanging out of an open vent, a little Huki-like arm had him by the topknot.

Tomokato hurled himself across the stateroom, but with a last violent jerk, Huki was yanked from view. Dropping his sword, Tomokato jumped on the desk, reaching into the vent. His outstretched fingers just brushed Huki's feet.

Tomokato leaped up, forcing himself into the hole, but his armor made it too tight a squeeze; he could not crawl quickly enough. Ahead, there was total darkness; he heard bumpings and boomings and metallic slitherings, growing fainter and fainter with distance.

He climbed back down from the vent and started to take his armor off; but he had not even removed his helmet when he heard Shiro groan. The kitten turned his head towards him. For the first time, Tomokato noticed a small green tendril running out of Shiro's mouth, down under the far side of the bunk.

Heart in his throat, Tomokato got on his paws and knees, looking beneath the bunk.

There lay another Shiro, Shiro clothes and all. It was even holding a little Mauser Broomhandle in its paw.

How had it happened? Had the kittens let someone in? Had Shimura and Hanako had more plants than he had thought? Surely, if a coffee cup could fit so inconspicuously beneath an officer's hat, who could tell

how many would fit in a kimono? Especially Shimura's kimono, which had room for roughly all the Colt .45 automatics ever made?

Tomokato looked under the other bunk and the desk and the chairs. Empty cups under each of them.

Shiro groaned again—the Shiro under the bed. He opened his eyes and looked at Tomokato. Tomokato noticed that the tendril entered *his* head through the topknot.

"Uncle-*san*," the second Shiro said groggily.

Kill it, screamed a voice in Tomokato's head. He was sure this must be the replica.

But . . .

Shiro reached for the topknot, tugged on the tendril. "What *is* this?"

"Perhaps you could tell me," Tomokato said.

"I had such bad dreams," Shiro said numbly. "I dreamed there was another Shiro, and he put me under this bunk, so that no one would realize he was fake . . ."

Torn by doubt now, Tomokato looked back at the topside Shiro. Was there any way he could tell which one was real? He peered under the bunk once more—

—just as Shiro number two chambered a round in his Mauser. Tomokato rolled aside as a vicious spray of full-auto fire rattled from under the bed. Scrambling to his feet, he jumped back up onto the desk.

"You don't hop too badly, for an earth creature," said the thing under the bunk. "But you really are a menace, and so . . ."

Broomhandle leading the way, the replica popped out into view. Tomokato hurled his sword.

The point caught the thing directly in the crown,

passing out through its throat, pinning the replica to the deck.

The real Shiro began to cough furiously. He sat up, tugging at the tendril in his mouth. Its pale green darkened swiftly, almost to black; he pulled it out and tossed it on the floor, gagging.

Getting down off the desk, Tomokato examined it. There was a bulb at one end, with many slimy shoots. He noticed raised lettering on it, and bent closer, squinting. *"Suck-A-Form Deluxe,"* it read, *"Patent Pending, Squashstyles, Inc."*

Hardly had he finished reading when the bulb and the tendril disintegrated into extraterrestrial ick. His nostrils filled with a skunk-cabbagey stench.

He looked back at the replica. It was not disintegrating, but seemed oddly shrunken; an immense pool of green ichor widened beneath it. Tomokato wondered if the body was simply deflating.

"Why are weird things always full of ichor, Unc?" Shiro asked, looking over the edge of the bunk.

"Standard pulp usage, though technically incorrect," Tomokato replied. *"Ichor* properly refers to the blood of the gods, not monster blood. But it really sounds rather more monstrous than divine, doesn't it? And besides *gore,* there really aren't too many other words for blood. Sometimes you just have to give the author a break."

"Gore . . . gore," Shiro mused. "Isn't that a fantasy world?"

"Yes. One we will *not* be visiting."

"What if someone on your list goes there?"

"They can have him."

Suddenly Shiro looked around wildly. "Where are my brothers?"

"They got them, Shiro," Tomokato answered.

"Are they . . . do you think they're . . . ?"

"Dead?" Tomokato asked. "No. The replicas have been taking all the originals and hiding them somewhere. I saw the Marx brothers stuffed into a couple of laundry carts down on E deck. Along with W. C. Fields."

Shiro gasped. "Fields is aboard too?"

Tomokato nodded. "It's turning into quite a voyage, isn't it?"

"So what do we do?" Shiro asked.

"Head down to E deck, see if we can't save your family."

"Yeah," said Shiro, climbing off his bunk, skirting the pool of green blood. Thrusting his Mauser into his belt, he picked up the AUG bullpup, which was lying on the other bunk.

Setting his foot on the replica, Tomokato pulled his sword out, the deflating body giving squishily beneath his weight, the wounds in the neck and throat bubbling juicy Bronx cheers. He and Shiro went out the door.

Two children, a boy and a girl, were running down the passage towards them. The pair screamed and stopped when they saw Tomokato and Shiro, eyes wild.

"It's all right," Shiro said. "We haven't been taken over."

Shivering, the children grabbed each others' hands.

"It's not th-th-th-that," said the little boy.

"We've just never seen such big cats before," said the girl.

There came a muffled thudding from behind the children. A thirtyish man and woman emerged from an adjoining passage, both of them hopping in perfect unison, feet pounding the carpet. Swinging from the woman's arm was a purse stuffed with greenery; a plant nodded in the water-stained breast pocket of the man's sport shirt.

"Gotta split," said the children, and took off.

The couple bounced near Tomokato and his nephew. "It's all right," they said. "We're their parents."

"Unc," Shiro whispered, "you're not going to let them go after those kids."

The man and woman pogoed by, smiling all the while, heads swiveling round; even after they were some distance past the cats, they continued to peer at them, looking straight back like owls.

"Shoot them," Tomokato said.

Shiro raked them with the AUG, high up across the shoulders. Dark syrupy liquid flowed from the round holes, pouring to the floor in unbroken continuous streams. The replicas' faces registered a certain mild discomfort; bodies swiveling under their heads, the couple staggered back at the felines, making naughty-naughty at Shiro.

The kitten drilled a dozen more slugs into them. Draining rapidly, the replicas' upper bodies began to collapse. The heads shriveled, slumping forward. Legs buckled, and the bodies struck the carpet with a wet-raincoat sound.

Tomokato noticed small pale ovals in the fluid that splashed over the carpet, and looked closer: seeds. One cracked open even as he watched, a tiny white growth uncurling from the shell.

"You think the Burpee people might be interested?" Shiro said. "There's gotta be a use for these things. We could make a mint."

"Shiro, how can you—"

"You're right," Shiro said. "This is more Kaddafi than Burpee. Now if we can just keep the West Germans from getting to him first—"

Snarling, dropping his sword, Tomokato slung him over one arm and was about to give his upraised butt a savage spanking when the kitten asked, quite casually:

"Hadn't we better go find my family?"

Simmering, Tomokato set him back down. Smirking at him, Shiro straightened his kimono, uncricked his neck with an uncannily Jimmy Cagney–like movement, and set off towards the nearest elevator.

"What are you waiting for, Unc?" he cried.

Tomokato followed him, muttering. Shiro jumped, slapping the down button.

"If there are replicas inside, just act like we're already taken over," Tomokato said. "If they're not duplicates of cats, they can't read our minds."

The lift arrived.

"Now smile."

The doors opened with a blast of Muzak, turned way up. Two maids stood inside, smiling, snapping their fingers listlessly to the insipid beat of a string rendition of "Pressure." With the maids were two large covered laundry carts.

207

Tomokato looked at Shiro, began to snap in time. Shiro nodded, picking up the beat. They entered the elevator. The doors closed behind them.

Eyeing the laundry carts, Tomokato remembered the Marx brothers and Fields.

"So," he said, "you're headed for the designated place?"

"Yes," the maids replied. "But why aren't you and the kitten speaking in unison?"

Tomokato hazarded a guess: "Because we replicas don't always speak in unison."

"Very good," the maids replied.

"Perhaps you'd better jot that down," Tomokato added.

Whipping out pens and pads, they did just that.

"Pressure" faded into "Sympathy for the Devil." The elevator stopped on E deck. Stepping out, Shiro and Tomokato held the doors open for the maids, then followed them.

Straight to the engine room.

Two grungy-looking oilers stood guard on either side of the entrance, holding huge wrenches. The maids went through without question. But the sentries halted Tomokato and Shiro.

"What is your business in the designated place?" they asked.

"The captain sent me to count the originals," Tomokato answered.

"They were just counted," the oilers replied.

"It is not my place to question my orders."

"True," said a voice from inside the engine room. "That is our place."

Shimura's replica appeared in the hatchway.

Tomokato and Shiro remained motionless, smiling.

"Honorable Brother," 'Shimura' said. "Have you forgiven me for impugning your word?"

"Completely," Tomokato said.

"Shiro," 'Shimura' continued. "How do you like your new existence?"

"It's peachy."

"Don't you mean squashy?"

"That too."

"Strange," the duplicate said. "I don't recall seeing your originals down here."

"They've started a second designated place, up in the galley," Tomokato said. "It's very nice."

"And, no doubt, you and Shiro were both damaged while you were growing, and that's why I can't read your minds, even though you are certainly within range."

"Unless *you* were damaged, and you can't read minds at all," Tomokato said.

"But I *can* read minds," the replica objected.

"Can you be certain of that? How do you know you're not simply hallucinating?"

"Who ever heard of a squash hallucinating?" 'Shimura' asked.

"Who ever heard of a squash reading minds?" Tomokato rejoined.

"You're trying to confuse me."

"Don't feel bad. It is the nature of squash to be confused."

'Shimura' shook his head. "Not *this* squash, earth creature. How do you say it? The up is jigged?"

Tomokato sliced at him with a draw cut.

209

Nimbly avoiding the stroke, the replica hopped back into the engine room. The thing certainly had Shimura's reflexes.

But the oiler on the right did not. Green blood fountained like, well, emerald ichor.

Shiro lifted the AUG. The oiler on the left took three hits, spun round, and with a terrific *bong!* slammed face-first into the bulkhead beside the hatch. Little tweeting winged squashes circled over him as he slid to the deck.

"You don't hear tweeting when you're dead," Shiro corrected.

Instantly the winged squashes merged into one big ghostly squash with a halo and harp which promptly vanished through the ceiling.

'Shimura' and Tomokato stood watching each other through the hatchway. Shiro's duplicate had reproduced Shiro's Mauser. Was the Shimura-thing's kimono filled with innumerable braces of Colt autos? If the replica had the pistols, Tomokato knew he would never be able to cross the distance in time. But why then hadn't the duplicate shot him already? Tomokato thought of throwing his sword, but Shimura had always been fast enough to deflect that move.

Out of the corner of his eye, Tomokato saw Shiro standing against the bulkhead flanking the hatch.

"Just give up," 'Shimura' said. "The process is painless. And then you're reborn in one of us. Minus your emotions—and your aversion to Muzak, of course. Honorable Brother, please, for your own sake, surrender. We want you. We need you—"

Shiro popped out from beside the hatchway. "But

210

you're never going to love us!" he cried, and cut loose with the AUG.

The duplicate ducked, paws darting into its kimono, reappearing with .45s. The guns barked twice.

Shiro was already shifting. One bullet banged into the AUG, hurling it from his paws. The second caught him in the right lung and sent him sailing back from the hatch like a beautifully punted pigskin.

Tomokato retreated, crouching by his nephew. 'Shimura' advanced, pistols leveled, a crowd of duplicates following him from the engine room.

"Surrender," 'Shimura' said.

Tomokato looked down at Shiro. The kitten was gasping, blue kimono spotted with purplish bloodstains.

"Don't worry, Unc," he said, coughing up pink spittle. "The author wouldn't dare kill me off."

But having just witnessed such a horrendous display of the author's capriciousness, Tomokato was in no mood to be comforted; rising, he let out a ferocious scream and charged Shimura's replica.

"Pity," it said.

"That you have to try and kill me?" Tomokato demanded.

"No, that I'm completely emotionless. Because otherwise I'd get a real sadistic rush out of this."

The pistols began to roar.

Tomokato deflected sixteen shots.

The other two hammered into his left shoulder and right thigh.

The replica dropped the emptied pistols, reached for two more. Tomokato closed in, *katana* whistling. A Colt

211

dropped. Tomokato raised his sword, brought it down at the duplicate's forehead. But before it could connect, the other pistol flamed, sending a bullet crashing into his helmet.

His mind went white for a instant.

When vision returned Shimura's replica was sinking to the floor, still smiling, paws clapped together above its brow. Beneath them, Tomokato's sword was buried inches deep in the duplicate's head.

Tomokato grunted. The double hadn't absorbed Shimura's memory completely—Shimura would never have tried to save himself with that *Shogun Assassin* try-to-catch-the-blade stunt, especially with a wounded arm.

The other replicas had halted; but more reinforcements were coming out of the engine room. Tomokato's eyes riveted on one shouldering its way to the front—

Another Shimura.

Tomokato turned. Wounded as he was, he could not expect to cope with a second duplicate of his brother. And he had to try to get Shiro somewhere safe, if any place on the ship was safe.

He limped back up the passage, sheathing his sword, picking Shiro up in his arms. Behind him, a rhythmic booming started up; he had no idea what it could be, but didn't dare pause for a look back.

He found a stairwell and dragged up to D deck. There he had to stop, wincing at the pain in his shoulder and thigh.

Doors banged open below. Booming filled the stairwell, the landing trembling beneath his feet.

"Could you stop that noise, Unc?" Shiro wheezed. "I really could use some rest. You don't want to take chances with a sucking chest wound . . ."

Tomokato resumed his agonized ascent. He was only halfway to the next landing when he heard more booming from above.

He went back down to D deck, stumbling from the stairwell. He reeled towards the end of the passage, where a door stood open; a maid came out pushing a cart full of plants.

Do you really want to go in that room? he asked himself.

The booming was muffled by the stairwell doors, but grew steadily louder; suddenly the sound exploded into the corridor, and he knew the barriers had been thrust aside. At last he looked back.

Hopping in perfect unison, rank after rank, dozens of uplicates came bouncing out of the stairwell like Easter Bunnies from Hell, 'Shimura' leading the way, holding his .45s straight out in front of him.

With a speed unthinkable in such a wounded kitten, Shiro pulled out his Broomhandle and capped off six rounds. Never expecting such utter implausibility, Shimura's doppelgänger shot backwards, riddled in mid hop. The duplicates directly behind him went over like dominoes.

Tomokato turned. Ahead of him, the maid was standing in front of her cart, trying to shield the little plants.

"They're only babies," she said.

Shiro coughed. "That's what people used to say about

213

me," he said, and hosed her and the cart down with the Mauser.

Behind Tomokato, the booming began once more. Ears ringing, the cat stumbled into the open room. The door was heavy reinforced steel; he closed it and dogged the bolts, then sat on the deck. Shiro slid from his grasp.

Tomokato eyed his surroundings, head reeling. The room was lined with shelves. The shelves were lined with plants.

He got back to his feet, sweeping the coffee cups to the deck, stamping on the growths as they spilled out of the shattered vessels. Thinking he'd gotten them all, he went back by Shiro and painfully lay down beside him.

"Unc," said Shiro weakly. "Unc . . ."

Tomokato reached out to him.

"I don't think you got them all," Shiro said.

Tomokato gaped in horror as a green tendril appeared from behind Shiro's profile and dipped into his mouth.

The cat tried to pry himself up off the deck. The effort was too much. He blacked out.

3

Tomokato drifted slowly upwards from the darkness. Oblivion gave way to a weird dream.

He was lying on a table in what appeared to be a surgical theater. Wobbling about the chamber were two huge squashes in nurse's uniforms, white caps concealing their stems; surgical masks were stretched below the caps. Leafy creepers hung from slack sleeves. Beyond the nurses were tier upon tier of intern-squashes, observing from behind a wall of plate glass.

Three surgeons entered, pale rubber gloves slipped over the ends of their creepers. One came up beside the table and leaned over Tomokato. Even though there were no eyes above its mask, the cat had no doubt that it was examining him. The other two surgeons came up, prying his mouth open; the first sliced a tendril off one of its creepers with a scalpel, then stuffed it into Tomokato's mouth. Tomokato nearly retched.

The squash with the scalpel cut a crescent through its mask, spitting a moon-shaped section of rind onto Tomokato's cheek.

"Don't like the greens, eh?" the thing said. "They're better with dressing." It turned to one of the nurses. "Oil."

"Oil," the nurse said, slapping a bottle into its glove.

The surgeon sprinkled the greenery in Tomokato's mouth. "Vinegar," it said.

"Vinegar," the nurse replied. Tomokato began to cough furiously when the liquid dripped through the leaves onto the back of his throat.

"You would have preferred Tangy Avocado, perhaps?" the surgeon asked.

Nodding, Tomokato coughed the salad out. The surgeon stuffed it back in.

"Don't worry," it said. "You'll feel better soon."

Without warning, two orange paws pushed out of

215

the surgeon's mouth, hooked on opposite lips, and slowly forced the top and bottom apart. There was a gruesome wrenching noise, and the whole top of the squash, everything above the mouth, cracked off and flipped backwards. Up rose a dripping felinoid in Japanese armor. Staring down at Tomokato, it asked:

"Has anyone ever told you how much you look like me?" it asked.

Tomokato awoke. His face was still turned towards Shiro. He tried to look away, found he couldn't. He was completely paralyzed.

Something was stuck in his throat. No doubt that was why he had been dreaming about the salad. But unlike his dream-self, he was not very concerned. He thought it peculiar that the obstruction bothered him so little; he did not even know if he was breathing, not that it seemed to matter.

He heard gunfire outside in the passageway. Who was fighting the replicas now? The Tamil Tigers, perhaps? Members of the QLF? Whoever they were, he guessed they had prevented the vegetables from breaking into the chamber.

He studied Shiro's face. Hadn't he seen something going into Shiro's mouth? Yes, a tendril. Suddenly, but without any force, it struck him that the thing down his *own* throat was probably a tendril too.

But why doesn't that worry me? he asked himself.

The noise outside faded. The combat seemed to be moving to another part of the ship. Finally the sounds vanished altogether.

An indeterminate time passed. He began to entertain

216

the possibility that he might actually be dead. Would the afterlife consist of gazing at his nephew forever?

Certainly isn't Nirvana, he told himself. *But at least it isn't Hel—*

A second Shiro sat up behind the first.

I suppose it's about time, the cat thought.

The duplicate reached up and unplugged the shoot connecting it to Shiro.

Wouldn't have guessed it would come out so easily, Tomokato thought. *How convenient.*

Something tugged on the tendril in *his* throat; his face jerked away from Shiro. He found himself staring into a puss that might have been his own mirror image.

Such attention to detail, the cat thought. *Absolutely meticulous!*

His double ripped its umbilical out of the top of its helmet and tossed it away; but the tendril in Tomokato's mouth had not gone slack. He felt another jerk, and another. A second double appeared behind the first, and helped it to its feet. They made a gesture that looked suspiciously like the Phi Beta Kappa secret signal, then hopped on one foot, and gave each other five. They repeated this strange ceremony in the direction of Shiro's double. Finally the three replicas bent over Tomokato and said, very clearly, "Woggeda woggeda woggeda."

I suppose it must mean something, the cat thought, more than willing to give them the benefit of the doubt.

His duplicates disarmed him and picked him up by the shoulders. Shiro's double dragged a chair past him. Tomokato heard the doorbolts squealing; he guessed the little replica was standing on the chair, unfastening them. The chair scraped aside; then came the creak of the door opening.

The neck guard of his helmet kept his head from lolling; his field of vision included the upper quarter of the double holding his legs and a lot of bulkhead and ceiling.

A shadow stirred behind a high-up ventilation grate. There was a hollow thump.

The double twisted, looking over its shoulder.

A pistol spoke. Wires peeled back from a bullet hole in the grate.

With true Miaowara speed, the doubles loosed Tomokato and reached for their hilts. Whirling, the one in front almost had its sword out when the slug took it. As he fell, Tomokato saw the bullet splash through; the side of the replica's helmet opened like a can of ichor soup.

Chunky style.

With the replica dead, Tomokato snapped instantly out of his trance. Striking the deck, he began to gag at the tendril in his throat.

The dead replica sagged towards him. He hurled it aside, yanking the tendril out of his mouth.

The grate banged away from the vent, a smoking Desert Eagle 44 mag. thrusting through. The gun spoke again. It had quite a lot to say, none of it nice.

Bullets spanged off steel, deflected by the second replica. Paint flew from the bulkhead around the vent; none of the slugs went inside. Apparently the duplicate did not have perfect control over the richochets.

Tomokato scooped up his *katana*. The gunfire paused.

The cat heard a clip drop, then the snick of another being rammed home.

The second duplicate's eyes darted to him, then back to the vent. The Desert Eagle's action clacked, chambering a round.

The duplicate turned and fled, slamming the door behind it. Two bullets tore shiny-rimmed holes in the door as it closed.

Tomokato nodded, approving the thing's judgment. Faced with himself *and* a gunman, he would've fled too.

Shiro was gone—the kitten's replica must have dragged him out.

Have to kill it, Tomokato thought. He opened the door.

His duplicate was standing outside. The point of a *katana* shot in at his face. He parried it upwards. The blade licked back. He slammed the door.

"Step aside!" cried the guy in the vent. Tomokato obliged, and the man put six more rounds through the door. "Lock it!"

Tomokato dogged it tight.

His benefactor climbed out of the vent and lowered himself to the deck. Tomokato's jaw dropped.

It was Carlos LaFong—and undoubtedly the real one, this time.

"What's your name?" LaFong asked.

Tomokato said nothing. LaFong's gun was empty; now was a perfect chance to kill the man—not that LaFong would've had much chance if the weapon *was* loaded. But Tomokato let him slide a new clip in.

219

"You saved my life," the cat said. Like it or not, he owed LaFong a debt of gratitude. He had no idea what to do. This was going to require some hard thought.

"We're all in this together," LaFong answered.

"Very true." Feeling a slight stiffness, Tomokato worked his shoulder. Only then did he remember that he had taken a bullet in it; one in the thigh, too, now that he thought about it. But he was hardly in any pain at all. He looked at his shoulder guard—there wasn't even a hole.

"I was wounded," he said, puzzled.

"So was I," LaFong said, lifting the lapel of his sports jacket. The cloth was covered with grime from the inside of the vent; the bloodstain was hard to see, but Tomokato picked it out. There was definitely no hole though. "I was shot by a kitten when I made my second escape . . ."

"Kitten?"

"Little black-and-white one. Relative of yours?"

Huki, Tomokato thought, nodding. "You said your *second* escape?"

"Yes. I escaped three times. Once last night, twice today. When I came round the third time, the bullet hole was gone. Part of the duplication process. The plants purge the originals of injuries and disease before they copy them. I don't even have my postnasal drip anymore."

"But why should it extend to repairing our garments?" Tomokato asked.

"I tried looking that up in this manual of theirs," LaFong answered, pulling a booklet from his jacket. "It said, 'If you have to ask a question like that, you're

220

obviously not a squash; please put down this booklet immediately.' "

"Why do they have manuals at all? They seem to operate purely on instinct."

"Right," LaFong agreed. "They evolved beyond the need for manuals a couple million years ago. But they've got some kind of an agreement with a typesetter's union, back on Altair."

"How did you learn that?"

"It's in the *other* manual."

"Ah," Tomokato said. "So how did you manage three escapes?"

"My duplicates must've been killed. I kept waking up down in the engine room. The first time, the replicas weren't expecting any of the originals to be up and around, and I managed to slip out."

"And the second time?"

"They *still* weren't expecting anything. I suppose they thought lightning wouldn't strike twice. They wised up after that, though. The third time I came round, they were watching me pretty close. But there was an accident with the big vat. I jumped up in the confusion, pulled a pistol off one of them, and busted loose again."

"Big vat?"

"That's where they're putting the originals. They're melted down somehow. Seems the replicas have to follow up with a couple shots of liquefied protein from the duplicated species. Otherwise, they start to lose their form." LaFong held up the manual, cracked open to a sequence of photos showing what appeared to be E.T. turning step by step into a bloated squash, with Drew Barrymore looking on aghast.

221

"One more question," Tomokato said. "There's a replica of me still alive. Why did I wake up?"

"I must've shot the first duplicate off the tendril. Just works that way when there's more than one bud."

"Isn't that a bit arbitrary?"

"Are you complaining?"

"Certainly not."

LaFong went to the door and looked through one of the bullet holes. "A lot of dead replicas out there. I wonder who killed them?"

"Any sign of my double?"

"It's down by the stairwell. Waiting for reinforcements, if you ask me. I think we'd better leave by the vent."

"I have to get down to E deck. Can you show me the way?"

"I was going to suggest we snatch a lifeboat."

"I have to rescue my kin. And destroy that vat, if possible. Prevent the squashes from passing themselves off as human. If they're going to coexist with us on this planet, they'll have to succeed on their own merits. If we don't massacre them first, that is."

"Save the world, eh?" LaFong asked.

"Does the idea appeal to you?"

LaFong scratched his cheek, nodding. "Might make up for some past sins. Particularly if I sacrifice myself in some really spectacular fashion."

Tomokato studied him. "Guilty conscience?"

"I'm tortured day and night," LaFong answered. "What would you say if I told you that I'd led a life of extreme brutality, which I believed was justified by my

222

political ideals, but which slowly came to sicken me, especially after I had to personally back my car over a box of baby mice belonging to Amin Gemayel's son Bucky, as a *quid pro quo* for Hezbollah investment in a Quebec Liberation Front combination training camp and sixplex theater?"

"I'd say that was quite a convoluted question."

"I used to be incapable of sentences like that," LaFong said, and sighed. "But once I became involved in the murky world of international terrorism . . ." His eyes sought Tomokato's, full of aching, earnest regret. "Terrorism stinks. Really."

Tomokato nodded thoughtfully.

"And if anyone ever asks you to become a terrorist," LaFong replied, "just say no."

He rubbed his hands, then smiled, apparently in anticipation of the coming ordeal of atonement. "Now. Let's get into that vent before your alter ego comes back with a mob."

LaFong first, they climbed up the shelves and through the opening. Tomokato had little difficulty in the conduit; the vent was larger than the one in his stateroom.

"The system's quite extensive," LaFong explained, illuminating his way with a penlight. "It's really thoroughly in excess of function, if you ask me. Unless it was *designed* for clandestine travel as well as ventilation. But that's probably the simplest explanation for the people movers, I suppose."

They came out in a well-lit, spacious corridor that looked rather like a tunnel between airline terminals, complete with conveyor belts going both ways. An arrow on the opposite wall pointed to the left: RESTROOMS and newsstand were printed in block lettering underneath. A second arrow pointed to the right, labeled SNACKBAR and ELEVATORS. Tomokato and LaFong stepped onto the belt trundling that way.

Midway between them and the lifts, a figure crawled out of a conduit. It rose slowly, outlined against the lights farther up the passage. Stepping onto the other conveyor, it glided towards them.

"Brother-*san*," came Shimura's voice. It sounded dull and flat.

Suddenly both people movers stopped.

"What happened?" Tomokato asked.

"I don't know," said LaFong.

The figure strode closer on its now-motionless belt.

"Stop right there," Tomokato ordered.

The figure complied. Tomokato tried to scan its face, but there was still too much light from behind.

"I woke up in the engine room," it said. "There was gunfire outside, and all the replicas went through the door. I found a dead duplicate of myself by the threshold, and took its guns. Did you kill it?"

"Just listen to it," LaFong told Tomokato. *"It's* a replica. It's trying to fool us."

"Then why hasn't it fired?" Tomokato asked.

"I haven't fired because you're my brother," it answered.

"Your voice sounds strange."

"I'm a little woozy. I went up on D deck, looking for you. I found a whole horde of them up there. One had a pistol. A bullet grazed my head."

It was possible; that would explain the gunfire Tomokato had heard back in the storeroom. But it still didn't ring true.

"One of *them* managed to graze *you*, Brother-*san*?" he asked. "Even though you had your forty-fives?"

"Not mine. *Copies* of mine. Very good ones, but a bit too much play in the action."

"Don't listen to it!" called a voice from behind.

Tomokato looked back. Some distance away stood five more figures. He couldn't see their faces either, but recognized the silhouettes.

Huki, Duki, Luki, and Agamemnon.

And Hanako.

"It's a double!" Hanako continued. But *her* voice sounded as strange as Shimura's.

"Don't trust it, Uncle-*san*!" the kittens cried.

"They're the duplicates!" answered Shimura. "My family's still down in the engine room. I had to leave them."

"We had to leave Daddy!" Huki replied. "He woke up and unplugged us, but they got him again!"

"They were already unplugged when I woke up," Shimura said. "But they were still asleep. I couldn't wake them."

"Tomokato, do you believe the *real* Shimura would've left us?" Hanako demanded.

"Do you believe the real Hanako would've left *me?*" Shimura asked, moving closer.

"Stop where you are!" Tomokato answered. "You already admitted you left *them.*"

"I couldn't carry them."

"We couldn't carry Shimura," Hanako retorted.

"If they're the replicas, why haven't they started shooting?" Tomokato asked Shimura.

"Because they know they can't win that way," Shimura answered. "If they're *not* the replicas, why are they armed? The squashes disarm the originals."

"Why are *you* armed?"

"I told you already."

"He's lying!" the kittens cried.

"What kind of guns did the kittens have?" Shimura demanded. "They must've been disarmed. But if they were disarmed, only the replicas would have the kind of guns the kittens were carrying."

Tomokato looked back at them once more. Agamemnon was holding an AUG.

But Shiro had picked Agamemnon's AUG up, back at the cabin.

"There was a second set of duplicates," Hanako answered. "They were still attached to us. Shimura killed them. We took their guns."

"But the kittens had been disarmed before they were dragged from the cabin," Tomokato pointed out.

"The squashes might still have duplicated the guns," LaFong put in. "Says so in the manual. Something about 'lingering resonance.'"

"So you've been following all this, eh?" Tomokato asked.

"Yes."

"Would you kindly explain it to me?" Tomokato asked, looking back and forth from Shimura to Hanako. She and the kittens were edging nearer now.

"Halt!" Tomokato barked.

"It's simple," LaFong said. "They're *all* duplicates, and they're just trying to wear you down."

"Hmm," Tomokato answered, considering this. "Hanako," he called, "if *that* Shimura's a duplicate, why haven't you opened fire on it?"

"We still couldn't handle it," she replied. "We were hoping you'd take care of it."

"Shimura," Tomokato cried, "why haven't you shot *them?*"

"I can't. They look too much like my family. You'll have to kill them."

A likely story, Tomokato thought. *LaFong's right.*

It was a frightful situation. If Tomokato turned to attack Shimura, Shimura's family would mow him down. If Tomokato went for *them*, Shimura would do the honors.

"Take cover," the cat told LaFong.

LaFong leaped behind a convenient fallen log.

Shimura's replica was the greater threat—Tomokato knew that turning his back on it was one hundred percent rock-solid papal-infallible certain death. He had no choice but to try and kill it first. He was *almost* sure the other replicas would fill him with lead, but there was some tiny chance that La Fong might distract them, just long enough. Tomokato charged.

Behind him, the Desert Eagle cracked. 'Hanako' and the 'kittens' cut loose—all towards La Fong, apparently.

Tomokato neared 'Shimura.' Inexplicably, the duplicate never reached for its pistols. What was it waiting for?

Tomokato raised his sword to strike. The replica just

227

shrugged. Not even when the edge sang down did it go for the guns.

Tomokato checked the blade an inch from the double's shoulder.

"It *is* me, you know," Shimura said, with a hint of impatience, scratching dried blood from his face.

"I do believe you're right," said Tomokato.

The shooting had stopped. He pivoted.

Huki's replica lay motionless. LaFong was stretched out over the log. Hanako, Luki, Duki, and Agamemnon were reloading.

Tomokato started towards them. Finishing, they met him with a hail of lead. He was hard put to handle it.

The sight of Tomokato in such danger conquered Shimura's reluctance to attack the replicas; he had to help his brother. Two forty-fives practically leaped into his paws.

"Shimura!" 'Hanako' cried, taking a hit.

"Daddy!" 'Duki' wailed.

"We'll be good!" 'Luki' screamed.

"They'll take us away from you!" 'Agamemnon' shrieked.

Shimura lowered his guns. Shaking his head, he came up beside Tomokato.

"This really is dirty pool," he said. "Just the thought of social workers . . ."

Tomokato had tangled with several once. He understood completely.

Staggering, the wounded replicas aimed their weapons once more.

But at that moment LaFong raised himself from the log and snapped off four shots. 'Hanako,' 'Duki,' and

'Luki' rocked off their feet. 'Agamemnon' dropped the AUG, facing LaFong.

"They'll take us away from you too," the replica said.

"Fine," LaFong answered. "I'm a dog person. Eat my wadcutter, squash-for-brains."

Bloowie.

"That was my last clip," LaFong said.

Tomokato pointed to the replica-kittens. "Take a gun from them."

LaFong picked up 'Luki's' Owen gun, plus ammo, then came over to Tomokato and Shimura.

"You were just pretending to be dead, eh?" Tomokato asked.

"No, I was taking a nap," LaFong replied. "You know how Thomas Edison never slept, but only took short naps? Said it improved his mental efficiency? That's how he beat Alexander Graham Bell at the O.K. Corral. Bell hauled out his scatter-gun; Edison just lay down and went napper-byes. When he woke up, he kicked butt."

"I thought it was the Earps and the Clantons at the O.K. Corral," Tomokato said.

"Bell *was* Ike Clanton. Alias, of course."

"And Edison was Wyatt Earp?"

"Doc Holliday."

"Tomokato," Shimura said, "when did you decide to make common cause with Mr. LaFong here?"

"Tomokato?" LaFong demanded. "Miaowara Tomokato?"

"Yes," Tomokato answered, keeping an eye on the Owen.

"Why haven't you tried to kill me?"

"Because you saved me back in the storeroom. And

also, because you promised to die spectacularly at the climax of this story, to expiate your sins."

"What if I *don't* die then?"

"Then I'm afraid I'll be obligated to kill you."

LaFong thought this over. "That's fair," he announced good-naturedly.

Shimura tapped Tomokato on the shoulder. "Company," he said.

Beyond the dead replicas, out of every conduit in sight, bodies were wriggling.

"We'd better get to the elevators," Tomokato said. He and the others took off at a sprint.

More replicas appeared ahead, worming into view like human snakes, snaking into view like human worms, or snaking and worming like humans into view, the remainder birding and fishing like dirigibles, but only with considerable difficulty, as might be expected.

"Don't shoot!" Tomokato told LaFong and Shimura. "You might touch off the hydrogen!"

But some of the replicas ahead had firearms, shotguns from the ship's armory, apparently; blasting a couple rounds at Tomokato and his colleagues, they succeeded only in touching off their dirigiblelike cohorts themselves. Four hydrogen explosions blossomed in the tunnel, leaving only one squash on its feet. LaFong and Shimura gasped as they approached it.

"We had no idea Fields was on this boat," they told Tomokato.

"All things being equal, I'd rather be on Altair," 'Fields' replied, coming at them with a dental drill. Tomokato winced, remembering some of the more painful bits from *The Dentist*. Utilizing all its purloined

230

juggler's coordination, the double gave the cat a surprising amount of trouble. Then Tomokato's sword whickered past the drill and sank home.

"Wasn't he in *Marathon Man*?" LaFong asked.

Tomokato shook his head. "That was Laurence Olivier."

"The Olivier from *Fatal Glass of Beer*?"

"I thought Thomas Edison was in that," Shimura broke in.

A tremendous booming arose. There was no need to look back. They raced to the lifts and pushed the down button.

"Don't you just hate elevators?" Shimura asked as they sweated it out, the human veggies bouncing nearer and nearer.

"Just be thankful this isn't a science fiction convention," LaFong answered.

On hopped the replicas under a huge squash banner, looking like a commercial for an all-bunny version of *Les Miserables,* humming their hideous anthem.

"Is that 'On Wisconsin' or 'Do the Freddy'?" Shimura asked.

An instant later, for some reason known only to themselves, the replicas stopped hopping and continued their advance in an odd teetering gait, swaying side to side and flapping their arms up and down in unison.

"*'Do the Freddy,'*" Tomokato said.

The elevator opened. Inside were two full sets of Marx brothers, both Grouchos performing a disturbingly spiritless version of "Hooray for Captain Spaulding." Grinning vacantly, twin Harpos came front and center, trying

231

to light the pilot jets on their flamethrowers. Tomokato struck them down. Shimura and LaFong greased the rest.

The Freddying mob closed in. Tomokato pushed the button for E deck, but the dead Harpos were blocking the doors. He and Shimura tossed the corpses outside. A last glance showed Tomokato that the replicas had broken ranks, a lounge lizard entertainer-type outstripping the rest.

Tomokato ducked back. The door began to close once more. But at the last second, a hand thrust between them. They bounced back again.

"Going down?" the lounge lizard asked.

"You are," Shimura said, and gave it three in the face. As it fell, arms flapping in the spastic Freddy of Death, the replica knocked over two more behind it. The elevator shut up tight and descended a floor.

Armed with fire-axes, Martin and Lewis were waiting at the bottom.

Tomokato's sword bit left and right.

"But they weren't replicas!" Shimura said, noticing a red smear on Tomokato's blade.

"Couldn't take the chance," Tomokato answered, as LaFong led the way to a conduit on the far side of the passage. "Besides, have you ever seen any of their movies?"

4

In the engine room, blissfully unconcerned in her trance-like state, the real Hanako had watched the building of the great protein vat from various vat materials the replicas had found lying about the ship. She had seen originals delivered, by the dozens, by the scores; laundry cart after laundry cart was unloaded on the upper catwalks, the bodies lowered in cargo nets. When the duplicates ran out of room on the deck, they had begun to hang them from pipes, from the catwalks, to attach them to the bulkheads, all with gobs of sticky gunk they extruded from their fingertips.

Glue in one's fingers, she had thought to herself. *What won't they come up with next!*

When every inch of available space was occupied, the originals began to go into the vat. The end result was something looking kind of like vanilla milk shake, which went into bottles, cans, cleaning buckets. Some of the containers were carried from the engine room; others were drained on the spot by duplicates slurping greedily through straws. They certainly seemed to like the stuff. Hanako wondered what it tasted like.

After a time replicas of Huki, Duki, Luki, and Aga-memnon deposited their originals around her. She didn't mind one bit; indeed, she was dimly pleased that the kittens had been reunited with her and Shimura. If anything troubled her it all, it was that Shiro was missing. But she guessed he'd be along soon.

Before long, so many of the human originals had been

233

liquefied that new deliveries no longer had to wait their turn, but went directly into the hopper. For some reason, none of Hanako's family had been taken; she wondered placidly when this oversight would be corrected, secure in the belief that the duplicates would eventually see to it. They seemed very thorough.

She was mildly irritated when the gunfire erupted beyond the entry hatch, distracting the replicas from their work. The whole bunch rushed up the stairway and disappeared.

That was when Shimura sat up, pulling the shoot from his mouth. Seemingly quite unreasonably agitated; he tried to rouse her and the kittens, but she remained resolutely uninterested, and she noted with some satisfaction that the children did too. Finally Shimura abandoned the family altogether.

Not that Hanako cared much.

Replicas began to come back into the engine room. The deliveries of originals resumed, but soon slacked off. The last to arrive was Shiro. Shiro's double brought it personally. Hanako thought that was a nice touch.

The replica laid him down with the other kittens, then knelt beside Hanako and took her paw.

"Mama-*san*," it said. "So good to see you."

Such a fine son, Hanako thought.

Stroking her fur, the replica continued: "Soon we'll have processed the last human originals. Then we can drain the vat and put you and my brothers in. Just think. In no time at all, I'll be sucking your protein through a straw."

Hanako wanted to smile.

If only my face would work.

234

"Bye, Mom," said the duplicate, and went over towards the vat. As it walked off, Hanako noticed something sticking out of the back of its neck, protruding above the collar of its kimono: a little semiformed kitten head, with a smaller, even less developed head-bud protruding from *its* temple. Would they grow up into still more Shiros?

Hanako wished she could smile yet again.

The last humans were liquefied, the fluid drained. Replicas opened the side of the vat; shaking bottles of champagne, they popped the corks and began hosing the interior down.

The cleansing was well along when Hanako woke from her trance; LaFong had just killed her duplicate.

Tranquillity vanished. Cold rage filled her.

Threaten my kittens, will you? she thought, her eyes narrowing slightly.

She could feel that she no longer had her hideout rigs inside her sleeves; the replicas had taken them. But that still left the twenty-shot USAS 12 auto shotgun concealed in her hair. She had almost not opted for replication-proofing on the weapon, but the salesman had been so charming that she'd relented—it was Shimura's money anyway. Now the duplicates had no idea she was still armed; she'd chosen well. She usually did, whatever her reasons.

She eyed the replicas by the vat, sneering. For an instant, she almost felt sorry for them.

They'd picked on one baaad mother.

"Mama-*san*?" Agamemnon whispered.

"You're awake?" she asked.

"Us too," said Huki, Duki, and Luki.

"Be quiet for a few moments, darlings," Hanako answered. "Mommy's got to think."

Tomokato, Shimura, and LaFong came out in the passage leading to the engine room. Spotting them, the guards at the hatch immediately transmitted a telepathic condition red.

With the exception of the conduit Tomokato's party had just emerged from, every hatchway and vent in the corridor vomited a torrent of replicas, as though the ship had just been force-fed a titanic overdose of squash-strength ipecac.

"What an image," Shimura said.

"You liked it?" LaFong asked.

"I didn't say that."

"Take the ones in back," Tomokato cried.

"But if we turn," LaFong answered, "they'll be the ones in front!"

"You know what he means!" Shimura growled, spotting a firehose. "Tomokato! Seawater destroys them, right?"

"How did you know?" Tomokato asked. "You weren't at the pool when LaFong's replica melted!"

"No, but the Collective Unconscious was," Shimura said. Grabbing the nozzle, he unreeled three yards of hose. LaFong gave the valve a good spin before rushing to back him up. Together they advanced behind a pummeling stream of brine. The replicas facing them were torn limb from limb before they could even strike the deck. Smoke billowed.

Coughing, Shimura and LaFong pressed forward,

soon finding themselves ankle deep in something about the color and consistency of floured beef gravy.

Eventually the miasma cleared. A beige swamp stretched all the way to the closest stairwell. There wasn't a living replica in sight.

Suddenly the stream from the hose slowed to a trickle. They turned, swearing when they saw the reason.

Tomokato had pressed some distance towards the engine room hatchway, leaving a wake of dead replicas; but between him and his companions stood another Tomokato. All Shimura could think was that it had crawled out of the conduit they themselves had come through. It had shut off the water; now, with a powerful sweep, it sliced the wheel from the valve.

Shimura let go of the hose, reaching for pistols. "Tomokato!" he screamed.

Having just finished the last duplicate in front of him, Tomokato wheeled. His double rounded upon him.

Gunfire echoed, from back by the stairwell. LaFong shrieked in pain. A bullet plucked at one of Shimura's sleeves. For an instant he was torn by indecision. But having alerted his brother, he opted to deal with the new menace.

A group of officers in hip boots were wading through the swamp, pistols blazing. A hippo got one; a croc took a second; crouching, Shimura and LaFong ripped into the rest. Bodies struck with huge dark splashes. Some staggered back up, sheets of smoking fluid cascading from their disintegrating forms. Two started forward at a clumsy run, then tottered and rolled, breaking up like combers in the shallows.

237

Mark E. Rogers

"Tomokato," Shimura breathed, suddenly remembering his brother's plight.

Facing each other on opposite sides of the passage, Tomokatos met his gaze. Their blades met in a dazzling flurry, bounced back. The antagonists leaped, striking, changing places; it was like something out of an all-cat version of the mirror sequence from *Duck Soup*. Partners in a deadly dance, they whirled round and round, the drift of their movements taking them towards the engine room hatch.

Shimura had no idea which was which.

Led by Shiro's double, a group of replicas brought Hanako and her kittens to the vat. A transplanted metal staircase leaned up against the great receptacle. Welded to the top of the steps was a length of catwalk; stretching across the mouth of the vat, it had a gap in its railing through which originals could be given the old heave-ho. Two replicas carried Hanako to the opening. Two more waited behind, Agamemnon and the Ukis tucked under their arms, Shiro hanging from one duplicate's hand by the topknot.

Shiro's replica flicked a switch attached to the railing.

"Liquefication field," the duplicate told Hanako. "It was very difficult building it from the materials available on an Earthling cruise ship. But then again, I don't imagine you Earthlings ever dreamed of the more exotic applications of duct tape."

The replica had a bag over one shoulder; it pulled out a dead ship's cat and swung it into the vat by the tail. Six

238

feet beneath the catwalk, it entered the field, liquefying without any pyrotechnics or melodrama into a white rain of cat essence. Up on the walk, Hanako puzzled briefly over why she could observe this, seeing as how she was keeping her eyes fixed on the ceiling so as to best simulate a paralytic, squash-induced trance. Ultimately, she decided that the narrative must have switched unexpectedly from second to third person. That was fine with her; she had always thought Henry James was a moron anyway.

"Test successful, Mama-*san*," 'Shiro' said. "In you go."

But Hanako had no intention of going gently into that good vat.

"Now!" she cried; then, using the *matsushita panasonic,* or greased wild weasel roll, she and the kittens (minus Shiro) slipped from the grasp of the replicas holding them. The duplicates did not seem to realize what had happened; landing flat on her back, Hanako had plenty of time to pull the USAS 12 out of her coiffure.

The double that had been holding her shoulders caught the first blast just below the hip. Instantly rendered a unidexter, it began to topple towards her. A second blast hurled it through the gap in the railing, into the liquefication field. For the second time there was no way she could have observed the liquefication which then occurred, and which she somehow apparently saw, but this time she paid the anomaly no nevermind at all.

The third dose of buckshot cured the replica who had been holding her feet. Then Shiro's replica was standing over her, furiously trying to prime its duplicate Mauser. But the weapon was an imperfect copy; the doppelgänger succeeded only in yanking the whole action out. Yellow-green pus sprayed onto the front of the double's kimono.

Luki came sailing through the air, slamming into the duplicate and knocking it over. Scrambling after Luki, the replica who had been carrying him stopped short at Hanako's feet, staring down the muzzle of her shotgun. An instant later, it had nothing to stare with.

The fourth double simultaneously produced a white flag and pulled an improvised blowpipe made from rolled-up newspapers out of its pants. Hanako was not fooled. The replica went head over heels down the steps with a hole in its chest shaped exactly like the Great Meteorite Crater in Arizona, although somewhat smaller.

Hanako rose to find Luki hanging over the edge of the catwalk, Shiro's replica doing a rather hard variation of the old soft-shoe all over his paws. She was just about to cut the thing in half with the shotgun when its head swiveled round.

"Aww, Mommy," it said. "You wouldn't!"

"I really should save the ammo," she agreed. "Waste not, want not." She booted the double in the small of the back. Sailing into the field, it liquefied with a pale Shiro-sized splash.

Hanako pulled Luki up onto the walk.

"Why'd you wait till they brought us up here, anyway?" Luki demanded, none too pleased with his Harold Lloyd adventure.

"Better vantage," Hanako replied, going to the head of

the stairs. "And it was a lot more suspenseful this way, admit it."

Luki nodded ruefully. "Right again, Mama-*san*."

The catwalk was level with the other walkways; Hanako swept each one systematically, slaughtering replicas with fléchettes and deerslugs and old-maid popcorn loads, an invention of hers which had always served her very nicely.

And no matter how or where they were hit, every single one of the doubles took the high fall over the railings.

Hanako proceeded to clear the deck beneath; but by then Tomokato and his companions had arrived in the hall outside, and most of the replicas were heading up the engine room steps. Even so, Hanako nailed a lot of them before they reached the hatch. Then she reloaded.

"Drop the gun!" shouted a voice.

Hanako looked down to see another replica of Shiro emerging from behind the cover of a mint-condition '62 Ford Galaxy. The duplicate had the original Shiro by the scruff of the neck, and was holding a Mauser to his head. Shiro hung limply in the thing's grasp.

"Drop the gun or I'll shoot him!" the double cried.

Hanako rested the barrel on the rail.

"Now!" the replica insisted.

At that moment, a third Shiro came up beside her.

"Come on, Ma," he said. "I've been up here all along, remember? You woke me when you kicked that first one into the vat."

Spotting him with her, the replica below shouted:

"That's a duplicate too, Mama-*san*! I wouldn't listen to it if I were you!"

"I don't believe you would," said Hanako, and brought the shotgun up off the rail.

The double swept the Mauser away from the other double's head. The other double whipped out one of its own.

Hanako wasted 'em both with a single old-maid round.

The doubles, not the Mausers.

"Of course," said Shiro dully beside her, "maybe they *were* telling you the truth. . . ."

With a scream she trained the shotgun on him. But the grin on his face told her that he was the genuine article.

"Just fooling, Ma," he said.

"You little bastard!" she cried, stamping her foot. "I might have killed you."

"Nah," he said.

Snarling, she handed the shotgun to Agamemnon. Grabbing Shiro, she went down on one knee and put him over her leg.

"Is this going to hurt you a lot worse than it hurts me?" he asked.

"Not if I can help it," she answered, trying to compose herself. The situation really called for a true Zen spanking.

"Look!" he shouted before she attained the proper inner state. "It's Uncle-*san*! And *another* Uncle-*san*!"

Hanako signaled for her shotgun, forgetting all about giving the kitten the waling he so richly deserved.

Tomokato and his replica had staggered through the hatchway, each gripping the other's sword paw. They had wounded each other many times, but both were so splattered with each other's gore that it was impossible to tell which was bleeding the ichor. Following close behind, Shimura and LaFong still couldn't pick out the real Tomokato. The damn thing's speed and technique were so similar to Tomokato's own that even the original had instants of confusion, which the duplicate took every opportunity to multiply.

"*I'm* the original," it whispered. "If you kill me, you'll be letting your own double walk away scot-free."

"You're not me!" Tomokato answered.

"I am me," the double retorted. "It's a logical impossibility for me not to be me, and you know it."

"You're you!"

"Of course I am. My point exactly."

"But I'm me!" Tomokato growled.

"And what exactly does *that* prove, eh?"

"That I'd better punch you in the face, right now!"

"Just what I was going to say."

Each loosing the other's sword paw, they smacked each other powerfully in the chops. Both dropped their *katanas,* the blades clattering down the steps to the deck beneath. The opponents grappled, simultaneously going for the same judo-toss, a circle-drop; each planting a foot in the other's stomach, they hurled themselves down the stairs. Spinning over and over like a wheel, they bounced to the bottom, rolled a few yards, then toppled on their sides.

"You idiot, that was a terrible idea," Tomokato gasped.

"I take full responsibility," the duplicate replied, "as befits an original."

They rose, swaying.

"Don't we need a rest?" the duplicate asked.

"Are you out of shape?" Tomokato demanded.

"I'm in the same shape as you."

"I thought you *were* me."

"No. *I* think I'm me."

"Had enough rest?" Tomokato asked.

"Have you?" the double shot back.

Rushing over to their fallen swords, they resumed their epic struggle. Ultimately they worked their way behind a huge mass of pipes. And there the combat drew rapidly towards its murderous climax.

As Tomokato and the double vanished from view, Hanako and the kittens rushed down from the vat; LaFong and Shimura descended the stairway from the main hatch. All converged on the pipes.

A racket like a monkey wrench in a turbine ensued from behind the conduits; with his finely tuned samurai-ninja-feline ears, Shimura distinguished no less than a hundred clanging sword-on-sword blows in two scant seconds.

Then came the duller sound of a sword striking armor.

A Tomokato stumbled back into view, dripping green and red from head to toe like a melting Christmas tree.

"Brother-*san*?" Shimura asked.

"It's me," the other replied.

"Stay where you are," said Hanako, covering it with her shotgun.

"It's me," it replied. "I killed it." It stumbled a step nearer. "What can I do to prove who I am?"

"Put down your sword," Shimura said.

"All right," it replied. The sword dropped from its paw.

Shimura and Hanako relaxed.

The instant their weapons dipped, the replica pulled out a *shuriken;* Hanako began to dodge, but the spiked disc caught her in the arm. The USAS fell from her paws.

The replica ducked, snatching the sword before it could hit the deck. Shimura's first four bullets passed over its head. A second *shuriken* thudded into Shimura's shin.

The replica straightened and rushed towards them. Shimura tried to ignore the pain in his leg, but his aim was off. A head shot snapped one of the replica's helmet horns. The replica deflected another, swept both pistols out of Shimura's grip, then cranked its arm back for a sweep that would've split both Shimura *and* Hanako wide open—

If only the real Tomokato hadn't rushed out from behind the pipes and hurled his sword.

The *katana* struck the replica's neck guard just below the helmet bowl; a full foot of green-stained steel jumped out of the thing's mouth, passing between its clenched teeth with a screech. Its jaws opened, ichor drooling over its chin; then they shut once more, fangs clanking on the steel.

Tomokato staggered forward and pulled his sword out. The replica dropped at his feet.

"Left me for dead," Tomokato said, pointing to a huge bloody rent in his breastplate. "I would have. Knocked my breath out."

"But are you all right?" Shimura asked.

"Deflated lung, nicked left ventricle," Tomokato replied. "I've had worse."

The two brothers laughed heartily, for no particular reason. Shimura and Hanako pulled the *shuriken* out of themselves. LaFong went over to Shiro.

"Hello, Shiro," he said.

"Car-*los,*" Shiro said, under his breath, obviously none too pleased by this sign of recognition.

"You know my son?" Shimura asked.

"Yes," LaFong answered.

"Car-los, *please,*" Shiro said.

"From where?" Shimura demanded.

"Hadn't we better wreck the vat and get out of here?" Shiro asked.

"He's right," Tomokato told Shimura.

As it just so happened, there was a canister of DuPont Emergency Vat-Wrecker nearby, set in a niche in the bulkhead; breaking the glass with his sword, Tomokato pulled the pin and rolled the canister across the deck. It lodged under the vat, which collapsed in a sparkling gust of fairy dust a second later.

"Now let's go," Tomokato said.

There was some hard fighting in the minutes and weeks and months ahead, as not all of the replicas had perished; but as we've already had quite a bit of climax already, I'll skip over it. Suffice it to say that our protagonists made it to a lifeboat just fine. But LaFong snapped his fingers and halted before climbing into the launch.

"There might still be some alive," he said. "We've got to destroy this ship."

"What do you have in mind?" Tomokato asked.

247

"I've got just the thing, back in my cabin. Hold the boat. I'll be back in a bit."

Actually, he was back in two bits.

"Look what I found," he said.

Out from behind him came the children that Tomokato and Shiro had saved.

"Climb in," Tomokato said.

LaFong helped the youngsters up, then clambered over himself.

"Sorry about your folks," Shiro told the kids.

"Our folks were never on the ship," the little boy answered.

"Those were our stepparents," the girl added.

"Both of them?" Tomokato asked. "How did you manage that?"

"It's a long story," the children answered.

Once the boat was lowered, Tomokato started up the motor. Shimura at the tiller, they headed towards the setting sun.

"So, Brother," Shimura said, "What are you going to do about Carlos?"

"You're still alive," Tomokato told LaFong.

"Damn, you're right," LaFong agreed. "I really intended to die heroically, but they didn't give me a chance. Finally I just forgot about it."

Reaching for his sword, Tomokato stood.

"Don't stand up in the boat," Shimura said.

Tomokato sat back down.

"What are you going to do?" LaFong asked.

"Well, since I shouldn't stand up, and you saved me, and did your bit to save mankind, I think I'll just have to spare you."

"No," LaFong said. "I must pay for my career of bloodshed. I'm guilty as sin. I can't stand to live with it. For my own sake, kill me."

"No, Carlos," Tomokato said. "Every man, or cat, has something he simply must live with. In your case, it's life."

LaFong nodded. "I'll go to work with Mother Teresa."

"She doesn't hire terrorists," Tomokato said.

"Then I'll lie to her about my past."

"She'd never approve."

"Then I'll tell her the truth."

"That's better," Tomokato said.

The *Gross Indulgence* steamed on southwards. The two vessels were perhaps six miles apart when LaFong looked at his watch and said:

"Ship's about to go up. Put on your sunglasses."

They complied, Shiro lending the kids a couple of his spares. Between the shaded lenses and the darkening eastern sky, the cruise liner could only pick out a few dim lights.

LaFong counted down:

"Five . . . four . . . three . . . two . . . one."

The whole horizon flashed yellow, the undersides of the clouds above painted briefly with the glare; then the clouds simply melted away. The flare faded; sullen orange, a titanic mushroom of glowing steam became visible against a black heaven. The sound rolled over the launch half a minute later.

"One kiloton device," LaFong said. "It fit in my suitcase. I stole it from my ex-colleagues in the QLF. I was going to chuck it in the sea."

"Where'd they get it?" Tomokato asked.

"Why don't you ask your nephew?" LaFong said.

Suddenly Tomokato remembered in full what Shiro had told him about those Québec Libre types.

"You actually *were* selling nukes to terrorists!" Tomokato cried.

"He was *what?*" demanded Hanako and Shimura.

Shiro lifted his paws and gave a sickly smile. "I have an excuse," he squeaked. Tomokato grabbed him.

And from that moment on, until they reached the Carolina coast two days later, it was one, long, acutely painful and utterly chastening Shiro spankfest.

"Wow," he moaned when it was over. "I'm just glad that we never sold any of those H-bombs."

Heart of Darkness

*Shiro fessed up to all manner of shady deals and
transactions; his parents saw to it that he returned
his ill-gotten gains. In exchange for immunity, he
testified in a number of crucial trials in Japan, the
U.K., and Canada. He became an instant celebri-
ty, his fame reaching its peak when he was
summoned before an American Senatorial committee investigating a particularly malodorous
scheme.*

> —from *Cat Out of Hell, A Biography
> of Miaowara Tomokato* by William Shirer
> and A.J.P. Godzilla

1

Could you please repeat that, Mister Miaowara?" said
Senator Blutarsky.

Shiro leaned aside to accept a few whispered words of
advice from his lawyer, Bernard "The Blowtorch"
O'Sullivan. Then O'Sullivan addressed the committee.

"Would it be possible for you to stop harassing my client?" O'Sullivan asked. "He's been making himself perfectly clear."

"Perhaps," said Blutarsky. "It's just difficult for me to understand how a consortium, even one involving Robert Vesco, John Pierpont Morgan, and Mao Tsetung, could possibly hope to corner the world market on fat."

"We didn't intend to corner the market, exactly," Shiro corrected. "We were trying to *patent* fat."

"What kind of fat?" Blutarsky asked.

"Any kind," Shiro said. "Although we were mainly interested in human fat. Humans would be most able to pay the royalties. We were, however, investing very heavily in genetic research to raise all animal species to sapience."

"Why?"

"So we could collect royalties from them too."

At that point, Senator Blutarsky was informed that his time was up. He turned the proceedings over to Senator North, who resumed the questioning pretty much where it had left off.

"You were trying to create rational animals?"

"Well, we already *have* rational humans and cats," Shiro said. "Our researchers discovered that the relevant genes were identical in both species. Electron photography revealed sections of human and feline DNA with the words 'IQ Here' tattooed on them."

"Were there any other tattoos?"

"On certain latent genes. 'Semper Fi,' and 'Death Before Dishonor.'"

"As an ex-Marine, I find that fascinating," North said.

252

"You mean, if those genes were activated, any creature could be turned into a Marine?"

"Almost, but not quite."

"A sub-Marine, then?"

"Yes. Exactly like a regular Marine in most respects, but with an uncontrollable desire to lie with its face under the water in bathtubs, bubbling."

"The enemy would spot the bubbles," North pointed out.

Shiro considered this argument. "Not if we turned the light off in the bathroom."

"He might have infrared goggles," North suggested.

"He might also be able to hear the bubbles," Shiro admitted. "You're right. Maybe we'd better rethink this one."

Before North could press the kitten further, Chairman Eastwood felt compelled to break in. "Don't you think this line of inquiry is running rather far afield, Senator?" he asked.

"Perhaps you're right," North said, and immediately turned the questioning over to Senator Dirksen. No one could understand him through the lid, but he seemed to get quite agitated whenever it was suggested he should cede his time to anyone else.

Next came Joe Tailgunner, the junior senator from Wisconsin.

"I notice that one of your coconspirators was Mao Tse-tung," the senator said. "Why was he investing in this scheme?"

"He felt that if anyone deserved the patent on fat, he did," Shiro replied. "We could hardly argue with him.

What a tub. I mean, when he sits around the Great Hall of the People, he really sits around—"

"Is he now, or has he ever been a member of the Communist Party?" Tailgunner broke in.

"Yes," Shiro admitted.

"I knew it!" the senator shouted triumphantly. In an excess of high spirits, one of his assistants kissed him loudly on the cheek.

"Not here, Roy," Tailgunner said, then returned to Shiro: "Are *you* now, or have *you* ever been a member of the Communist Party?"

"This is pure McCarthyism!" Shiro cried indignantly.

"Answer the question!" Roy snarled, leaning over to the senator's mike.

"I simply must protest!" O'Sullivan growled.

"Fill your hand, you son of a bitch!" Roy answered.

Rising, they both slapped leather.

"You're out of order!" cried Senator Eastwood.

They paused just long enough for him to shoot them both. Heads blown *clean* off, they toppled like a pair of decapitated lawyers.

"Now then," Eastwood said, slipping his .44 mag back under his jacket.

"Are you a Communist?" Tailgunner asked Shiro.

"No," Shiro said. "As a matter of fact, I was personally involved in the assassination of Lavrenty Beria—which led, in turn, to the death of Joseph Stalin. I understand that you, on the other hand, served in the U.S. armed forces during World War Two."

"Proudly."

"But wasn't the U.S. allied to Stalin then?"

"What are you driving at?" Tailgunner demanded, as

though he couldn't possibly understand how his service record could be used against him.

Shiro leaned forward, paused for effect, then released his thunderbolt: "Are *you* now, or have you ever been, a member of the Communist Party?"

The chamber hushed. Tailgunner mopped his brow.

"Well?" Shiro prodded.

"I only joined to meet girls!" Tailgunner shrieked.

The whole chamber drew a single gasp.

The onlookers made some kind of noise too.

"Girls, eh?" Shiro asked. "Is it not true that you once exchanged naked photos with Lev Davidovich Bronstein?"

Tailgunner thrust his handkerchief back into his breast pocket. "Who?"

"Lev Bronstein—aka Leon Trotsky."

"But there was no frontal nudity!" Tailgunner wailed.

"No frontal nudity," Shiro sneered. "I rest my case."

Tailgunner picked up Roy's fallen gun. "I think it's only fitting that I, who have driven so many others to suicide with Communist smears, should kill myself in the very same hearing room where I committed my crimes against democracy." He put the pistol to his head.

"Don't do it!" cried Senator Blutarsky.

"Ah, let him," said North. "Idiot set anti-Communism back thirty years."

Tailgunner pulled the trigger.

Click.

Eastwood handed him a bottle. "This is how you're going to do yourself in."

Tailgunner smacked it against his skull. It didn't break. Two guards dragged him out.

"I have a list, somewhere," he muttered.

Eastwood said: "Seeing as how subsequent hearings will simply be anticlimactic, I move to close these proceedings. Any objections?"

Samantha Foxe raised her hand.

"What are you doing on this committee?" Eastwood asked. "You're not even an American citizen."

"Yes, but I do have an enormous chest," she answered breathily.

Senator Benatar bopped her with McCarthy's bottle.

"Voice vote!" Eastwood cried.

"Let's split!" the others replied.

"Motion carried," Eastwood announced, and banged his gavel. The senators left the panel, all but Dirksen, who seemed quite content to rest where he was.

As the hearing room cleared, Tomokato came up to Shiro.

"Shame about Bernard," he said, nudging O'Sullivan's corpse with his foot.

"He was a good Blowtorch," Shiro said. "And he would've wanted it this way."

"Roy, too, I think," said Tomokato.

"Will someone bury them?"

"Can't be sure," Tomokato said. "I've heard they leave dead meat around here for years and years."

"Well, I suppose we'd better take Bernard, then," Shiro said.

"That is, *I* should take him, right?" Tomokato asked.

256

Shiro nodded. "I may be a media superstar with a frightful past, but I'm still just a little guy."

Tomokato shouldered the burden. There was a lawyer's field somewhere on the Capitol grounds.

"So what do you think of American democracy?" the cat asked Shiro.

"I liked the gunfight."

"And the rest?"

"Bor-ing. Still, I suppose it's better than blood dripping from the ceiling."

"So you've lost your taste for such things?"

Shiro weighed the question. "As long as it's the *wrong* people's blood," he said. "I've decided that it's immoral to admire mass murderers, no matter how good they are at it."

"Progress," Tomokato said.

"Aww, come on, Unc," Shiro said. "Not *much.*"

They inquired where the lawyer's field was and dropped O'Sullivan off in a convenient open grave. Going to their hotel, they packed for their trip to thirteenth-century China; Tomokato's next target was Genghis Khan. The cat was rather looking forward to leaving the twentieth century; he had no idea that the trip was going to be indefinitely postponed. But as Shiro was stuffing ammo belts into his bag, he suddenly blurted out:

"I have one last confession to make, Uncle-*san*!"

"Well?"

Shiro toed the carpet. "It's the thing I've been most ashamed of."

"Then get it off your chest."

257

Shiro took a deep breath. "You know how you put me in charge of your financial affairs? Gave me power of attorney?"

"Did you use any of my money in your schemes?" Tomokato demanded.

"Nothing like that," Shiro said. "But I knew you probably wouldn't approve."

"Why wouldn't I?"

"Because I know how you feel about the people in Hollywood."

"A pack of morons," Tomokato said. "Do you know what they did to Nobunaga's life story?"

"You've told me," Shiro said. "Many times."

"Changed the setting to Scandinavia," Tomokato gritted. "Liv Ullmann as Nobunaga dying of a drug overdose just before her comeback concert! Bette Midler as *me*!" He looked sidelong at Shiro, his eyes steaming. "Just what did you do, nephew?"

"I got you a great deal."

"What did you do?"

"Optioned the *bzzt . . . bzzt . . . bzzt,*" Shiro whispered.

"Optioned the what?"

Shiro coughed. "Movie rights. To your life."

"To who?"

"Heliogabalus Pictures."

Tomokato exploded: "They're the ones that made that Nobunaga abortion!"

"They said they'd do a much more respectful treatment this time."

"And you believed that?" Tomokato cried.

"No, I didn't. And I started feeling really crummy

258

about it. So now I've told you. And that's the last bad thing you didn't know about." He paused, sucking his lip. "I think."

"This option," Tomokato said. "When does it expire?"

"Next week," Shiro answered. "But they want to extend it."

"Can we stop them?"

"Maybe. We can demand that they exercise the option. If they don't, the rights'll revert to us."

"But I don't want them to make this film under any circumstances."

"It could be a lot of money, Unc. Even the option money. And they might decide to exercise the option no matter what. In which case you'll only get half as much as you would if they weren't mad."

"They can do that?"

"Yeah. They can pretend they're only making a TV special, not a movie. So they pay you half as much."

"And you signed this contract?"

Shiro shrugged. "Standard deal."

"So what are you saying?"

"They'll probably exercise the option. The only question is how much money *you* make. Why don't we just ask them to fly us out, so we can see what they've been up to? Who knows? It might not be so bad. The director didn't work on the Nobunaga flick. Whole cast and crew is different. Maybe the film'll be okay."

Tomokato growled.

"Even you've said that Hollywood sometimes gets something right," Shiro answered. "And if it's a good movie, and you part on friendly terms with them, you'll make twice as much money. Besides, if it looks too awful, we can always massacre the bastards. And they'll have paid for our plane tickets."

Tomokato shook his head. "We signed a contract. I'm honor bound."

"You didn't sign it."

"I gave you the right."

"You mean you won't kill these guys no matter what?"

"Not when they're legally within their rights."

"Now look," Shiro said. "I think not doing bad things is fine. But they've *used* us. And wiping out a nest of scumbag movie producers is the least we can do for the world."

"They'll have to give me a better excuse," Tomokato replied. "But don't worry, nephew. If we get in their way, the people who made *Shogun of Sex* probably wouldn't draw the line at murder. We'll just have to let them make the first move."

"So some good might come of my badness after all?" Shiro asked.

"It is never a good thing to have to slaughter evil-doers," Tomokato answered.

"But meting out retribution is okay, huh?" Shiro asked, earnestly trying to understand Tomokato's moral code.

"Yes. We must fix our minds on the justice of our actions. We must not allow ourselves to be delighted by the splattering blood and the hanging viscera and the squirting bile and dribbling lymph and other bodily fluids. That is the reader's job."

"But why does the reader get to enjoy it? It hardly seems fair. We do all the work."

"Readers are hypocrites, Shiro. And if we start slaughtering people in a bad cause, or enjoying the killing, the readers would feel bad about it. Because they'd *realize* how hypocritical they are."

"So our job is to let them have vicarious jollies without feeling guilty?"

"Right."

"But aren't we encouraging them to have bad thoughts?"

"No, we're distracting them. Keeping them from having even worse thoughts. Have you ever met any of our readers?"

"No. What are they like?"

"Almost as bad as the author."

"That bad?" Shiro asked, with a shudder. Suddenly a question occurred to him. "But Uncle-*san*. I've been killing people with tremendous relish all along, and the readers haven't minded one bit."

"That is the fly in my argument," Tomokato admitted. "Perhaps they appreciate tremendous relish. Does it come in a tremendous bottle?"

"Merely adequate," said Shiro.

Tomokato canceled their travel arrangements; then Shiro called Heliogabalus Pictures, asking to talk to Ted Swill. Swill was out. Shiro had to settle for Swill's close companion, Ben Offal.

"Shiro-*san*," Offal said. *San* he pronounced *seeyan*. Offal was the only person Shiro had ever met who mispronounced the word. "How are ya, amigo?"

"Just fine, Ben."

"What can I do for you, bud?"

261

"My uncle's considered the offer."

"Don't keep me in suspense, pardner."

"He says no dice."

There was a hard silence at the other end.

"What are you telling me?" Offal asked at last.

"He doesn't like what Heliogabalus has done in the past. Deal's off. Unless you want to exercise the option, that is."

"You little piece of crap," Offal said. "I thought we had an understanding! We've already sunk a big piece of change into this project."

"So you'll just have to pay us the full amount, huh?" Shiro replied.

"You're going to do this without even seeing what we have so far?"

"Well, if you want to fly us out there . . ."

The tension left Offal's voice. "So *that's* what this is all about. I think we can arrange that. Let me talk to Ted."

"Anything you say, Ben." Shiro read him the hotel's number off a piece of stationery. Offal said he'd get right back to him. The phone rang fifteen minutes later.

"We'll wire you the tickets," Offal promised. "They'll be there in the morning. And by the way, I'm sorry about that 'little piece of crap' thing. I hope you didn't take it personally. I respect you. Really, bubby."

"You respect crap?" Shiro asked.

"Pays the bills."

After dinner, Shiro had a bath. Tomokato watched CNN.

"They're talking about you on *Crossfiring,*" he called.

"Who is?" Shiro cried, voice muffled through the bathroom door.

"Braden and J. P. Morgan."

"Is Buchanan on?" Shiro asked.

"Substitute. One of those TV wrestlers."

"Jesse Ventura?"

"I don't know."

"Turn the sound up," Shiro said.

Tomokato flipped the dial.

"Every word of that kitten's testimony was a lie," Morgan was saying. "I've never paid illegal gratuities to the head of the Patent and Trademark Office, and I never even *heard* of Robert Vesco and Mao Tse-tung. I died in 1913."

Braden pounced: "If you're dead, what are you doing on this show?"

"What are *you* doing on this show, Braden?" the beefy guest host demanded. "How many tana leaves does it take to get *you* up and around?"

Within moments, the proceedings degenerated into a veritable World Wrestling Federation shouting match. Braden tried to punch Buchanan's substitute. Morgan got in the way. Braden belted him good. As if to protect a tag-team partner, Mao lumbered onstage to bail Morgan out.

Drawn by the bad vibes, a horde of skinheads parachuted in. Skidding to a stop in their mucous trails, several talk-sleaze kings appeared. À la Hope and Crosby, Morton and Geraldo did "patty-cake, patty-cake" to Phil, complete with the double pop to the face.

263

Screaming like harpies, Oprah and Sally Jessie rushed onto the scene, guns blazing. Blood splashed across the camera lens—

Cut to an editorial. Ted Trunner was explaining piously why *Singin' in the Rain* needed to be colorized. Tomokato watched just long enough to see him yanked off with a hook.

There came a rap at the door. Tomokato looked out through the peephole. Three very salty-looking dudes in sharp suits and shades stood outside.

"Who's there?" Tomokato asked.

"Room service," they answered.

"You know, I can see you through the hole. You don't look like bellmen to me."

"You didn't order the three hoods?"

Impressed by their ability to think on their feet, Tomokato opened the door.

A Browning Hi-Power and two Smith and Wesson automatics thrust into his face. The men pushed Tomokato back, the door shutting behind them.

"Where's your nephew?" the thug in the middle snarled.

"He's having a bath," Tomokato answered. "Shiro, visitors."

"Hit men?" Shiro called.

"Right."

"Aww, come on, Unc. I'm in the tub. You waste 'em."

Tomokato considered the request. "You're from the consortium, aren't you?" he asked the thugs, as the man in the middle backed him across the room.

"J.P. and Mao send their regards," the other two answered, shouting for Shiro's benefit.

"Shiro," Tomokato said. "You got yourself into this situation, and I think you would profit more if you got yourself out of it."

"But I don't even have my pistol, Unc!"

"Shiro, Shiro," Tomokato replied sadly.

One of the men by the bathroom kicked the door open. They went inside.

"Bubble bath?" one laughed.

"Great stuff," Shiro said. "You'd be amazed at what you can hide in it."

There was a rattle of full-auto fire. Bullets tore through the bathroom wall in puffs of plaster dust. One of the hoods sailed out and crashed into the panel doors of the closet opposite.

The man covering Tomokato began to squeeze the trigger on his double-action. He was not very fast.

Not even deigning to pull his sword, Tomokato had time to take a scrap of stationery, make a spitball, wad it into the barrel of the gun, get behind the man, and stuff his fingers in his ears. The exploding Smith and Wesson turned the thug into a very nasty project for Consuela the next day.

Shiro came out of the bathroom, swathed in foam from the neck down. The thug who struck the closet doors looked up at him, hand wandering towards his fallen gun.

"I said I didn't have my *pistol*," Shiro told him, and finished him off with the watercooled Browning Thirty he was holding. Blowing gunsmoke away from his face, he looked thoughtfully at Tomokato.

"You were right, Uncle-*san*," he said. "That certainly *was* a learning experience. I feel I have grown."

2

The following day, three o'clock Pacific Standard Time, they arrived at LAX. Just outside the exit ramp, a muscular young blond man stood holding a card with Tomokato's name markered on it. As the cat and Shiro came up, he bared his teeth in such a perfect and furious smile that Tomokato felt he was being irradiated.

"Unc, this is Craigie Catamite," Shiro said. "He's from Heliogabalus."

Craigie extended his hand. Tomokato did not take it, instead bowing curtly. Shiro shook Craigie's mitt, but only after slipping on a surgical glove. Trashing it once they were done, the kitten took the added precaution of spritzing his paw with Lysol.

"Hey, Shir, what you need is Nonoxynol-9," Craigie laughed, going through his pockets. "Got some here, I think."

"That's okay," Shiro said.

"That nephew of yours, what a card," Craigie told Tomokato. "Come on. Limo's this way."

Before long they were on the highway, cruising towards Tinseltown.

"You're booked in the Hollywood Howard Ramada," Craigie said. "Mr. Swill's putting his card down, of course. We'll just let you unwind tonight. Big day tomorrow."

"What do you have planned?" Tomokato asked.

"There's a morning screening we want you to see. And

after lunch, we'll take you over and show you the boards."

"Boards?"

"Storyboards. And you can meet the director and the writers." Craigie paused. "So. How much do you know about Heliogabalus?"

Tomokato replied icily: "I know your company made a total mockery of my lord and master, Nobunaga."

"You're talking about *Shogun of Sex,* aren't you?" Craigie said. "Well, don't worry. We've learned our lesson. Total shakeup. Everyone connected with that is long gone."

"Mr. Swill and Mr. Offal weren't involved?"

"It's hard being hands-on when you're being detoxed, you know?"

At that moment, Tomokato spotted a huge billboard from FAD—Filmmakers Against Drugs. Highlighting the movie community's recent conversion to the antidrug crusade, the photo showed a huge number of Hollywood figures not engaged in substance abuse. The picture appeared to have been snapped with a very quick shutter.

"So, what has Heliogabalus done lately?" the cat asked.

"Well," Craigie began, "we had a bit of a dry stretch after *Shogun.* Backers were pretty hard to find. That's over now. We've got two musicals, just about wrapped. First, there's an all-grown-up remake of *Bugsy Malone.* Originally we were going to do a nonmidget version of *The Terror of Tiny Town,* but we couldn't reassemble the original cast.

"Then there's *Three Thousand Scots.* Hershell Gordon Lewis's first musical. Sawney Beane's clan comes back from the dead and kills some modern tourists—it's sort of a cross between *Brigadoon* and *Two Thousand Maniacs.*

"We also just finished a ballet version of *The Magic Flute.* Sets and costumes designed by Leroy Neiman. Captain Lou Albano and Roseanne Barr as Papagena and Papageno. Sandra Bernhard as the Queen of the Night. You should see her in a tutu. It's pure dynamite.

"We're taking a stab at the kiddie market, too. We've got a live-action flick called *Old Saint Nick and the Ice Cream Rabbit.* Santa's sleigh gets caught in a tar pit and the Ice Cream Rabbit has to pull him out before he sinks. They don't make it. Sad, huh?"

Tomokato winced.

"Hey, kids gotta learn about death sometime," Craigie said. He counted on his fingers. "Let's see. We sold an afterschool special to HBO. It's called *Just a Regular Kid with AIDS.* These parents want to take their kids out of school because there's this boy with AIDS, see? Only the kids all go and catch it themselves, just to show solidarity. Heartrending.

"We also did an animated feature. It's called *The Courageous Tiny Tampon.* But we're having trouble getting that one distributed . . ."

Looking out the window, Shiro had listened to little of this. But slowly he became aware of a distinct warmth on the back of his skull; he turned to find out who was staring at him. Off in an alternate universe, Craigie was

269

going on and on about other Heliogabalus projects; it was Tomokato's eyes that the kitten had felt. They were like lasers. Shiro had never seen him look so murderously steamed.

"Unc, I've made every effort to atone, really," Shiro said, heart aching. "If you want my little finger, my head, anything, when this is all over, you've got it."

"I might settle for the finger," Tomokato said. "But ask me again tomorrow. After I see the boards."

They crossed the boundary of Hollywood. Tomokato had expected at least a certain amount of surface glamour. Instead, the city was intensely sleazy, as though 42nd Street had been transplanted from New York, stretched out over miles, and dotted with palm trees, oil wells, and tar pits.

At least, he *thought* they were tar pits—until he saw the muck putting out long, dripping pseudopods. The arms held things resembling black satellite dishes. Twisting like rubber bands, the arms would rotate the dishes through several 360-degree sweeps, then pull the receivers beneath the goo once more.

"What is that stuff?" Tomokato asked.

"Geologists used to say it was asphalt," Craigie said. "It's started bubbling up all over the city—not just staying in the pits anymore. Turns out it's alive. There's a huge pool of it underlying Hollywood. We call it the Crapmos. Kind of like the Matmos in *Barbarella,* except it doesn't feed on evil."

"What then?"

"Stupidity. Those receivers pick up stupidity waves. The Crapmos had this quantum growth-spurt when they

270

made *Temple of Doom,* and things have never been the same."

"Are they better or worse?"

"Depends on whether or not you think stupidity is a bad thing."

Hearing that, Tomokato decided not to carry the discussion any further. But Craigie continued:

"Long-term exposure to the Crapmos fertilizes our minds. It's kind of a stupidity farmer. But I've never had less trouble paying the bills, so I'm not complaining. Actually, the worst thing about the Crapmos is what it does to traffic."

Tomokato saw a red Ferrari sinking butt first into a bubbling sinkhole; a saber-toothed cat nailed to its hump by the fangs, a trumpeting mammoth was struggling to extricate itself from another, larger basin. The limo driver slowed as he approached the pools, slaloming lazily between them.

But beyond lay a dead wooly rhinoceros, full of spears and bullet holes, the focus of a savage fight between two detachments of Bloods and Cripps mounted on dire wolves. The chauffeur tried to speed up, but drove directly over a seam of Crapmos that had bulged up only seconds before; the front wheels plowed through, but the car slowed enough for the rear tires to stick. Other autos began piling up behind it, caught in the channel between the pits. Horns began to blare.

"Shit," said Craigie. "We're in for it now."

The gang members had noticed them. The trapped limo was far more interesting than the rhinoceros; declaring a temporary truce, the hoods reined the dire wolves round, reloading their weapons.

271

Shiro clapped with delight. "Look at all the assault rifles!"

Craigie, very agitated, snorted something. "That's illegal!" he said.

As if to show their contempt for gun control, the miscreants raked the bolts back on their weapons. Even through the windows, the vicious snap stung Tomokato's ears. Craigie fumbled for a cellular phone, hastily punched in a number.

"Send the Ninja, now!" he cried.

"Hadn't you better tell them where we are—" Tomokato broke off as a figure in black, contrasting most startlingly with the brightly daylit buildings nearby, swung into view on a line attached to nothing conceivable.

It was the Hollywood Ninja, beyond a doubt.

Awe plain on their faces, the Cripps and Bloods reined their lupine mounts to a halt.

Lighting before them, the Ninja drew his sword; and drew it and drew it and drew it. It was a full ten minutes before it came clear of the scabbard. Tomokato was impressed by its prodigious length, though he did not think it could possibly be a very serviceable weapon.

But the gang members compensated by sitting very very still on their mounts, long enough for the Ninja to swing it laboriously round, beheading every single one of them. Their severed necks erupted in perfect unison, like fountains in one of your more sanguinary Esther Williams movies. Bleeding gratuitously at the mouth, the dire wolves all just lay down and died.

The Ninja slid his blade back into its scabbard without even wiping it. If he had the slightest idea that he was a ludicrous figure, there was no hint whatsoever in the pride-drenched arrogance of his body language.

"Boy, that was stupid," Shiro said in disbelief.

"Wasn't it?" Craigie said, adoringly.

"How did he get here so soon?" Shiro asked.

"Hollywood time," Craigie said. "Ever wonder how the alien beat Sigourney Weaver back to the atmosphere generator with the little girl when Sigourney had a spaceship? How the Ewoks threw all those booby traps together? How Luke Skywalker became a Jedi knight after studying with Yoda for a day and a half?"

"Heed what he says, Shiro," Tomokato said. "We are in a place where even time and space are stupid."

The Ninja finally finished resheathing his weapon and came near. Looking in at Tomokato, he acknowledged him with a nod, then suddenly ripped the mask from his face, revealing that he was an utterly round-eyed Western person. Tomokato rolled down the window.

"Ah, so," said the Ninja, in a thick Swedish accent. "I told you we would meet again."

Tomokato eyed him narrowly.

"No thanks for saving you?" the Ninja demanded.

"I could've dealt with them," Tomokato said. "And without using the quick and easy way."

"The Dark Side of Absurdity?"

Tomokato nodded.

"And where would ninjas be if they did not do absurd things?"

"There is nothing wrong with absurdity," Tomokato replied. "As long as the omnipotence it conveys is used properly: To get laughs."

The Ninja smiled wickedly. "But why shouldn't omnipotence be a goal in itself?"

"Because it's less funny that way."

"You speak like a weakling," the Ninja sneered.

"I speak as one who knows his limitations. Have you ever sat through a serious Woody Allen film?"

The Ninja began to tremble. "I don't know what you mean."

"Your antics are fit only for comedy. Yet you have made many serious films. You have persuaded many children to try to leap backwards up onto thirty-story buildings. Little boys have broken bones going boing-boing-boing, bouncing up and down on one finger with their feet up in the air. You have induced other ninjas to wear white at night and black in the daytime, to charge machine guns in thoroughly useless slow motion."

"I get away with it," the Ninja insisted.

"Yet in the end," Tomokato said heavily, "it will destroy you."

The Ninja laughed, replacing his mask. "We shall see." Grabbing his line, he swung off. Tomokato closed the window.

Having seen the Ninja dispatch the gang members, the drivers behind had stopped honking; now they started again. Rolling down the partition, Craigie ordered the chauffeur to lure the Crapmos away from the tires. Beckoning with a videotape of *Sergeant Pepper's Lonely Hearts Club Band*, the driver backed away from the car. Tomokato felt the vehicle's rear end settle as the sludge released it. The chauffeur laid the cassette down near a crack in the road, out of which the Crapmos promptly resurfaced. A pseudopod lashed out and snatched the cassette.

The driver hopped back into the front seat, slammed the door, and hit the gas.

"Gotta get out of here," Craigie told Tomokato. *"Sergeant Pepper*'s a grade-A Crapmos fix, but the high doesn't last long. And then the Crapmos gets real mean for a while. It's started eating people, you know. Got Jack Valenti just last week."

As they pressed deeper into the city, Tomokato saw scores of derelicts on the sidewalks, tap-dancing arthritically or shambling after people with what appeared to be scrapbooks, trying to make them look at their clippings.

"They're the forgotten people," Craigie said. "Ex–kid stars, Charlie's Angels who've lost their looks, leading men from failed Gene Roddenberry pilots . . ."

"Isn't that Flipper?" Shiro asked, pointing to a dolphin on a dolly, the handle of a pencil cup hooked over its snout.

"No," said Craigie. "Rin-Tin-Tin. Just shows you what that fall from the pinnacle can do."

They began to pass vacant lots stacked with mountains of has-beens, some still alive—if just barely. Hollywood sanitation men wearing gas masks climbed into the backs of medieval-looking carts and began hurling withered old studs and eighty-year-old starlets onto the heaps.

"What are they going to do?" Shiro asked, horrified. "Burn 'em, like plague victims?"

"Then there wouldn't be nearly as much fever," Craigie said. "And without fever, there'd be far less brain damage. And without brain damage . . ." Craigie shivered. "I'd hate to think what would happen if the Crapmos got really hungry."

They passed a cart stopped in front of a run-down pink-stucco boardinghouse. A recorded voice blared from a loudspeaker mounted on the vehicle's side:

"Bring out your stars. Bring out your stars."

Out of the building came a melancholy procession, carrying a huge mass that was either Orson Welles, a California grey whale, or some hideous combination of all three.

"I thought Welles passed on a while ago," Tomokato said.

"Just what he wanted everyone to think," Craigie said. "He was so ashamed of what he'd become. Merv Griffin's pet intellectual, providing occasional serious insights . . . *c'est la vie,* eh?" He paused. "By the way. Does *c'est la vie* mean what I think it does?"

"Does anything?" Tomokato answered.

Craigie snapped his fingers. "Gotta learn Spanish one of these days."

They arrived at the Howard Ramada. Craigie made sure everything was okay with the reservations, then took his leave. Tomokato and Shiro went up to their room.

Shiro checked out the movie offerings on the TV. One was *Three Thousand Scots.*

"Isn't it a bad sign when a movie winds up on TV before it's even released to the theaters?" Tomokato asked.

"Unc," Shiro said, "it wound up on TV before they even finished it."

"We can just catch the next show," Tomokato answered, morbidly curious.

276

Shiro set the dial to Spectrevision. Ernst Stavro Blofeld came on and said a few words about how they were about to enjoy the finest in hotel entertainment and/or lonely businessmen's emergency date flicks. Then *Three Thousand Scots* began.

Several unmistakably American Deep South yokels, not very well disguised in kilts, capered out of a cyprus swamp and began switching road signs around, all to the accompaniment of bagpipes, plunking banjos, and an American Deep South yokel vocal group singing something about "EEEE-hah! The Scots gonna rise again!" As the credits rolled, two guys bearing an uncanny resemblance to Van Johnson and Gene Kelly took the fake detour to a picturesque out-of-the-way village; there they fell for some local babes and were afterwards tortured in ghastly clinical detail for the whole second quarter of the movie, with breaks for musical numbers.

The Van Johnson look-alike bought it, but Tomokato never did find out if his companion escaped; the fumes from the film knocked him out midway through. Shiro lasted a bit longer; but the combination of pornographic grisliness, *Pithecanthropus erectus* technique, and roller disco blitzed him shortly too.

3

They rose shortly before nine the next morning. A Spectrevision logo occupied the TV screen; the movies had gone off long before. Tomokato and Shiro washed up and went down to breakfast. Craigie was supposed to return for them at ten.

A movie crew was on location outside the restaurant. The film was some kind of period piece, apparently set in the early 1950s, to judge by the cars and most of the costumes; but some of the clothes seemed to have wandered in from the Civil War, and there was at least one spacesuit. A large statue of Benjamin Franklin had been placed in front of the hotel, between two stone lions.

The shooting preparations took forever. Tomokato and Shiro finished their meal and went outside to wait for Craigie. He appeared shortly; the limo was parked some distance off to the right, well away from the movie crew.

"This is one of our productions too," Craigie informed them. "Teen comedy. Ricky Schroder and Alyssa Milano. It's about the Rosenberg trial. It's called *Ethel and Julius's Excellent Adventure.* We're shooting it here because this hotel's absolutely a dead ringer for the Federal Courthouse in Manhattan. All it needed was Ben Franklin and the Lions, you know? That was a problem for the set dresser, but it turned out we had just what he needed. Statues were left over from *Food Fight on the Planet of the Apes—*"

"Action!" cried the director through a bullhorn.

A door swept open. Out rushed Ethel and Julius. Ed Asner's Judge Kaufman begged them to stop, afterwards trying to plug them in the back; but they managed to get into their car in time, and sailed over a Gestapo roadblock with the aid of the vehicle's rocket pods.

"Cut!" the director shouted.

"What do you think, huh?" Craigie asked Tomokato.

"Are you going to film my story with the same kind of attention to historical detail?" Tomokato inquired.

"Absolutely," said Craigie proudly.

Tomokato looked at Shiro. "Is there any point in going forward with this?"

"Maybe not," Shiro said. "But we're already out here. We might as well find out what Swill and Offal have in mind, right from their own lips. After all, Craigie might not know anything."

To which Tomokato replied: "Far be it from *me* to accuse him of knowing something."

Lowering his shades at this perceived compliment, Craigie gave him a wistful I-want-to-have-your-child smile.

The limo took them to a small screening room. There Tomokato met Swill and Offal.

Swill was a thin, elegant fellow. Dressed in intensely expensive casual wear, he resembled nothing so much as a lead from any number of British films about witty Cambridge lads driven to spy for Stalin by the insensitivity of others.

"Miaowara Tomokato," said Swill. "I've heard so much about you."

Tomokato bowed.

Offal nodded towards Tomokato's *katana*. "Not for us, I hope."

"I only kill evildoers," Tomokato replied.

Offal laughed. "I like that," he said. "Evildoers. Great."

His casual wear was a good deal louder than Swill's; but in face and build the two men resembled each other closely. To judge by the small scars, both had recently had plastic surgery so that they might resemble each other still more.

"Well," said Swill. "Let's see the film."

Craigie went up to the projectionist's booth. Tomokato and the rest entered the auditorium. The lights went down, and *Paths of Glory* came on. Tomokato was deeply impressed.

"So," Swill said when it was over, "that's what Hollywood is capable of."

"Hollywood should be congratulated," said Tomokato. "But did Heliogabalus have anything to do with it?"

"Not exactly," said Swill. "But Stanley Kubrick did spit on me once."

Offal held up a casual shirt swimming listlessly in a plastic bag full of clear fluid.

"He must have been very angry," Tomokato observed.

"Actually," Swill admitted, "it *was* more than once. But I really respect him."

Tomokato shifted uncomfortably in his seat. "Mr. Catamite said something about storyboards?"

Swill nodded. "After lunch," he replied.

They went back out into the lobby. There they discovered that a huge crack had opened in the floor; a seam of Crapmos came bubbling up.

"Hold it," Swill told the others.

A small receiving dish thrust into view, training on him, Offal, and Craigie. Instantly Swill shoved Craigie toward the crack. Sensing the onrushing mass of stupidity, the Crapmos sent a pseudopod up beside the dish.

Craigie somehow managed to stop before reaching the fissure. He turned, gasping.

"It's for the good of Hollywood," Swill told him. "Really."

The pseudopod arched into view above Craigie like the neck of an elasmosaur. Darting forward, it splashed into the back of his head. The various plops, slops and arcs of the splatter curled round to his face, entering it through every available orifice. The pseudopod lifted him off the floor, shaking him. His loafers flew from his feet. He reached up, fingers sinking into the pseudopodlet that had invaded his mouth. The Crapmos banged him once against the floor. Tomokato heard a dim rattle that might have been the sound of Craigie's seed-sized brain bouncing about in his gourdlike skull. Then Craigie vanished in the crack.

"Now!" said Swill. Tomokato and the rest tried to slip round the fissure.

But the Crapmos had already finished with Craigie. Two pseudopods slid forth.

The projectionist was coming out of his booth; Swill turned and grabbed a reel of *Paths of Glory* from him and advanced upon the tentacles like Van Helsing with a cross. The Crapmos gave a little bubbly cry; the pseudopods whipped from sight like recoiling rubber bands.

It was only after the sludge was gone that Tomokato noticed Swill's hand smoking; the producer shrieked, hurling the canister across the lobby, his flesh severely burned.

They scooted outside, dashing for Swill's stretch Caddy.

"Hey Ted," Shiro cried. "Who are all those guys in there?"

The limo's doors sprang open. A horde of hit men poured out like clowns from a circus car. Fifty Uzis trained on Tomokato and Shiro.

The cat looked at Swill. "Yours?" he asked.

"No, Unc," Shiro said. "They've got Morgan, Vesco and Mao written all over them."

Tomokato scrutinized them more closely. Indeed it was written all over them, in bright Day-Glo letters. He wondered how he had missed it before.

"Get lost," the hit men told Swill and Offal, who were only too eager to run. Tomokato wondered briefly why the killers were allowing two witnesses to flee; then the shit hit the fan.

"Where did all that shit come from?" the assasins cried, looking about wildly.

"Take the ones on the right," Tomokato told Shiro. And as his nephew whipped out his Browning Thirty, Tomokato leaped snarling among the gunmen on the left.

It was sheer butchery at its finest. Hollywood hadn't seen that much gore since, well, *Three Thousand Scots.* When it was over and Tomokato stood surveying the carnage he and Shiro had wrought, he was reminded of the scene where the Van Johnson look-alike suffered the death of a thousand cuts while being simultaneously raked with 20-mm Vulcan fire; only this was not in such good taste.

Looking on from behind a palm tree just on the border of Beverly Hills, Swill said to Offal:

"We should send for the Ninja."

"Why?" Offal asked.

"In case they don't like the storyboards."

Offal tiptoed over to a pay phone, told the Ninja to meet them for lunch, then snuck back to Swill. All before Tomokato and Shiro could look round: Offal was particularly adept at handling Hollywood time. Then the pair rejoined the felines.

The limo's chauffeur had been shot; Offal unceremoniously dumped him on the sidewalk and got behind the wheel.

A cop car rolled up. Swill lowered his window.

"Something wrong, Mr. Swill?" a policeman asked, eyeing the corpses and corpse fragments and the vast, crawling Mississippi-size rivers of blood.

"Not at all, officer," Swill replied.

The cops drove off.

"Company town," Swill told Tomokato.

Offal pulled away from the curb.

The limo had a well-equipped emergency room between the bar and the TV; by the time the doctors had treated Swill's burn, the car had arrived in a trendy urban-reclamation section of L.A. The restaurant was a former meat-packing plant duded up in New Wave motifs; the inside was a marvel of sterility, quite perfect in its own way. As Tomokato entered, he had an uncanny feeling that every microbe on the surface of his body was dropping off, stone cold dead.

The Hollywood Ninja was waiting at a table in the back.

"Tomokato, this is—" Swill began.

283

"We've met," Tomokato answered.

A waiter resembling Conrad Veidt in *The Cabinet of Dr. Caligari* wafted up, deposited a single handwritten all-pilaf menu, and stood silently with a slightly pained expression on his face, waiting for someone to order a drink. Offal and Swill asked for cherry seltzer. Tomokato and the Ninja requested nothing, but sat staring, sizing each other up. Shiro ordered a Coke.

"We don't have—" here Cesar the Somnambulist sniffed with contempt *"—Coca-Cola."*

Shiro sneered right back at him. "What else don't you have?"

Cesar drifted away like a vapor. Offal handed Shiro the menu card.

"What is this pilaf crap anyway?" the kitten asked.

Swill explained.

"Well, okay," Shiro said. "But for fifty bucks a plate?"

"Don't worry," Offal said. "We're paying."

"You'd better believe you are," Shiro replied.

When Cesar returned, the kitten and Tomokato ordered the tuna pilaf; Swill and Offal decided to split a pilaf salad, while the Ninja ordered the Ninja pilaf.

"What exactly is he doing here?" Tomokato asked Swill. "Who do you need protection from?"

"More hit men," Swill answered.

"But they were after Shiro," Tomokato said. "And they seemed most unusually happy to let you go."

"That *was* startling, wasn't it?" Swill asked.

"You wouldn't be worried about how I'm going to react to your presentation, would you?" Tomokato asked.

The Ninja's hand flew to his hilt; Offal and Swill both vanished under the table.

"Whatever would give you such an idea?" Swill asked, his voice perfectly composed—no mean trick at E above high C.

"You needn't worry," Tomokato said. "I am a cat of honor. I intend to live up to my contractual agreements. As long as you are within your rights, I will not scatter your guts from here to Midway Island, even though you will almost certainly be asking for it."

The Ninja studied him closely. "He's speaking the truth," he announced, hand slipping from his hilt. Slowly he removed his mask, revealing a ferocious triumphant Ninja smile that said to Tomokato: *We have you, fool.*

Tomokato smiled in return, clearly replying: *You think so?*

To which the Ninja's smile answered: *With very good reason, purest kitty bozo.*

Whereupon Tomokato's responded: *And what is that reason, oh thou son of thine own Ninja mother, also known as Patty, who swims out to meet whole continents?*

The Ninja's smile tightened: *You leave my mother out of this.*

Tomokato's widened: *But I have proof.*

Oh yeah?

Tomokato began to lift his copy of Patty Ninja's *Greenland, North America and Me.* But at that moment the various pilafs arrived, and the ugliness subsided.

"So how's your lunch?" Offal asked Shiro after an interval.

"Fabulous," Shiro said unenthusiastically. He noticed a rat creeping across the floor toward the table.

"Psst," said the rodent. "What happened to the meat-packing plant?"

"Why should I tell you?" Shiro whispered, leaning over. "Rats and cats are mortal enemies."

"Us animals gotta stick together," the rat replied. "Especially in a joint like this. But really. Where am I going to go to get my scraps?"

Shiro checked to see if anyone was looking, and lowered his plate to the floor. The rat stuck his snout over the rim. Sniffing, it looked up at Shiro with a pleading expression.

"You got anything besides this pilaf crap?" he asked.

4

After lunch, they went to Heliogabalus Studios for the storyboard presentation. The boards had been set up along a wall in the art department, but before Tomokato could inspect them, a round of introductions began. The cat met a series of Heliogabalus executives. Then Swill came to Larry Abortionist.

"He's the director on *Tomokato/Tomokata*."

"*Tomokato/Tomokata?*" the cat asked, suddenly queasy.

"Once you see the boards, you'll understand," Abortionist said.

A couple of studio flunkies rolled up a fellow in a wheelchair.

"This is our top screenwriter," Swill said, indicating the invalid, an old man, staring vacantly and drooling. Tomokato was sure he had seen him somewhere before. Suddenly he realized where. Hadn't the oldster been the proprietor of the True-Value store, back in Boston?

"Totally brain-dead," Swill said. "The shining light of our script department. And people thought Chris Columbus was as dumb as you could get! We caused quite a stir when we brought this guy here. Kicked off this whole brain-dead writing craze. You should have seen the stampede last month—the other studios heard about this whole truckstop full of basket cases back in Maine. Super treat for the old Crapmos. It's been all we could do to make it settle for the stupidity waves. Script department at Universal nearly got swallowed yesterday."

Swill looked at his watch, then at Offal. "Where's Smeazie? He should be here by now."

"Smeazie?" Tomokato asked.

"Smeazie Ringlets," Swill said. "He's signed for the lead."

"That singer who tried to buy Rondo Hatton's body?" Tomokato asked, his nausea now reinforced by a splitting headache. "The one with the rabbit?"

"Bitsy-Boo," Offal said.

"I beg your pardon?"

"The rabbit's name is Bitsy-Boo," Offal replied. "Now remember. When Smeazie arrives, you and Shiro have to give Bitsy a kiss."

"On the mouth," Swill added.

"We'll do no such thing," Tomokato answered.

"Bitsy's had his shots—"

287

The doors opened. In swarmed a crowd of plastic surgeons, an automated gurney humming along in their midst.

"Smeazie!" Swill and Offal cried. All the Heliogabalus people except the Ninja went over to fawn; abandoned by his attendant, the scriptwriter made a pathetic basket-case attempt to join the rush, laboring along in his wheelchair.

A hand the color of coffee with too much milk in it thrust out from between the doctors, holding a bloated bunny.

"Kiss, kiss!" cried the occupant of the gurney.

Swill and his creatures fell all over each other to get to the bunny lips. Ignoring the pandemonium, the surgeons kept up a steady *snip-snip-snip,* sending unwanted Smeazie bits flying through the air.

When at last the bunny kissing subsided, the patient motioned the doctors aside. Revealed was a person of indeterminate race and gender, face a mass of stitching, nose pared down to a little tiny near-nothing, painfully thin body covered by a sequined sheet. Its ringlets were smeazie indeed. It thrust Bitsy-Boo straight in the direction of Tomokato and Shiro.

"Kiss, *kiss!*" it shouted insistently.

All the Heliogabalus people turned to Tomokato, signaling him toward the bunny with desperate jerks of the head.

"I will *not* kiss that pestilential rabbit," the cat said.

"You'll kill this whole deal!" Swill cried.

"Kisskisskisskiss!" Smeazie shrieked.

Tomokato stamped his foot. "SILENCE!" he roared.

Smeazie's hand opened. The swollen rabbit dropped

to the floor and flattened like Silly Putty. Offal and Swill scrambled to shove it back into Smeazie's grip.

"You were saying?" Tomokato asked Swill.

"Do you want Smeazie to pull out of this project?"

"Will it fold if he does?"

Swill nodded.

Tomokato thought he had him. "As I said. I will not kiss that—"

Smeazie's emaciated form jackknifed into a sitting position. Smoothing Bitsy-Boo's fur, he dangled his matchstick legs over the edge. Huge cartoon-bug eyes shining with pure malice, he smiled at Tomokato with far more teeth than anyone had ever been born with.

"I'll play him anyway," he announced.

"All right," Tomokato said. "That's it. Exercise the option. Or surrender the rights."

"Don't you even want to see the boards?" Swill asked.

"I've seen enough."

"It's entirely to your advantage," Swill went on.

"How so?"

"Because if you refuse to extend the option, we get to kill you."

"What?" Tomokato demanded.

Swill approached him with a sheaf of papers peeled back to the last page. He pointed to a clause in the fine print. Tomokato read it in disbelief.

"Shiro, what have you done to me?" he asked tonelessly.

"Uncle-san," the kitten breathed. "Oh Uncle-*san.*" Kneeling in front of Tomokato, he pulled out a *wakizashi,* and prepared to open his belly.

"I forbid it!" Tomokato cried.

289

Shiro looked up, green eyes welling with tears.

"What would your parents say?" Tomokato asked.

"That I had it coming!" Shiro wailed. "If they have any sense of justice at all!"

He tried to plunge the blade in.

Tomokato kicked it from his grasp.

"No," the cat said. "Not yet." He trained his eyes on Swill. Swill looked as though his skin had suddenly grown too tight for him.

Still, the moviemaker had Tomokato where he wanted him, and he knew it.

"Would you like to see the boards, Honorable Tomokato-*san*?"

"San means honorable, redundant barbarian bunny's-lip licker," Tomokato replied.

Swill ran his tongue over his lips. "Do you want to see the boards?" he repeated.

Tomokato looked down at Shiro. "If there's any way out of this, we must take it," he said, then told Swill: "Do your worst."

Swill, growing bolder, scuttled near. "I don't think you know what you're asking for. But, since you insist . . ." He snapped his fingers at a flunky. "The chairs."

A switch clicked. Two oral hygiene seats, one adult and one kitten-sized, rose from the floor beneath Tomokato and Shiro, scooping them up.

"I was in Moscow recently," Swill said. "With the Butch Cassidy Institute, you know? There was this garage sale at the Lubyanka. That's where I picked the chairs up. I understand you've been in the little one before, Shiro."

Shiro started to stand up. The flunky thrust him back down and moved to strap him in.

"No need for that," Swill said. "His uncle's under contract. They *have* to watch. Isn't that right, Tomokato?"

"Yes," Tomokato answered, voice choked with rage.

"Well then," said Swill, rubbing his hands. "Showtime. Miaowara Tomokato, This is Your Life."

Tomokato steeled himself. Offal danced over to the storyboards. *"Tomokato/Tomokata,"* he said. Picture by picture, he ran through the story.

Tomokato soon discovered that Swill had been telling the truth, and then some; the cat hadn't known what he was asking for. The travesty they had come up with was worse than anything he could possibly have imagined. Even though he had spent his life in ferocious conflict with evil, there yet remained in him a vast streak of pure innocence; there were depths he could not conceive of until he actually glimpsed them.

In his naïveté, he had thought that Smeazie was at least going to play him as Japanese; but no such luck. The character had been transformed into a willowy young American.

"Audience won't identify with an Oriental," Offal explained.

Yet if that weren't bad enough, the character wasn't even a cat.

"People can't identify with cats," Swill put in, smirking at Tomokato.

The character *did* remain a samurai; but from a stuffy samurai family in Orange County.

291

Mark E. Rogers

"He feels compelled to rebel against the masculine stereotype he's being forced into," Offal went on. "He confronts his father. His father doesn't understand. Tomokato leaves for life on the road. There are many musical numbers. Finally he has a sex change—"

"That's why Smeazie's ideal in the role," Swill broke in. "He can do before *and* after. Without makeup."

"Tomokata's family cuts off her funds," Offal continued. "She embarrasses them further by appearing in a transsexual revue in New Orleans. Their ninjas attack. Rejecting violence, she allows herself to be fatally wounded in mid striptease. Falling on some convenient barbed wire, Tomokata dies, cuddling her pet bunny and intoning a haiku about farting."

Offal lapsed into silence.

Finally, Tomokato thought, thanking Buddha. No matter what happened next, at least the presentation was over.

"Then, after the intermission . . ." Offal resumed.

Flunkies tacked up a whole new set of boards.

Tomokato gritted his teeth, determined to bear it all. He had told Swill to do his worst; that much punishment at least he was going to absorb. And that much punishment he triumphed over.

At last the presentation was *really* over.

"Ah," Tomokato said. "Soon we will be with Lord Buddha, Shiro. And things like this will trouble us no more."

"Well," said Swill, approaching. "What do you think?"

Tomokato rose from the seat. So great was the dignity and power within him that Swill and all his minions

292

drew back, receding like Hell in the presence of Farinata; calling on their hideous Hollywood deities, they kissed their crystals and little toy pyramids and icons of Shirley MacLaine and Ramtha. He sneered at them, spat once, then took off his helmet and knelt, baring his neck.

The Hollywood Ninja strode forward. Swill and company followed like curs behind a wolfhound. Drawing his sword, he lifted it for the beheading stroke—

"Hold it!" Shiro cried, jumping up, the Browning Thirty slung over one arm.

The Ninja's sword froze in space.

"We have a contract!" Swill protested.

"There's nothing in it that says *I* can't fight back!" Shiro replied.

Swill grinned. "Actually . . ." He came almost to the muzzle of the Browning, holding up the contract. "Clause 42b."

Shiro studied it. As he read, he noticed Swill reaching behind his back with his free hand.

"Got you dead to rights, haven't we?" the producer gloated.

Shiro nodded. He could've kicked himself. Why hadn't he read the contract closely? Atypically clear for legalese, the language did indeed forbid him to defend his uncle.

"How about that?" he asked.

And unloaded five inches of belt into Swill's forehead.

Arms flailing, contract flapping, Swill took three steps backward before he fell. As Shiro had thought, the producer had been hedging his bets all along; there was a pearl-handled purse pistol in Swill's left hand.

Mark E. Rogers

The Ninja turned on Shiro, preposterous sword whooshing round.

"Any of your enemies ever think of this one?" Shiro asked, taking full advantage of Hollywood Time.

He moved.

The sword missed him.

The Ninja's eyes popped wide with surprise. Grudgingly he produced a smaller, much more wieldy sword.

Even so, he was not about to give up on the Dark Side of Absurdity. As Shiro opened up with the machine gun, the Ninja leaped up onto the continuous stream of bullets and came tiptoeing swiftly toward the kitten like Mikhail Baryshnikov in a frying pan.

Shiro released the trigger.

The Ninja dropped to the floor, snapping his fingers in frustration.

Swill leaped back up. Above his eyes, all that remained was fragile arch of skull; his whole brain had been reamed out by Shiro's blast.

"But," as he explained cheerfully, aiming his little gun, "that's my least vital organ."

Shiro hit the trigger again. The Browning was jammed.

Tomokato bounded to his feet just in time to deflect three bullets from Swill's pistol.

"But—" Swill began.

"Contract or no contract," Tomokato said, "I'm not going to let you kill my nephew. And if it'll make you any happier, I'll commit seppuku after I've slaughtered you."

Dissatisfied with that proposal, Swill turned and ran. So did his minions, the scriptwriters struggling along at

294

the rear. But the Ninja stood eyeing Tomokato and Shiro, rubbing his chin.

"We don't have to answer your absurdity with absurdity, you know," Tomokato told him. "The Dark Side can be defeated with the least ounce of common sense. If your sword is big and slow as a glacier, we will dodge. If you run on our bullets, we will stop firing. If you come at us in slow motion, we will move quickly. If you bounce boing-boing-boing on one finger, we will laugh our medieval Japanese butts off and then slice you up for dogmeat. We are not from around here, David Carradine–breath. And if killing you means not going for laughs, we will do it. And still get laughs in the meantime."

Doubt showed in the Ninja's eyes.

"Wimping out, Ninja-*san*?" Tomokato asked, with a smile.

To his credit, the Ninja began to advance.

But before this particular boil of potential violence could burst, a chorus of screams interrupted the proceedings, easing the antagonists' collective grip on the metaphorical quat.

The Heliogabalus folks were pouring back into the room. Pursuing was a huge mass of Crapmos, flowing viscously through the entrance.

"Must've sensed the storyboards," Shiro guessed, watching it wolfing down illo after illo.

"But I don't think it's going to stop with them," Tomokato said.

A bizarre crest of black, beautiful cursive script rose on the Crapmos's back. *"No shit, Sherlock,"* it read.

A pseudopod whipped around Offal's neck and

295

yanked him into the depths of the goo. Vast transparent paisleys and other hallucinogenic motifs appeared above the Crapmos, and the script shifted shape.

"What a rush," it declared.

The Heliogabalus crowd fled for another exit. All but Smeazie: getting down from his gurney, his flock of surgeons still snipping away at what was left of him, he gave Bitsy-Boo to one of them, and stood facing the Crapmos defiantly, apparently inspired by the new macho persona he had adopted on his last album.

The Crapmos paused, scanning him with two receiving dishes.

Repeating the most famous move from his *Wretched* video, Smeazie cocked his hips forward, reached down, and flicked his crotch at the living tar.

So inflamed was its stupidity lust by this sight that the Crapmos lunged without even bothering with pseudopods.

Smeazie yelped. Bitsy-Boo leaped back into his arms. Then the Crapmos took them, surgeons and all. All that escaped was a teeny hurtling shred of Smeazie's pointy chin, and that only for a moment; the Crapmos snatched it before it struck the elegant hardwood floor.

Whereupon the script on its back formed yet a third message:

"Who's Bad?"

Tomokato, Shiro, and the Ninja bolted from the room, hanging a right in the corridor outside; the Crapmos did not appear to be following. Tomokato thought it was probably downing the rest of the storyboards.

The three emerged in a sunwashed parking lot. There

296

they halted; ten thousand hit men awaited them, mounted on surrounding buildings and palm trees, on horses, armored cars, tanks, mechanical bulls, very large hand puppets, Swedish knee-rocker chairs. And in front of this legion stood John Pierpont Morgan, Robert Vesco, Mao Tse-tung—

And Ted Swill.

5

"You always showed such inspired financial judgment, Shiro," Morgan cried. "You really impressed us. So we kept very close tabs on you. Watched your investments outside the consortium. And when you decided to commit your uncle to *Tomokato/Tomokata,* we figured you were probably onto something."

"We bankrolled the entire project," Vesco said.

To which Chairman Mao added some thoughts of his own, but since they were in Chinese, which I can't understand, I won't give them here.

"But why did you try to kill me outside the screening room?" Tomokato asked. "Why didn't you wait until I'd seen the boards?"

"We were after Shiro," Vesco replied. "But if we'd gotten you both—well, the project could've proceeded anyway."

"That doesn't make any sense at all!" the Ninja cried suddenly. "What a stupid subplot!"

"Since when does stupidity bother you?" Swill cried. "Come, take your rightful place among us."

"Better still, kill Tomokato and Shiro," said Morgan. "I mean, we might very well have ten thousand hit men here, but you're closer."

Tomokato and the Ninja faced each other, the Ninja's outfit changing most startlingly from black to white to black as he considered the evil he had dedicated himself to. Finally it settled on a kind of polka-dot pattern.

"I can feel the good in you," Tomokato said. "Indeed, it has manifested itself visually in a most silly way. Abandon the dark and easy path. Or as I said—"

A blur of speed, Tomokato swung his edge, halting it a fraction of an inch from the Ninja's throat.

The Ninja pulled his mask off. "You'll slice me into dogmeat," he said.

And smiled a joyous smile of repentence. Heavenly light washed over them. A celestial chorus burst forth with "Be a Clown."

Or was it "Make 'Em Laugh"?

The Ninja sheathed his sword.

"Shades of Carlos LaFong," Shiro said. "Two repentant baddies in one book."

"Three if we count you, Nephew," Tomokato answered, lowering his weapon.

A troubled look replaced the Ninja's smile. "Three?" he asked.

"Yes," Tomokato replied.

The Ninja's outfit suddenly returned to black against the bright sunlit background. "That is too many repentant baddies," he said, and launched into a furious if highly implausible ninja attack involving break dancing, bolos, and Ethiopian cuisine.

Sighing with regret, Tomokato emptied the Ninja's

insides onto the steps with a single swift stroke, the very height of elegance.

"That was a stupid reason to throw your life away," the cat told him.

"I felt I should die as I lived," the Ninja replied, collapsing. Two shuddering breaths, and he was gone.

"Get up!" Swill cried to the corpse. "Get up and fight!"

The body didn't move. Swill turned to Morgan, Vesco, and Mao.

"Never let it stop him before," he said.

Morgan pointed to the cat. "Fire!" he shouted to his assembled legions.

But even as he spoke, the Uzis were whisked magically from their hands by legislation passed just a moment before.

"Great Buddha," Shiro said. "Gun control really does work!"

"I notice you still have yours," Tomokato answered.

Shiro tucked the Browning under one armpit and fished out a license. "I'm a collector," he said. "I'm going to donate all my guns to a museum some day. A very *big* museum."

But the legislation didn't exempt just Shiro. The tanks still had their cannons, 120-millimeter Rheinmetall smoothbores. The gunners cranked the tubes down, point-blank.

"Fire!" Morgan cried once again.

Ten muzzles roared, belching flame.

"Strange," Shiro said. "We heard and saw the blasts at the same time. Isn't light faster than sound?"

"Not in this town," Tomokato said.

Gleaming cannon shells moved lazily towards them in Hollywood Time. The cat and Shiro charged forward from the steps, pausing only to unscrew the projectiles' fuses.

"Don't you feel kind of bad?" Shiro asked, as he raced along, trying to clear the Browning's action.

"About what?"

"Exploiting Hollywood Time this way. I mean, after the way you lectured the Ninja . . ."

"Shiro, as I told Wisconsin Platt, we're *supposed* to be funny," Tomokato explained. "We are the rightful masters of Hollywood Time. It is Hollywood that abuses it. It is Hollywood itself that sucks."

"Thank you for clarifying that," said Shiro. "But aren't you setting me a bad example by using swearwords?"

"Shiro, the reason young kittens should not use bad language is that they might wear it out. There is a place for bad language. And this town is it."

Shiro unjammed the Browning. By then, Morgan, Swill, and company had vanished into the army of hit men.

Some of the torpedoes held their ground as Tomokato and Shiro approached; they pulled out switchblades, Swiss Army knives, real butch keychains. But these availed them little against Shiro's collector's piece. And still less against Tomokato's sword. The two felines swiftly peeled back the first four ranks of thugs, revealing Swill and the Consortium before they could flee farther into the crowd.

By then, the surviving hit men were all too anxious to let Tomokato and Shiro settle their bosses. Those with tanks and armored cars wheeled the vehicles around. The cavalry galloped away. The hoods mounted on hand puppets and knee-rockers fled however a person flees on such things. The rest had to settle for their standard-issue hit man scooters, desperately knocking the kickstands out from under them and hopping aboard.

Swill and the Consortium were left high and dry. It never seemed to occur to them that Tomokato and Shiro had had no real interest in killing them. Up till then the felines had simply been acting in self-defense. Tomokato would have agreed to a deal, provided it ensured Shiro's safety.

But the corpses behind Tomokato, all three thousand of them, made him look perhaps more unreasonable than he actually was; the fact that he seemed to be wearing most of their blood only heightened the effect. Swill and the Consortium made their last miscalculation; and as a result, the massacre which follows was all quite moral and aboveboard, you'll be happy to know.

Vesco tried to smash Tomokato over the head with Richard Nixon. Now Tomokato had never been sold on the Nixon-as-monster theory; nonetheless, with the ex-President screaming down at him, he had no choice but to slice him through at the waist.

The earth shaking beneath his elephantine tread, Mao rushed to bail Vesco out, priming a portable minigun loaded with victims of the Cultural Revolution. Fortunately Shiro's Browning chewed into the Chairman before he could bring that near-inexhaustible ammo supply to bear.

Mao just grinned, apparently believing his fat would insulate him from the slugs. The minigun swept towards the kitten. But Mao hadn't counted on any of Shiro's slugs being incendiaries.

All that tallow made for a very dramatic blaze.

Circling around behind Vesco and Mao, Morgan lunged at the cat with a huge combination in restraint of trade. It was a formidable weapon, in the right circumstances; but these called for a sword. And Tomokato's left Morgan looking like an explosion at a ketchup factory.

Tomokato turned to see Shiro jumping down from Vesco's back. The kitten's machine gun was knotted around the financier's neck. How Shiro had accomplished that, Tomokato had no idea. The cat had tried such a maneuver once, but the water-cooling jacket had frustrated him utterly.

A bullet clanged from Tomokato's armor. The cat whirled.

There stood Swill, raising his pistol, aiming for Tomokato's face. Tomokato thrust his sword forward, sinking it in Swill's heart.

But Swill didn't go down. "Another of my least vulnerable spots!" he crowed.

Tomokato took his gun-hand off. "Then I suppose I'll just have to totally dismember you," the cat said.

"That won't work either," Swill snapped.

Events proved otherwise. While he still had a face, Swill looked genuinely surprised.

"Unc!" Shiro said. "The Crapmos!"

It was finally coming out of the art department. It was also coming up out of the asphalt. Tomokato and Shiro looked round wildly. The stuff was surfacing everywhere. They were completely surrounded by bubbling cracks.

Pseudopods whipped out of the nearest, snatching what was left of Swill. Paisleys exploded above the parking lot; for a minute the sky looked like a flower garden in bloom. Then the Crapmos needed a new fix.

The asphalt heaved and bulged. Black gleaming ridges thrust out of fissures. Tomokato saw the surrounding buildings and palm trees beginning to sway; then a pitchy wall crested over him and Shiro, blotting out the heavens.

"It's been good to know you, Unc," Shiro said.

"Likewise," Tomokato answered. "Better this way. At least I won't have to commit—"

A vast weight settled on him. He was completely enveloped. Breath spewed from his lungs, squeezed out by the pressure.

But it could not escape; the Crapmos was too thick. As the bubble expanded, he felt the ooze peeling back from his face. He opened his eyes, gasping. There was nothing but darkness.

He inhaled. The bubble collapsed, the heavy stinking fluid pushing back into his face, sealing against his features.

Something solid touched his chin; he had no way of knowing, but he found himself certain that it was a bit of undissolved Swill. He wondered what would kill him first: the digestion process, or suffocation?

A shudder passed through the Crapmos. A series of rapid spasms followed. Tomokato felt as though he were being squeezed repeatedly by a giant fist.

There was distant barfing noise. After one last mighty twinge, the Crapmos expelled him into the blessed air.

Gulping, he sailed perhaps fifteen feet, straight up from the living tar. Shiro was hurtling along beside him.

"Uncle-*san*!" the kitten cried. "I guess it couldn't stomach us at all!"

As they dropped back down, Tomokato saw a patch of Crapmos changing color beneath them, wrinkling, bunching up; he and Shiro landed unhurt on a thick brown leathery surface, apparently generated to keep them from sinking into the depths again.

The patch began to move. Up and down over the billowing Crapmos crests it slid, like a raft on a black ocean.

The sludge was rapidly engulfing all of Tinseltown. Pseudopods climbed the sides of buildings, flowed into windows, burst out through roofs in explosions of shattered masonry. Black waves rolled down broad avenues, splashing towering walls. Hotels and theaters crumbled and vanished in the ravenous muck.

In the midst of it all, Tomokato spotted Ten Just Men tobogganing along on their own protective scabs; but if anyone else was being spared for their sake, he saw no trace of it.

Tomokato's patch soon neared the border of Hollywood. Black letters thrust up beside him:

"Don't Come Back!" they read.

The scab rolled over the top of a wave and careened down the dark slope toward an oil field just beyond the boundary. Tomokato and Shiro slid off at the bottom.

Shiro tried to look back at the city. But Tomokato stopped him.

"No," the cat said. "Don't."

There was no sign of the Ten Just Men; Tomokato guessed they had been deposited elsewhere. But moments later, Rin-Tin-Tin went skidding past them on his dolly.

"Rinty!" Shiro cried, running up to the dog-cum-dolphin. "You made it! Rinty!"

Rinty nodded wearily, avoiding Shiro's glance. The kitten sensed some kind of turmoil going on within him. The dolphin began to tremble. Slowly he pressed his flippers against the ground and began to turn the dolly.

"Don't do it!" Tomokato cried, still some distance behind them. "Don't look back!"

It was too late. A flash of light seared his retinas. When his sight returned, he saw that Rinty had been turned into a dolphin of salt.

Shiro backed up for a look. "Whoa, boy," he said, awestruck. "When it rains it porpoise, huh?"

Tomokato reached his side. "Try not to make too many more jokes like that, nephew. I won't be there to protect you."

Shiro laughed. "Where will you be, Uncle-*san*?"

Tomokato slipped out of his armor and knelt. He unsheathed his *wakizashi*.

"Uncle?" Shiro whispered.

"I have completely dishonored myself," Tomokato replied.

"What?"

"I broke the contract."

"All you did was defend me!" Shiro cried.

"And if I hadn't, I *also* would have dishonored myself. I made the right choice, seeing as how I would dishonor myself no matter what. But still, I must pay for my transgression." He looked at Shiro and smiled. "I love you, Nephew-*san*."

Gripping the *wakizashi* in both paws, he pointed it towards his stomach.

"Farewell," he said.

"Uncle!" Shiro shrieked.

The razor-sharp shortsword plunged inwards.

And howling at the top of his lungs, little Zork Arggh sat bolt upright just in time to see a vast glowing Hollywood crash into the sandpit just the other side of the hill.